SEVEN WAYS
TO SEDUCE A MARTIAN

Cynthianna Appel

Triskelion Publishing
www.triskelionpublishing.net
All about women. All about extraordinary.

Praise for ***Seven Ways to Seduce a Martian***

"Ms. Cynthianna Appel has written a witty account of the foibles of dating in the twenty-first century. Jodi is the quintessential modern woman with her independent ways, while Brent has an extremely vulnerable side he hides with his aloof manner. They both show remarkable tenderness towards each other once the barriers are breached and the underlying motives are exposed. The typical office setting creates a great backdrop filled with varied characters that people the story nicely. I enjoyed this book." -Kathy, Reviewer for Coffee Time Romance

Triskelion Publishing
15327 W. Becker Lane
Surprise, AZ 85379

ISBN 1-933471-91-3

Printing History
First e Published by Triskelion Publishing
First e publishing March 2006
First printing by Triskelion Publishing
First trade paper printing May 2006

Cover design Triskelion Publishing 2006

Publisher's Note. This is a work of fiction. Names, characters, and places and incidents are a product of the author's imagination. Any resemblance to a person or persons, living or dead, business establishments, events or locales is purely coincidental.

Chapter One

TO: ShaynaE@wazoo.com
FROM: jbaker@hit-on-us.com
SUBJECT: What gives?

Hey, Girlfriend!

Like, you haven't emailed me in over six hours…What gives? You know how I hate being put on hold. You're the only person I can "talk" to right now – really talk to. You're special. You lived with me for four years in a dorm room and didn't kill me – or yourself. And you even let me borrow your toothbrush on more than one occasion! ☺

Let me catch you up on the latest victim to be cast into our cubicle prison here at ***H****olliday's* ***I****nternational* ***T****ravel* ***ON****line* ***US****. He's a quiet one. I really don't know much about him yet, and he's been here a whole half day already. Yes, before you jump down my throat, our newest employee is a "him". I'm pretty sure he's male, as no one has noticed the slightest hint of electric pink lipstick on him. He dressed in conservative blues unlike our former partner-in-crime, Mr. Frankie "Floral" Fernandez. BTW, I hear Frankie is doing quite well in Vegas. If there's one thing you can say about dear ol' Frankie it's that his Cher impersonation* *can't be beat!*

But I digress. Don't I always? ☺

About our new inmate... His name is Brent Davison. He's tallish, has thick, dark brown, semi-wavy hair, deep brown eyes and is rather quiet. That's about it as far as descriptions go at this point. From what I overheard of his interview (and who couldn't hear it with the way Mr. J keeps his door open all the time?) this Brent guy strikes me as being overqualified to sit at a computer terminal all day working with mindless business-types who want a cheap airline ticket from Boise to Boston with a side-trip to Bermuda. But who am I to judge? I have a magna cum laude attached to the bottom of my diploma and a third grade education is all you need to work at this place.

I know what you're thinking. "You idiot, get over that jerk-off ex-fiancé and get on with your life." You're absolutely right. I am a first class idiot. I really regret not going directly into grad school now. But when "Mr. I-Can't-Make-A-Commitment-But-Can-You-Still-Do-My-Laundry?" walked out of my life last year I was really shook up. Life-altering decisions shouldn't be made under the influence of severe depression – and ten strawberry daiquiris – and we both know it.

But what's done is done. My dad put a good word in for me with his golfing pal Mr. J. and I've landed here for better or worse. I'm just glad I can afford a decent apartment and food and a Bi-State bus pass what with my Toyota being in the shop for major surgery again.

Luckily our receptionist, Melody, lives near my apartment and I can catch a ride to work with her. (Can you imagine being just twenty-one and still living at home? I can't imagine living with my folks now – it wasn't so great before I left for college.)

Yep, things could be mega worse and we both know it. I'm glad you stayed in school. I can't wait to call you "Dr. Easton" and read your doctoral dissertation on the mating habits of the Colobus monkey – or have you come up with a better animal? I'm sure that beefy, brown male body that warms the other side of your bed qualifies as an "animal." You could use the electric shock thingy on Jamal like we did in that psych experiment with those lab rats. Knowing how twisted Jamal's mind is, I'm sure he'd love it! ☺

God, my mind is wandering…Here it is only 2 PM and I'm losing it. I just now remembered that tonight is Ladies Night at the club downstairs in the plaza, too. I'd better get the important stuff off my desk so I can afford to be partially hung-over tomorrow. You know how I can't resist those "two for one" specials!

Later,
Jodi

*****

"He loves my muffins!"

Jodi Baker traipsed blissfully unaware into the break room at the same time her animated co-worker shrieked the good news.

"Excuse me?"

"I said, 'He loves my muffins,'" Raheesha Tate pronounced deliberately as if Jodi were deaf. "He said he really likes my homemade muffins."

"We all do. You're a great muffin maker, Raheesha."

Grinning, Jodi reached into the break room refrigerator, retrieved a diet Coke and popped the tab. "So, who is this person who's in awe of your culinary prowess?"

"Brent, of course." The big-boned, well-fleshed woman breathed out a proud sigh with her head held high, her enormous chest practically filling the closet-like room. "You know who I'm talking about—our newest member of Hit-On-Us Incorporated?"

"Sh!" Jodi lowered her voice. "Don't let Mr. Johansson hear you say that. Remember how bent out of shape he was when the bakery abbreviated our company's name on that sheet cake last Christmas? I thought he'd have a stroke."

"I thought he'd have a stroke when he realized our Frankie was a bit 'different' than your average male." Raheesha chuckled then turned to place her empty plate into the small sink. "Never have I seen a white guy turn so pale before. I didn't think it was possible."

"Neither have I. But let's not hold Mr. J's lack of judgment against him. He hired us, didn't he?"

"That he did. And he hired Mr. Brent Davison, too. So Mr. J's judgment can't be all the whacked. You see all the diplomas and certifications Brent has on his wall?"

Jodi shrugged and took a swig of her Coke. "No, I

haven't made the obligatory cubicle visit yet. I take it you have?"

"Yes I have—and so have all your fellow co-workers. Babs is already working on the man to sign him up for her regular Friday morning half court b-ball game at the Y."

Jodi quirked an eyebrow. "This guy is a jock?"

"No, I don't think so, but she's hoping to change his mind."

"Well, if Babs could get Frankie out of his spike heels and skirt for an hour to run up and down the court with her, she stands a chance with our new inmate. He actually wears pants."

Raheesha slapped her ample thigh and hooted. "Oo, girlfriend! You kill me with that wicked sense of humor of yours. And speaking of the afterlife here on earth, Lotus muttered some mumbo-jumbo and gave his cubicle a pagan blessing of some sort. To ward off bad files or bad karma or something so she said."

Rolling her eyes, Jodi took another sip of her drink. "Lolo is a sweetheart, but I withhold judgment on how crazy that sounds. Who else has visited our gulag's newest prisoner?"

"Well, Keryn got his computer set up and made a big deal out of passing him one of her flashy business cards—the one with the hologram on it. Melody shuffled in and said hello and shuffled out without raising her head once, as usual. And last, but certainly not least, Ms. Gabriela 'The Femme Fatale' Roget waltzed in and practically propositioned the man while he was organizing his pencil drawer."

Jodi cringed. "Ugh. I swear Gabby reminds me of

my parents' cocker spaniel. You think getting her fixed would help?"

"All right, Ms. High-and-Mighty." Raheesha placed her hands on her broad hips and laughed. You better get your lily-white ass in there quick and say hello so he don't go on thinking you're a snobby bitch. Heck, we all know you are, but we love ya just the same."

"Ha, ha. I love you, too, you overbearing mama." Jodi gave her a quick hug. "You're the only woman I know under the age of thirty-five who still believes the way to a man's heart is through his stomach."

"But it is," Raheesha insisted as they exited the break room and strolled down the narrow hall leading to the cube farm. "Sex is dessert, but food truly nourishes the soul. I should know, being well nourished myself."

"You finished off all the muffins already?" Lotus Blossom poked her head around the opening of her cubicle, the first on the block. "I only ate a couple."

"I didn't finish them off, Flower Child. Our newest co-worker did."

Lotus's thin face crumpled like a used paper cup. "Oh, but honey-bran is my favorite."

"I'll make some more tonight just for you. Promise." Raheesha crossed her heart with a plump finger. "Besides, Jojo here couldn't be pried from her computer during lunch to have even one, remember?"

Lotus scooted her desk chair to the doorway and prayerfully pressed her hands together in front of her bright green paisley-printed, butterfly-sleeved top. "You starting a diet, Jojo?"

"No, I just didn't feel hungry today," Jodi admitted. Thoughts of her two-timing ex-fiancé suddenly rushed into her consciousness further depressing her appetite. "I stayed in my cubbyhole and e-mailed my college roommate instead."

"I see." A Zen-like look of understanding washed over their resident hippie's petite features, her expression made even plainer by a complete lack of cosmetics. "You enjoy electronic correspondence more than interacting with your fellow humans."

Good grief! The office psychiatrist was really hitting her stride now.

"Sometimes. It's also been a while since I'd heard from Shayna, and I wanted to know how her latest animal behavior experiments were coming along."

Lotus lifted a thin, blonde eyebrow. "Behavior experiments?"

Got her! Jodi felt a surge of pride in being able to use her co-worker's interests to her best advantage.

"Yes, I'll have to tell you all about Shayna's experiments sometime. Right now I have to go introduce myself to Brad or whatever his name is."

"His name is Brent," Raheesha corrected her. She breezed past Jodi and squeezed into her playpen next door. "Be nice or else, ya hear?"

Jodi laughed. "Yes, Mom."

Lotus raised her other eyebrow then scooted back into her office. Jodi marched down to the last cubicle on the left and summarily knocked on the aluminum door frame.

"Hello?" No answer. Jodi was about to return to her own pen when a grunt halted her in her tracks.

"Oh, hello," came a monotone reply. "You can come in."

Jodi took a step inside the cubicle and quickly scanned its contents. Raheesha was right about the certificates—about six were framed and already hanging on pegs set in the coarse fabric-covered walls. Her new officemate sat with his backed turned to her at his perfectly organized desk complete with blotter, flip calendar, stapler and a paperclip holder. Odd, nothing as personal as a hand-painted vase, a child's colored picture or even a small framed family photo interrupted the otherwise sterile surface.

"You're one of my co-workers, I take it?" His eyes never left the computer screen.

"Yes, I'm Jodi—Jodi Baker." She held out her hand then on second thought lowered it. "I'm in the cubicle right across the hall. Sorry I didn't make your acquaintance at lunchtime like the others. I was…busy."

He continued to scroll down the spreadsheet he was engrossed in. "Same here."

So cold, so abrupt. She wouldn't have to worry about winning the "most unfriendly cubicle denizen" award again this coming Memorial Day at the annual company picnic. Jodi slowly reversed her steps.

"Well, I'll let you get back to your work now. Nice to meet you, Brad."

He turned halfway in his chair, observing her from the corner of his eye. "Brent. The name is Brent Davison."

"Of course it is. How silly of me," Jodi blabbered, trying hard to make light of her faux pas as she backed out of the cubicle blindly. "Ooo!"

Jodi's backside bounced off the doorframe. She toppled over onto her hands and knees. Brent materialized next to her, kneeling at her side.

"You okay?" His tone signified concern.

Jodi slowly nodded, her gaze immediately captured by his closeness. His eyes glowed with an amber tint that she hadn't noticed when he entered the office yesterday afternoon. A shock of thick, chin-length, wavy, brown-black hair fanned across his cheek, giving him a guarded and dangerous look. Her palms dampened. It couldn't be because her small hands were cradled in his large, strong ones, could it? Mesmerized, she momentarily forgot to breathe.

"Can you stand?"

"Uh…sure."

Once she regained her feet, Brent released her and returned to his desk. "You have to be careful moving about in these cages. They're practically closet-sized." .

Gasping for air, Jodi forced her gaze away from his noble profile of aquiline nose, strong chin and broad cheekbones. The guy had to be at least six foot four, too. He could be a *GQ* model.

"You're not kidding," she managed at last. "These things are not even as big as a walk-in closet ."

He sat back in his desk chair, a wisp of a smile dangling on his full lips. "Just watch where you're going from now on, Ms. Baker."

"It's Jodi," she reminded him, returning his shy grin. "Jodi. I promise you won't jinx yourself if you say it."

His smile instantly disappeared. "Of course not.

I'm not superstitious."

Smack! She saw stars. Their easy camaraderie evaporated just as quickly as it had been established. What happened?

"I didn't say you were." Jodi immediately headed for her own private sanctuary.

"From cover model to creep in seconds flat. How the hell did he manage that?" she muttered, plopping down at her desk. Where had that brick wall come from? Was it her or him? Most likely him.

Sighing, Jodi shook her head clear of the cobwebs of unrewarding human interaction. She pulled out the next work order in her in basket, forcing herself to focus on her next exciting task…arranging air travel for a visiting delegation of Japanese businessmen.

*****

TO: MrBoJangles@crapster.net
FROM: bdavison@hit-on-us.com
SUBJECT: Send in the rescue squad

Yo, Bo –

You were right. I'm not into this sort of thing. An all woman office may be a dream come true for you hyperactive playboys, but it's about to send me over the edge…I've already been propositioned, stuffed with goodies, asked to play basketball (which you know I despise), prayed over by a retro-hippy, told in excruciating detail what kind of computer set-up I'm using and then accused of being superstitious. The closest thing to a normal person we have around here is the receptionist, and she's the original, "Don't look at me, I'm not worthy" type. At least Ms. Superstitious has a nice smile and curvy, well-padded back side. Yeah, right – stop drooling on your keyboard!

I'm tempted to throw in the towel after six hours on the job, but I don't want to hear it from Gramps again. He keeps telling me I have to "let her go" and get on with my life, but I can't. I won't. Nothing will ever make me forget her. Nothing.

Sorry to get dismal on you. How's the music business treating you these days? You ever get a gig at that music festival you were talking about? Come on up to St. Louis sometime and I'll take you to one of the jazz bars. Or a hockey game – your choice.

Back to the rock pile now. I miss U bro –
B

*****

"The man's gotta be gay." Gabriela Roget rolled her eyes, leaning closer to the Zodiac Café's women's room mirror as she reapplied a thick coating of her shocking mauve lipstick. The hideously bright color perfectly coordinated with her short skirt, sequined halter top and platform sandals. "There's just no other explanation for it."

"What makes you say that?" Barbara "Babs" Calloni, attired in loose, black silk pants and matching tank top, sat cross-legged in the corner, braiding her long brown hair into twin pigtails to pin onto the top of her head before she headed to the dance floor for some serious dancing.

Gabriela tossed her straightened bleached-blonde locks over one shoulder and sniffed loudly. "How do I know he's gay? Why, I made it easy for him to ask me out tonight and he completely ignored me. Can you imagine that? He's either gay or from another planet."

"His aura was a bit off now that you mention it." Lotus thoughtfully rearranged the many strands of wooden beads about her neck. "It could mean he's not human. But then again, it could mean he simply isn't eating enough fiber."

"Fiber? The man has been eating more than enough fiber," Raheesha called out from one of the stalls where she sat straightening her queen-sized panty hose. "He polished off my honey-bran muffins quick enough. Isn't that right, Flower Child?"

Lotus sighed. "Yes, he did."

"You're crazy if you think our new playmate is some kind of alien, Roget," Keryn Wiseman chided, emerging from the other stall. She adjusted her crisp, gray blazer, dusted off her matching slacks and tilted her chin high, admiring the swing of her straight black hair arranged in a bowl cut. "Brent's an intellectual, and intellectuals don't care for vapid females fawning all over them. He respects intelligence and ingenuity. And there's simply no competition in that department in our office, now is there?"

"Yeah, none whatsoever," Jodi said under her breath, struggling to get her hair pick through her mass of thick, dishwater blonde curls that seemed to have taken on a life of their own tonight. "Ow! God, I hate this fuzzy mane of mine."

"Break another tooth in your comb?" Melody quickly finished her primping and handed hers to Jodi without a second thought. "Your hair gets real ornery on humid days, doesn't it?"

Jodi accepted the comb, smiling at her bashful co-worker with mousy-brown, shoulder-length hair. Melody's lime green, polyester pantsuit looked like something she turned up after raiding her grandmother's closet.

"Thanks, Mel. You're a lifesaver and you're absolutely right. Humidity and my hair is a lethal combination. I should just pull it up in a clip or something. What'd ya think?"

Melody nibbled at a well-chewed nail. "It's cooler to pull it up on top and it does make you look more 'dressy' in a way."

Jodi frowned at her rather crumpled appearance in the vanity mirror. Her slim-cut denim skirt and light blue peasant blouse displayed the more crumbly remains of her hastily devoured dinner of McDonald's French fries and a chocolate shake. "Yes, I could stand to look a bit more 'together' here, couldn't I? Grab me a paper towel, will ya, so I can sponge this spot off my skirt."

"I'm ready to hit the 'meat market'," Gabriela announced to no one in particular. "Who all's coming?"

"I'm there," Babs replied. "Keryn, you ready to strut your stuff?"

"Why the hell not?" The computer tech sighed as she followed behind the others. "It's not like any of these assholes are worthy of my valuable attention."

The stall door banged opened. Raheesha tugged her caftan-style dress into place and rolled her eyes. "I think the 'assholes' as Keryn calls the male population of this office complex, are entirely too worthy of her and that's one reason why the woman can't ever get a date."

Lotus stifled a laugh behind her hand. "Oh, Rae. You may be right on the money, but I can't believe you said such a thing."

"I can." Jodi winked at her generously proportioned friend in the mirror. "It's her attitude that turns them off. If Keryn could only stop acting like she's some kind of Miss-Know-It-All and admit she's as scared and lonely as the next person then she'd come across as being halfway human and get lucky occasionally."

"It's her pride that does her in," Melody added. "Too much pride puts men off. That's why I try to act as humble as I possibly can all the time." She slumped against the mirror shelf, frowning. "I wonder why it doesn't seem to work."

Raheesha put an arm around Melody's shoulder, giving her a friendly squeeze. "Humility is one thing, but you don't have to act like a doormat, Honey."

Melody eyebrows knitted together in puzzlement. "Doormat? I act like a doormat?"

Jodi, Lotus and Raheesha exchanged meaningful looks and shook their heads.

"We'll explain it to you later, Mel," Jodi said. She disposed of the damp paper towel she had used to blot her skirt clean and quickly pulled her wayward curls atop her head with a banana clip. "Okay, I'm ready to trip the light fantastic and get some great two-for-one drink specials. How about you guys?"

"Go for it, girlfriend." Grinning, Raheesha pointed to the door.

Bellying up to the bar, Jodi ordered their usual round of drinks—three light beers and lemon-flavored mineral water for Lotus—then joined her comrades at their usual big round table in the back, close to the dance floor. Gabriela and Keryn sat calmly sipping their drinks watching Babs gyrate and jump about on the raised dais beneath the swirl and splash of lights, oblivious to the fact that not a single person—male or female—had yet joined her.

"Our Babs is a one woman dance machine," Lotus shouted over the booming music as she twisted off the cap on her bottled water. "I can't figure out how she possesses so much energy when all she eats is processed food."

"Some people were just born to dance." Gabriela's eyes glowed as the first few men left the safety of the bar area and made their way toward the dance floor. "And some people were just born to do the wild thing." She put down her drink and stood. "Excuse me, ladies. I see a few familiar faces I need to become reacquainted with."

"Only a few?" Keryn laughed.

Gabriela pretended to pout. "Don't worry. I'll steer the extras over this way."

They watched in silence as the man-eater in pink sauntered to the middle of the dance floor. True to her word, Gabriela was soon encircled by four left-footed, office-types with ties askew and shirt collars unbuttoned.

"One with too many, one without." Melody rested an elbow on the table. "Too bad we couldn't get Brent to come down and dance with us. He seems like such a nice guy."

"Nice?" Jodi felt the hairs on the back of her neck bristle. "Nice isn't the word that comes to mind when I consider our latest fellow employee."

"Didn't Gabriela say maybe he was from outer space?" Lotus interjected. "That could explain his odd manners. Maybe it's okay where he's from to ignore his co-workers and consume large quantities of muffins."

"Maybe," Raheesha drawled, "but I sure wish he'd eat less of my homemade goodies and take a big bite o' me instead."

Jodi put her hands to her throat and stuck out her tongue.

"Yeah, he isn't half-bad looking," Keryn remarked casually. "What do you think of his hair? Too rock star or just right?"

Lotus sighed dreamily, settling her thin face into her bony hands. "I'd say just right."

"Me too," Melody said, giggling.

"I'll take 'em with long hair or short as long as they got what it counts in the trouser area." Raheesha grinned and rubbed her hands together. "And with that height and those big hands of his…Well, I bet he's more than okay in that department."

Jodi started to cough. "You guys make me sick. The man is a loser with a capital 'L'. He's a snob. Just forget about Brent What's-His-Face ever wanting to go out with any one of us."

"Who wouldn't want to go out with any one of us?" A flush-faced Babs collapsed into an empty seat next to Jodi. "With all we have to offer, any fool who'd frequent this dive would be happy if we'd gave him the time of day."

"Ain't that the truth," Raheesha concurred.

Gabriela breezed to her seat and took a long sip of her beer. "God, some of the creeps who walk into this place."

"What, no crumbs to cast to us poor dogs?" Keryn teased.

"Hell, no. I wouldn't send those jerks to chat up even my worst enemy."

"What happened, Gabby? Weren't any of them interested in taking you out?" Melody asked wide-eyed.

"No, they *all* were interested. That's the problem."

Melody shook her head, confused. "The problem?"

Keryn took pity on their youngest and most naïve group member. "She means they all wanted to head over to the Marriott and share a room with her."

"Well, it is cheaper the more people share," Melody began, the light slowly dawning in her brain. "Oh…It would be one girl and four guys sharing a room."

"Exactly." Raheesha shook her head sadly. "Uhm-uhm. What is the world coming to these days?"

Lotus absentmindedly counted her beads. "You know, we really should invite Brent to accompany us next Tuesday night. He could always act as our bodyguard and scare off the deviants."

"Hey, I'll pound those assholes into the ground if you want me to, Gabby." Babs slammed down her Manhattan Iced Tea. "Just give the word and I'd be happy to practice my kick boxing technique on their flabby ab walls."

Gabriela grinned. "Thanks for the offer, Babs, but I don't want to cause a scene. It wouldn't be good for my image."

"It wouldn't be good for any of our 'images,'" Keryn agreed.

Lotus took a sip of her bottled water and nodded. "That's why I think we should invite Brent. He wouldn't have to necessarily 'date' any of us, just be our companion."

"But why wouldn't he want to date any of us?" Gabriela raised her chin and put her hands on her hips. "Aren't we good enough for him?"

"No, we're not." Jodi crossed her arms. The finality of her words caused everyone at the table to turn and stare at her.

"Why are you so anti-male, Jodi?" Keryn took a long sip of her drink, considering her through narrowed eyes. "It's not like you to be so negative."

Jodi squirmed in her seat. She usually wasn't the naysayer of the group, but something about Brent Davison rubbed her the wrong way. All she sensed about the man was trouble... Why should she encourage her friends and coworkers to walk into a hopeless situation?

"I'm not negative. I just don't get good vibes from

the guy, that's all."

"Well, he *is* from Mars after all," Melody said, supporting her friend's conclusion.

"Mars?" Raheesha quirked an eyebrow. "You mean like we women are from Venus and men are from Mars?"

Melody giggled, sloshing her beer over the sides of her glass as she placed it on her coaster. "Oh, I was being silly. I meant he seems like he comes from another planet like Gabby said in the bathroom, but that works, too."

"Yes, he's definitely a Martian." Lotus looked off into the distance, idly twisting her strand of beads. "Maybe this is his first reincarnation as an Earth man?"

"And you think just because Brent comes from another planet he wouldn't want to date any of us?" Keryn asked. "I could go along with that line of reasoning provided we dropped the flaky part about him being a Martian. He's just an asshole—that's all."

Babs briskly tapped her drink stirrer on the tabletop. "I don't know about our newest Hit-On-US inmate being a space alien, but I'll bet you guys a round of drinks that I can get Brent to take me out by next week."

"You're on." Keryn took a sip of her drink and leaned back in her chair. "I'll bet I can get Mr. Brent Davison to go out with me before he agrees to go out with any of you. Any takers?"

Lotus dropped her beads and wrapped her knuckles on the table. "I'm not much of a gambler, but I'm sure I can get him to be our companion to Ladies' Night. I'll buy you all a round of mineral water if I can't."

A group grumble gave credence to the popularity of that idea. Lotus threw up her hands in defeat.

"Oh, all right. I'll buy everyone a drink—alcoholic or not—of their choice if I can't get him to accompany us."

"You all are wasting your time," Jodi warned. "The man's impossible."

Gabriela stroked her chin thoughtfully. She leaned toward the others, lowering her voice as the dance music faded.

"You know, I think we all should attempt this 'impossible task' as Jodi terms it. First one to successfully seduce our resident Martian and go out on a date with him gets free drinks from everyone for an entire year's worth of Ladies' Night at the Zodiac Café."

Raheesha looked askance at her co-workers. "I don't know. That's a bit rich for my pocketbook. I can imagine how much some of y'all would drink if the drinks were on someone else's tab."

"That's what makes the bet so fun." Babs grinned and wiggled her eyebrows. "High stakes—high risk."

"My dad would kill me if I spent all my paycheck on booze." Melody bit her bottom lip. "But this bet thing sounds sort of fun to me. Count me in."

"Mel!" Jodi gasped. "You can't be serious."

"Of course she's serious." Keryn placed a protective arm around their inexperienced office receptionist then scanned the others' reactions. "What about it, Raheesha? I've never known you to run from a challenge before."

The big woman tapped a finger to her fleshy, mocha-tinted lips. "I don't usually. You're right. I like a good challenge, and I'm curious about how those full lips of his feel on any number of erogenous zones. All right, I'm in, too."

Jodi sighed, rolling her eyes. "The whole world has gone mad."

"You're the only one who's not playing. What's up, Jojo?" Gabriela pouted playfully. "Ah, come on and be a sport and give it a try."

"Actually it's better if Jodi doesn't join in on our little bet," Keryn said. "We need a 'control group' for this experiment anyway. Six of us with six different methods to seduce our Martian against Jodi who will do absolutely nothing. Right?"

Jodi finished her beer and put down her empty glass. "You're damn right about that. I'll be in 'control' and that's all I'll ever be."

"Good. It means less competition for the rest of us," Lotus said under her breath.

"Yeah, that could only help," Melody agreed.

Babs pounded a drum roll on the table. "And so the race begins…"

Jodi slapped her forehead in disgust. How could her otherwise reasonably sane office mates suddenly turn into a pack of drooling idiots? Were they all so hypnotized by Brent Davison's great looking ass and his sexy, dark, good looks that they couldn't understand the man wouldn't cooperate with their plans in the least?

"Well, good luck on your bet, ladies," she said, sighing. "You're sure as heck going to need it."

Chapter Two

TO: ShaynaE@wazoo.com
FROM: jbaker@hit-on-us.com
SUBJECT: All is fair…

Hey, Woman!

I'm glad you answered my on-my-knees-groveling emails at last. Sorry to hear about your grad advisor's asinine attitude. Can you get a new one at this stage of the game? I'll keep sending positive thoughts your way. I know you can handle the work load and come through with flying colors. Keep your chin up.

In the meantime, I'll cheer you up with the latest gossip around here. ☺

Remember I told you about this "bet" all the double X chromosome inmates (excluding moi) made with each other to get this Brent guy to take one of them out? You wouldn't believe the amount of weirdness going on here lately. Raheesha has turned into Betty Crocker full-time, and she's playing right into Babs's hands. The poor guy is going to have to take up sports to get his waistline under control. I just hope he doesn't keel over from a diabetic seizure first. Of course, with our resident "herbalist" on staff, he may come out of it okay. I'm surprised at the professionalism Lotus displays while she dishes out her homemade tea mixtures to help soothe Brent's upset stomach. Maybe there's something to that herbal stuff she touts after all.

I'm not sure what the "suits" (aka Keryn and Gabriela) are up to yet. I think they're both trying a low-key approach, waiting for an opportune moment to dash in quietly for the kill. However, it does seem that Brent is experiencing more than his fair share of computer troubles lately.

Melody has contemplated taking herself out of the running. She confessed her fears on the issue to me while we were driving home last night.

*****

"It's no use." Melody sniffed loudly. She quickly floored the gas on her silver Kia and tore out of the parking lot. "What would a gorgeous guy like Brent ever see in me?"

Jodi bit her lip and growled. She felt royally pissed off with her co-workers for putting such a sweet thing like Melody up to this kind of nonsense. Couldn't they see what it was doing to the poor girl's self-esteem?

"What did you say?" Melody stopped the car with a jerk at the first traffic light.

Jodi composed herself then flashed a smile at her companion. "Nothing. I'm just angry with everyone for making you feel this way about yourself, Mel. You're a wonderful person. You're very warm and caring and beautiful and good. You shouldn't have to force guys to like you. They should love you for just the way you are—and if they don't, that's their problem not yours."

"But I'm a 'doormat'," she wailed, accelerating the car onto the I-270 expressway. "Rae said so. No guy likes a doormat. But what can I do? I'm no good at being assertive. I've tried—honest I have."

"Then keep on trying. But, most of all, be yourself and like yourself. It'll shine through. Keep your head up and believe in yourself. Trust me on this one, okay?"

Sighing, Melody absentmindedly fiddled with the radio tuner. "I will. You like yourself, Jodi. I can tell. You didn't let your world go to pot after that jerk-off dumped you at the altar last year. I should follow your shining example."

Jodi leaned away, shielding her pained face from her friend by staring out the passenger side window. Maybe she had bent the truth a bit when she told Melody how well she handled her disappointment concerning Cade. If she had managed her heartache better she wouldn't be working at Hit-On-Us and hitching a ride in Melody's car at this moment. She'd be studying for her MBA at Harvard or good old Mizzou. Anyway, she'd be doing what she had planned on doing with her life instead of hiding out in St. Louis and working at a dead-end job until she got her act together.

"I'm not sure I was altogether successful on that score, Mel." Jodi sighed. "But thanks for the compliment."

"You're welcome. I think you came through the horrid experience with flying colors. You're still here, aren't you?"

Jodi bit her lower lip. Suicide had never been an option. Her parents would have killed her if she had wasted the four years of schooling they had paid for with their hard-earned money.

"Uh, yeah, I'm still here. I wish I was in grad school sometimes, but I'm still here, and I'm gainfully employed—which isn't something to sneeze at in this day and age. Thanks for putting things into perspective for me."

Jodi took a deep breath and relaxed in her seat. Traffic had begun to thicken on the congested commuting trail. "You know it almost seems the whole 'Cade affair' is becoming a distant memory for me. Eventually, I may even forget the asshole's last name."

Mel signaled to change lanes—a rare gesture in St. Louis rush hour traffic. "What is Cade's last name by the way? I don't think you ever told me."

"It's..." Jodi's tongue froze in place. Was it possible? Had she forgotten Cade's last name?

"His name was Cade..." She ran a hand through her frizzy hair and furrowed her brow. *Think! Mr. and Mrs. Cade Something-or-Other.*

"Sears," she spit out at last. "That's it. His last name was Sears—like the department store. I dated the fool for years. How on earth could I ever forget his last name?"

A smile tugged at the corners of Melody's lips. "I think you already know the answer to that question. You're totally over Mr. Asshole—pardon my French. That's how you could forget his last name."

"Could be."

Jodi experienced an odd reaction just then, something that hadn't occurred in ages. She actually didn't feel scalding tears welling in the corner of her eyes at the thought of Cade What's-His-Name and their broken engagement. She didn't feel anything positive or negative about her idiot ex-fiancé anymore.

She was over the whole sordid affair at last.

"Maybe you ought to join us in the 'get Brent to take one of us on a date' bet," Melody ventured.

"No way. I'd never stoop to something so low—"

"I was willing to do it," her chauffer cut in. "You don't think I'd stoop to anything 'low', do you? I may be a 'doormat' but I'm not living in the basement yet."

Melody's hurt look cut Jodi to the quick. "No, of course you don't live in the basement," she explained. "You possess high standards. It's just different for me, that's all."

"How so?"

Jodi frowned. How was it different for her? In the past, she would have gladly taken on her drinking pals in such a silly and inconsequential bet, but something this time didn't feel quite right. Could it have something to do with the object of their bet—tall, dark and handsome Brent Davison?

Could it be she felt attracted to the man—the first man she'd felt anything for in a long, long time?

"I can't explain it," Jodi said. "Let's just stop talking about the whole thing, okay?"

"Okay. Still, don't you think Brent is dreamy looking? He's so tall and I can tell he's got muscles under that jacket and—"

"I thought you said you weren't interested in snaring Brent What's-His-Face," Jodi interrupted. "So let's not discuss the matter anymore."

"Oh, I don't know," Mel drawled thoughtfully. "I'm thinking of getting back into the race now and following your advice. I'll keep my head high and allow my true self to shine through for Brent. What do you think?"

Jodi's jaw dropped open in surprise. If sweet Melody Martz ever let her sweet, charming self shine through there wouldn't be a man on earth who could resist the young receptionist's charms. She swallowed hard. Why did the fact that Brent could easily fall for Melody cause a lump to form in her throat?

Jodi blinked several times and forced a grin. "If you show the world how truly great you are the others don't stand a chance."

Melody tossed her head back and laughed as they sped under the I-44 overpass. "Raheesha is so right. What a sense of humor you have, Jojo. I'm so glad you're my friend."

"I'm glad you're my friend, too."

Jodi sighed inwardly. She only wanted what was best for Melody—and catching a boyfriend might just bolster her friend's self-confidence. Still, Jodi felt an odd stabbing in the heart at the thought of Melody dating Brent.

TO: MrBoJangles@crapster.net
FROM: bdavison@hit-on-us.com
SUBJECT: Request for immediate back-up

Calling all squad cars!

Bo-man, you've just got to come out here and rescue me from these women.

Shut up and can the laughter. I know what you're thinking. It's not that. They're just absolutely insane, that's all. No, I'm not laying every skirt that crosses my path – since only two of my colleagues wear a dress on a regular basis anyhow. One shows her ass off all the time, which wouldn't be too bad actually if she didn't somehow remind me of a creepy reincarnation of an early Britney Spears. The other one wears long, flowing skirts and beads and practices witchcraft for all I know. I just wish they'd all leave me the hell alone!

A friggin' "good morning" is encouragement enough for some of these vampires. At least I'm saving money on groceries, what with all the great baked goodies one of my co-workers has brought to work on a daily basis this past week. I may even have to take up some kind of sport to burn off the calories if the Martha Stewart clone keeps up the cookie baking.

Gotta go. Something is screwed-up with my monitor – again. Our tech person knows what the hell she's doing sometimes.

Peace,
B

*****

Whack!

"Damn computer…"

Jodi startled and swiveled around in her desk chair. The smacking sound came from across the passageway, quickly followed by a long string of muttered curse words that only the male of the species could do justice to. She rose to investigate.

"Can I help?"

Brent twisted about at his desk. "Other than get me a new job? I don't think so."

Jodi understood the feeling well. She quirked an eyebrow, casually shifting her weight to lean a foot against his back cubicle wall.

"I can't believe your machine is acting up so much. I thought you got a brand new system. It must be a lemon."

"Purchased by our chief lemonade-maker and totally misnamed co-worker, Ms. Keryn *Wise*man, no doubt?" A slight sneer curled the corners of Brent's full lips, making him appear more sensual than cynical. "I guess that only goes to show the flaws inherent in the Equal Opportunity Act."

Frowning, Jodi crossed her arms. "What are you implying?"

"Nothing. It was wrong of me to say that. I apologize. After all, I am the 'token male' around here, aren't I? I shouldn't bad-mouth the government for protecting a single male's right to hold a steady job in this day and age."

Sheesh! He sounded worse than her older brother after he was downsized from his job.

"You've got a rotten attitude, Brent Davison. Has

anyone ever told you that?"

He tilted back in his chair, staring out of the corner of his eye at his sickly monitor. "Not in the last month or so. But I do appreciate being reminded from time to time. Thanks for caring."

"Don't mention it." She turned to leave.

"And I do mean thanks," he called out. "You've been very cooperative. I sincerely appreciate it."

Jodi froze in mid-step at the doorway then spun around to re-enter the cubicle. "Excuse me?"

Brent leaned forward and softened his tone. "I just wanted to tell you that you've been a wonderful cubicle neighbor. No plates of tempting desserts shoved under my nose, no awful tasting herbal remedies forced down my throat, no repeated attempts to sign me up for a sport I detest. I can't thank you enough for utterly ignoring my presence in the office this week."

So…the girls' plans to seduce Brent Davison were falling short of the mark. The idea brought a smile to Jodi's lips. She crossed her eyes and stuck out her tongue at him in mock disgust. "Gee, thanks. You're entirely welcome. It's been my pleasure."

He chuckled. "Please don't mention it—you know I sure as hell won't."

Brent flashed a wicked grin before slapping his computer again on the side. Miraculously, the distorted image on the monitor corrected itself.

"Hey, neighbor, I think you ought to put in for Keryn's job. Your mojo seems to work better than hers does. Yours even works from across the room."

"Ta-da!" Jodi snapped her fingers and wiggled her

nose. "I'm your magic genie next door. If you have any other problems that need fixing, you know exactly where to find me."

He scratched his chin, considering her for a long moment then nodded. "Yeah, you're right. I do."

Exiting, Jodi hummed a happy tune. Even wearing flats she felt ten inches taller today.

Chapter Three

TO: ShaynaE@wazoo.com
FROM: jbaker@hit-on-us.com
SUBJECT: Who could have seen that coming?

Hello…hello?

Is there an echo in here? I didn't hear from you yesterday and it got me worried. Don't turn into a total geekazoid who practically lives in the library! ☺

Things around here have been turned utterly upside down in the "Who will seduce the Martian first contest." (That's Lotus's name for all the insanity.) Guess what? It turns out our token male has a heart after all…and he's escorting Melody to her cousin's wedding reception this Friday.

Who could have seen that coming? First off, Mel actually had the guts to ask Brent to be her date to the wedding reception and then Brent actually said yes. To say the mood in this office has transformed into one of totally "freaked out" is an understatement. Demoralized is more like it. I think even Gabriela is seriously contemplating becoming a nun.

I guess things will calm down now that this silly bet thing has been resolved and return back to normal—wherever the hell that is.

And I, for one, will be glad not to listen to all the incessant gossip about What's-His-Face anymore. It really gives me a heartache.

Gotta go now. It's "TGIF" night at the club tonight, and I need to get this stuff out of my inbox before five.

TTFN,
Jodi

*****

TO: ShaynaE@wazoo.com
FROM: jbaker@hit-on-us.com
SUBJECT: boo-boo

I was typing way too fast there... I meant to say "headache" not "heartache". Any way, I'm just glad this dumb bet thing is over.
J

*****

"Anyone wanna shoot some hoops with me tomorrow?" Babs scanned the silent ensemble. Each one shook her head no. The "TGIF" happy hour at the Zodiac Café was far from happy for the majority of the female denizens of Holliday's International Travel Online US.

"Sure, why not?" Keryn said at last. She picked up her half-empty glass of dollar draft beer, seriously studying the remainder of its sudsy contents. "Gotta get in shape for the next one who comes along and slips through my fingers. *Cie la vie.*"

"Well, I don't think our little contest is over yet, ladies." Gabriela crossed her arms across her chest and frowned. "We agreed that the first one of us to get Brent to take us out on a date was the winner. He's not really on a date with Mel. He didn't initiate it—so it doesn't count. It doesn't even come close to counting and—"

"Now, wait a cotton pickin' second," Raheesha interrupted. "We didn't say it had to be him who did the asking. In fact, I was about to ask Brent out to see that famous French TV chef do a demonstration of his new cookware over at the Galleria but Melody got to him first."

"That's only because she sits up at the desk by the front door. She waved that big, engraved wedding invitation at Brent first thing when he walked into the office," Lotus noted wryly, twirling her beads. "I was completely surprised to hear her initiate a conversation like that—particularly with a Martian. She acted self-assured, confident. I was amazed. Melody wasn't quite herself. Could she be channeling a more assertive spirit?"

"Could be. Maybe Melody's been taken over by an evil spirit or something?" Keryn's eyes narrowed. "That might explain all the monitor trouble we've been having lately."

Lotus almost choked on her mineral water. "Do you think so? It's not just faulty video cards in our machines? An evil spirit…I was thinking along the exact same lines."

"Oh, will you guys get off the demon possession kick." Jodi groaned. She hated watching Keryn bait poor Lotus who was easily led astray when it came to the supernatural. "I was the one who put Mel up to asking Brent out."

"You?" came a chorus of shocked voices.

"Yes, me."

Jodi banged her mug down on the table for emphasis then wiped her upper lip on the back of her hand. Somehow, instilling confidence into her shy friend and watching the results turned out to be more painful that she had assumed. Luckily, the numbing effects of massive beer consumption were starting to take hold.

"When Mel told me Tuesday on the drive home about her cousin's wedding and how everyone in her clan would be there with their spouses or dates and how left out she always feels at one of these things...Well, I sort of suggested she pop the question to our token male."

"Token male?" Babs' brows furrowed. "You're saying the only reason Brent got the job in the first place was because our office is almost one-hundred percent female? Why I ought to beat the crap out of him to show to Mr. J. just how useless males can be."

Raheesha placed a calming hand on Babs' shoulder. "No, of course Jodi isn't saying any such thing. Brent's more than qualified for the job—as are most of us."

"That's certainly true." Keryn leaned menacingly toward Jodi. "So, you're the spoiler in our little contest, eh, Baker? You said you were going to be our 'control' and not be involved in the bet. But you got involved, didn't you?"

"Not directly. I only wanted Mel not to feel bad about herself. I never wanted any of you to hate her just because she's sweet and kind..." She paused to sniff long and loud. "I mean, how could Brent have said no to someone with big deer eyes like Mel?"

Raheesha patted Jodi's hand. "How indeed."

Jodi swallowed a crying jag along with the remainder of her beer. *God, what on earth is wrong with me? I want Mel to be happy. I don't give a rat's ass about Brent Davison...So why does it feel like my heart is breaking?*

Gabriela rhythmically tapped a long hot pink fingernail against the table's surface. "It's not going to last, that's for certain. Melody hasn't got what it takes to keep a man's interest. He only went out with her because he felt sorry for her."

Keryn flashed an evil grin. "A mercy date, eh?"

Lotus shook her head and tutted. "That's not being quite fair to Melody. She's a very pretty girl with impeccable manners. Brent could very well be attracted to her."

Gabriela snorted. "Ha! I think not. She wears polyester pantsuits with visible panty lines, and she could stand to lose a few pounds."

"Couldn't we all," Raheesha mumbled.

Gabriela frowned. "And what's that suppose to mean, Rae?"

"Nuthin'. Just that some of us could stand to lower our hemlines a bit to hide our wide thighs."

"Why you—" Gabriela pounded the table with a fist. "You're certainly one to talk about weight, Raheesha Tate."

"Yes, ain't I." She stood and nodded to the door.

"And now I'm taking my fat backside into the little girls' room. Don't none of y'all start sippin' my beer before I get back, or I may decide to sit on top of you and squash you flat."

She turned to Jodi. "You wanna play chaperone?"

Jodi gained her feet slowly. The room seemed a bit wobbly. "Sure."

The two walked to the ladies' room, breathing a sigh of relief in unison.

"Man, I knew it wasn't going to be a picnic tonight, but I didn't think we'd go for each other's jugular." Raheesha sadly shook her head as she headed toward a stall. "Never let a man get between you and your girlfriends is the moral of this story."

"How true." Jodi slumped against the back wall. "I hate myself for even thinking it, but I'm so mad at Mel I could spit."

"Then find you a spittoon and share it with Babs. She's got that nasty habit, too." Raheesha's words were muffled behind the stall door. A second later her head popped over the top. "Hey, what are you mad at Melody for? She's your best buddy, isn't she?"

Jodi shrugged, slurping back tears. "Yeah, she is. I only want her to be happy, but…"

"But what?"

"But I didn't think she'd ever take me up on my advice."

"Why, Jodi Baker…You've got a thing for Brent Davison." Raheesha lowered back down.

Jodi crossed her arms and pouted. "No, I do not. I definitely do not have a thing for Brent Davison."

"Sure you don't, girlfriend. Anything you say.

You've just demonstrated all the symptoms of a broken heart, that's all."

"I do not have a broken heart," Jodi protested. But who was she fooling? Even to her own ears it sounded weak.

"Uh-huh. Why didn't you get in on the bet then?"

The sounds of flushing drowned out Jodi's sudden case of hiccups. "I don't believe in that sort of thing."

"Uh-huh."

Raheesha exited the stall, turned on the taps and began washing her hands. Jodi cringed. Was she so transparent? Did the rest of the gang suspect?

"Don't worry. I won't let on to the others," Raheesha assured her. "Heck, to be honest, I don't think I'm that interested in going after Brent's skinny white tail anymore myself. He just doesn't seem to genuinely appreciate good cooking. You ever see the junk food he stashes in his cubicle?"

"You mean the big bucket of Cheesy Poofs?"

The bigger woman straightened up and turned off the taps. "Ah ha—you do have regular contact with the man. You know what foodstuffs he stashes in his cubicle."

Jodi shrugged. "Only because his cell is directly across from mine and only because he's passed his bucket over to me once or twice. Just to be neighborly."

"Fraternizing with the enemy?" Raheesha arched an eyebrow and let out a belly-laugh. "No wonder he passed on my strawberry tarts today. What else you guys share? Already-been-chewed gum?"

"Gross! How can you think such a thing?"

"'Cause you're acting territorial…Like the man is your business and your business alone. You haven't been seeing him on the sly now, have you?"

"No, of course not. He's dating Mel, isn't he?"

"One outing to a cousin's wedding doesn't exactly constitute a date. He isn't sleeping with her, is he?"

Jodi felt her face turn beet red. "He'd better not. I'd…I'd…"

"Kill him?" Raheesha put her hands on her hips and narrowed her eyes. "Or would you rather kill *her*?"

Jodi's chin dropped toward the floor. She sighed. "Both of them."

Raheesha placed a comforting arm around Jodi and guided her toward the exit. They took their time strolling back to their beers.

"Don't worry, Jodi. I gotta strong feeling Mel and Brent won't be sleeping together."

"What makes you say that, Rae?"

"'Cause I can see Mel coming in the front door even now."

Jodi whirled about in confusion. "Huh?"

True enough, Melody was crossing the club floor, heading toward their table in the back.

Jodi scratched her head. "It's not even nine o'clock. What gives?"

"Maybe their date got cancelled?"

"Maybe…but they were going to a wedding reception. How can you cancel a wedding reception?"

Raheesha shrugged. "By canceling the wedding?"

Melody's racking sobs became audible as they reached the table.

"It was terrible, terrible…" Melody moaned into her tissue. "I'll be scarred for life."

"What happened?" Jodi asked. Concern for her pale, obvious distraught friend suddenly took precedence over her jealousy. She squeezed past the others and sat down beside Melody and gently patted her hand. "Did Brent say something rude to you? Did he hurt you? Should we call a hit man and have him rubbed out?"

Mel blew her nose like an elephant trumpeting its presence. "Oh, no, no. Nothing like that. In fact, Brent was the perfect gentleman when he met me at the church and even offered to drive me home after I told him about…" She shook her head and closed her eyes. "But I was just so embarrassed that I turned him down." She started hiccupping. "It was rather rude of me. I guess I should have invited him to come here with me."

"I don't know about that." Raheesha handed her an untouched beer to cry in. "If your date was such a fiasco, I'm not sure prolonging the disaster is wise."

"But the date wasn't a fiasco really. It's just that my cousin…" *Hiccup!* "My cousin, Ernie, he… he…"

"Ran off with another woman?" Gabriela suggested.

"Left the bride at the altar?" Babs wondered aloud.

"Decided to become a monk?" Lotus pressed her palms together in a prayer-like gesture.

"I know." Keryn leaned an elbow on the table, considering their young co-worker with a clinical, detached gaze. "Your cousin ran off with another man."

Melody's mouth dropped open into a perfect 'O' shape. Her hiccupping ceased. "How did you know?"

Keryn shrugged. "Lucky guess. It's an original option compared to the other possibilities. So, how long has your cousin been 'out-of-the-closet'?"

"Not very long." Melody sniffed and glanced down at her watch. "A couple of hours at the most."

Babs began cracking her knuckles in frustration. "What a shitty thing to do to the bride. That asshole needs his butt whacked with a two-by-four."

A titter of nervous laughter circled the table.

"Well put, Babs," Gabriela agreed. "Still, it's better he came clean, so to speak, before the honeymoon, or else the bride would have been really disappointed."

Another wave of tears overcame Melody. "The really sad thing is…she's four months pregnant."

"No!" The cry was universal.

"Yes. And it's his…At least that's what she's been saying all along, but I'm not so sure now."

Jodi put an arm around Melody's shoulder and gave her a hug. "All's well that ends well. So the reception was canceled, and Brent didn't care to be dragged into all the family intrigue, huh?"

"No, he was okay with it. He even said we could go to the reception if I wanted to. But, like I said, I was just so embarrassed and upset and…" She shrugged. "I just couldn't see myself there eating wedding cake and champagne after what Ernie did."

"The reception is still on?" Lotus arched a silvery blond eyebrow. "But you said there was no wedding."

"It seems that Ernie decided that since he'd paid for half the hall and the food, he'd go ahead and have a big party to introduce everyone in the family to Scott."

"Scott?" Babs spat out. "You mean his new boyfriend? That's just tacky."

Melody nodded mutely.

"Definitely sounds like a plotline from a soap opera." Raheesha rolled her eyes. "Still, Brent was nice enough to say he'd go with you. That was real supportive of him."

Melody smiled and wiped her eyes with the corner of a drink napkin. "Isn't it? Wanna know the best thing about the whole horrible evening?"

Gabriela furrowed her brow. "What's that?"

"Brent said he'd take me bowling with him and his grandfather sometime. Wasn't that nice of him?"

"Bowling... with his grandfather? Yeah, right." Keryn chuckled. "That's one hot date all right."

Jodi bristled at the remark. "Hey, at least he asked her out which is more than you can say. Mel is the decided winner of this little bet. And now the bet is over."

Melody perked up immediately. "Yeah, you guys have to buy me free drinks for the rest of the year."

"Well, I already gave you the first one." Raheesha pointed to Melody's glass. "And you've cried in it, so it's good and salty. Cheers."

"Cheers." Melody raised her glass. "What? Isn't anyone going to toast with me? Are you guys all just a bunch of sore losers?"

"Of course not." Jodi clinked her glass to Melody's and gave everyone else the eye. "Mel won the bet fair and square. Didn't she, ladies?"

Everyone raised their glass except Gabriela.

Arching a perfectly plucked eyebrow, she leaned across the table. "You're just glad it's over, Jodi, aren't you? You've been against this little game from the start. I wonder why."

Jodi felt her cheeks instantly warm. She wasn't about to spill her guts in front of this pack of wild hyenas and be torn to bits. Could she trust Raheesha to keep her trap shut?

"Because our Jojo is a person of integrity." Melody lowered her empty beer glass. "She doesn't play the field. She doesn't think men should be bounced about like a basketball or something. She believes in making a life-long commitment to one man and one man alone. Isn't that right?"

"Sort of," Jodi admitted quietly. "I've played the field long enough to know I'm no 'player' and I never want to be."

Raheesha nodded. "You gotta respect that sort of honesty. It's a rare commodity these days."

"Very true," Lotus concurred.

Babs stood, stretched and dusted off the front of her well-worn jeans. "Well, if our pity-party is over for the evening, I'm going to hit the dance floor. Anyone care to join me?"

"I'm there," Keryn answered, quickly downing her drink. "Time for us 'players' to get back on the court I guess. You coming, Gabby?"

Gabriela coolly considered Jodi for a moment then shrugged. "I guess. Still, I'm willing to bet you all a night on the town that I can get Brent Davison into my bed before any of you can even get him to remember your last names."

Babs became all ears. "Is that a bet?"

Gabriela rose, an evil grin spreading across her brightly painted lips. "Yes, it is. Who's on?"

Lotus nervously clacked her beads. "I'm not foolish enough to rush Brent into bed just to win a night on the town, but I bet I can get him to remember my last name before he'll even think twice about sleeping with you."

"My last name, too," Melody added.

Keryn nodded. "I'm with them." Gabriela glared at her.

"Piece of cake." Raheesha grinned. "Jodi?"

Smiling, Jodi stood, her hazel-green eyes locking hard with Gabriela's dark browns. "You definitely can count me in on this little bet. I'll guarantee Brent will know everyone's last name in the office by the end of the week except yours. Count on it."

Chapter Four

TO: MrBoJangles@crapster.net
FROM: bdavison@hit-on-us.com
SUBJECT: Getting friendly with the neighbors

Yo, BJ–

I can handle this job after all. Things really quieted down here this week. The computer is working okay, the muffin barrage has stopped and no one seems to be hassling me at all. My cell mate across the way–Jodi is her name, by the way–says she's taken care of everything. All I have to do is be polite to everyone and remember their names–first and last–before week's end. It's some kind of bet I think. You wonder what females do in the bathroom all day and now you know–they bet over stupid things like whether the new guy can remember your name. You'd think they'd learn to bet on something smart like hockey games.

Jodi's last name is easy to remember. It's "Baker" and Tom Baker was my all time favorite "Doctor Who." The others are coming along. "Lotus Blossom" is one I can't forget. It fits her all too well. Raheesha's name is Tate. I went to high school with a Tate who played tackle and was big like her, so no problem there. Keryn Wiseman thinks she's got the brains of a genius and the looks of pin-up girl, but I think it's the other way around.

Melody, the nice kid I almost escorted to her gay cousin's wedding reception, has a name that's a little harder to remember but I believe it's Martz. She keeps M & Ms on her desk up front, so maybe I can recall it by her initials. Babs is as Italian as they come...I think it's Macaroni or Cantaloni or something... I've got to work on that one. And last, but not least, is Gabriela Something-Or-Other. The one who wears skirts short enough to be outlawed in 150 countries and most parts of the lower 48. I don't even want to remember that vampire's last name. She irritates me more than my parents do. Lucky for me they're both living far out west.

Someone's beeping me here. Gotta fly.

Let me know when you're heading this way. B

*****

"Brent, could you come into my office, please?"

"Right away, Mr. Johansson."

Brent clicked out of the Excel file he was working in and disengaged himself from his phone headset. Why did the Boss Man want to see him? He'd been holding his own in this God-forsaken cubicle farm for the past couple of weeks now. No further incidents with bran muffins or herbal teas or freaky computers. He'd kept to himself and acted cool. It couldn't be a case of "last hired, first fired" could it?

He should have realized something important was up when he got an eyeful of Jodi Baker standing before

Mr. J's desk. And what an eyeful. She looked in flattering black slacks that accentuated her full, curvy hips and a rose-colored scoop-necked knit top that complimented her skin tone and lovely cleavage.

She piled her curly, sandy blonde hair on top of her head today with little wisps of it dangling against her swan-like neck. She wore her usual scent—something floral and musky at the same time. Sweet and sassy just like her. He wondered what her deliciously freckled skin tasted like…

Damn! He had to stop thinking about his co-worker like that. It was wrong. Jodi really was a beautiful girl, though. Correction, a beautiful woman.

But Helena had been beautiful, too.

"Good morning," he said, nodding to both. "What seems to be the problem?"

"No problem at all," Mr. Johansson said. "In fact, both you and Jodi are my top workers, and I want to reward your efficiency and talent. Why don't you two sit down and let me explain the project to you…"

Some reward! Brent gritted his teeth and listened politely to his employer. The man wanted the both of them to work overtime on some crazy scheme that would supposedly make Hit-On-Us the next Travelocity or Priceline or Orbitz. Brent smiled and nodded in the appropriate places, but it was all he could do not to scream, "Get me outta here!" and run for the door.

With Jodi's hand in his.

Damn! He was doing it again. He was thinking of Jodi as a woman and not as a fellow employee. He wanted to drag her into his bed and make love to her all night long. It just wasn't right.

And it wouldn't be fair to her or to Helena's memory.

"Well, Jodi, what do you think?" Mr. Johansson asked. Brent shook his head and tried to refocus his wayward thoughts on the conversation at hand.

"It sounds like a lot of extra work on top of our very heavy workload, Mr. J," Jodi said slowly and carefully. "I'm not sure I have the time right now to work overtime on a project of this magnitude. What about you, Brent?"

Brent perked up at the sound of his name dancing across her full, pink lips. Very kissable lips if he wasn't mistaken. He could see himself, feel himself, kissing those full, soft, luscious lips of hers...

"Uh, I have to agree with Jodi," he said a bit more brusquely than he intended. "I'm helping my grandfather renovate his home, and I really can't see myself working after office hours on this kind of thing at this point in time."

Sheesh! He sounded like the original bumbling idiot. No brownie points made with the boss there.

Mr. Johansson steepled his pudgy fingers and bobbed his balding head up and down like one of those turtle statues people mounted on their car dashboard. "I see, I see...Yes, I suppose it is a bit much to ask of you two when I've got you holding down the fort here most days, keeping the other troops in line."

Brent relaxed in his seat. Mr. J. felt sympathetic toward their plight and didn't remotely resemble the devil horned boss in the *Dilbert* cartoon. Lucky for them.

"I don't want you two burning out," he continued in a considerate tone. "I realize you're both over-qualified and very intelligent and that you only took these positions because of the economy..."

Yeah, the Boss Man was a human being after all.

"So, I guess that only leaves me one option." He pushed the intercom button on his desk phone. "Raheesha? Can you come in here, please?"

A sudden chill washed over Brent. From the corner of his eye, he noticed a slight twitch of Jodi's sensual lips...Those kissable lips. She was sweating this as well it appeared.

"Mr. J?" Raheesha knocked and stood patiently in the doorway. She took in her two co-workers sitting before the boss and raised an eyebrow. "You called me?"

"Yes, I did. Raheesha, how would you like to be our lead on the floor?"

The big woman took a bigger step into the office. "Our lead? What about Jodi? Ain't that her gig?"

"It is—or I should say, it was. I'm promoting Jodi to assistant manager for this office. And Brent will be helping her on a big new project."

Raheesha tilted her head, closely observing them both as they sat white-knuckled in their seats. "Hmm, I see. Do I get a raise then?"

Mr. Johansson thoughtfully scratched his bald spot. "Yes, I suppose you do. A small one. Jodi and Brent aren't going to be making much more unless this project really takes off. It's sort of a gamble for all of us."

"A gamble?" Jodi's voice sounded two octaves

higher than normal. Poor thing—she really was nervous Brent noticed. Both her bottom lip and her left foot were twitching.

"Jodi's not much of a gambler, Mr. J," Raheesha explained in that deep, motherly voice of hers, "unless it's going to pay out big time. What's this project all about?"

"It's going to put Holliday's International Travel Online US on the map." The older man chuckled, pleased with his witticism. "Get it? It's a pun since we're in the travel business and we deal with maps and such."

Raheesha nodded as if she understood. Brent knew she accepted the fact that her boss was a complete and utter moron, but she was cool with it. "Uh-huh."

"Can you take over as lead then, Raheesha?"

"Of course, Mr. J." She smiled and motioned toward the door. "Can I go tell the others the good news?"

Mr. Johansson looked long and hard at Brent and Jodi. "How about it? You two in? It could mean bigger and better things for the both of you. No more cubicles—you'll be sharing a real office with walls, a real door and even a window."

"Glory be!" Raheesha laughed and clapped her hands. "You can't pass up that offer, girlfriend."

"No, I can't." Jodi swallowed hard. "I accept your kind and generous offer then, Mr. J."

"Wonderful. What say you, Brent?"

Brent tried to gauge Jodi's true reaction to the news that they'd be sharing an office—one with a door and privacy and all—but it was difficult to tell. Her twitching seemed worse. Didn't she trust him to behave himself?

If that was the case, how could he convince her that he was an okay guy? He couldn't think of any other way except working beside her. It was risky letting her see a little more of his true self, but he felt ready to face the challenge. At least he'd be working alongside Jodi.

"All right, Mr. Johansson." Brent flashed a smile at his new officemate. "I can't let all those diplomas and certificates I have go to waste, can I?"

*****

TO: ShaynaE@wazoo.com
FROM: jbaker@hit-on-us.com
SUBJECT: Trapped!

Shayna, come quickly! I need your help!

God, I just don't know what to do…I mean I can't let an opportunity for advancement pass me by but—shit! I didn't bargain for it to happen so fast and for it to involve one Brent Davison.

Mr. J wants us to work together—side by side—on a big project. It involves re-working our web site, which is something Brent has previous experience and training in. And I have the background in business and the last year's experience working the "front lines" so to speak. We'd be perfect working together to whip this company around so we could compete on the level with the other big names out there. But I'm scared!

I don't know what it is about Brent, but whenever I'm near him, I feel like pulling him into my arms and kissing him senseless. Stop laughing—I know you're laughing at me but hear me out. He doesn't feel the same way about me. I'm 99.9% sure about that. He's never really given me any indication that he finds me remotely attractive as a woman. In fact, he's not given anyone around here any indication that he finds women attractive.

Could he be another Frankie without the dress and make-up? You never know.

I just don't think I can stand to work with him day after day the way I feel about him and not act on my hormonal impulses. I'm human after all. But I don't want to torture the poor guy, especially if he has a girlfriend somewhere that he's not letting on about. How do I get myself into these fixes?

I know, I know—I should have applied to grad school!

Glad to hear the monkey experiments are going well for you. What's this about Jamal? I thought you two had kissed and made up. Don't tell me the world's perfect couple is a thing of the past. I've gotta have something to console myself with whenever I think of my own dismal love life. You two gotta make it work, girlfriend.

Well, that's enough whining for now. I have to clear out my cubicle and move my junk into the office next to

Keryn's. Yeah, she has a hole in the wall with a door and a lock since she has a lot of valuable computer equipment in there. My new office actually is slightly bigger than hers with an honest-to-goodness window.

I guess if things get too difficult with Brent, I could always crawl out on the ledge, take a flying leap and splatter myself across Westport Plaza. That'd make the five o'clock news even in this jaded city.

Don't worry. I'm not jumping. I'll just crawl out on the ledge for a breath of fresh air every once in a while.

Take care of yourself and that hunk of yours,
Jodi

*****

"Nice set-up, Baker." Keryn Wiseman strolled into the office the following morning like a real estate agent pacing out the size of a living room. "Not bad. It's at least two square feet bigger than my digs."

"But I'm sharing it, so it's not like I'm hogging all the floor space."

Jodi opened the desk drawers and began filling them with her pens, pencils, paperclips and left over ketchup packets from McDonald's. "There. It all fits."

Keryn leaned against the open door, a smirk tickling the corners of her lips colored a burnt red today. "Aren't you forgetting something?"

"My computer set up? I thought you'd move it in here for me."

"Yes, I will. Don't worry. I'll get around to it after

Brent's off his machine."

"Brent is...Oh, yeah. You have to move his stuff in here, too."

"Bingo." Keryn touched the side of her nose. "Both your computers have to be wired up in here and both your shit has to fit into those desk drawers. You may want to ditch the ketchup packets."

"Right." Jodi began tapping a pencil on the edge of the desk.

Keryn's tone softened. "Have you ever shared an office before?"

Jodi shook her head. "I've never even shared a bathroom before I went off to college to live in a dorm. It was just my brother and me growing up. I'm sort of a drawer hog, too."

"Time to put those selfish instincts aside. Nothing's worse than sharing an office with a drawer hog. I know that from personal experience. That's why I insisted Mr. J give me my own office when I took this position. You can never be too careful sharing your office supplies...among other things."

"Other things?" Jodi blinked. Keryn's expression had changed from one of confident technocrat to little girl lost. Her gaze seemed to drift off into the past. It was so unlike Keryn to open up and share a part of herself. Was it a ruse? A ruse to trick her into becoming suspicious about Brent's every action that she'd drive him out of her office and into Keryn's arms next door?

"Just be careful with your ketchup packets," Keryn said, coming back to the present. "Number them. Count them every night before you go home. Be certain you always know where your stapler is and where your purse is. Keep the chat to a minimum—pretend you're still both working in your cubes. That helps with the...*closeness* issue."

"I see."

But she didn't really. Was Keryn intimating that she'd once gotten too close to someone she shared an office with? Maybe the idiot broke her heart in the process. It certainly would explain her cold, calculated way of approaching the opposite sex.

Perhaps Keryn Wiseman wasn't completely a cyborg, techno-nerd. Maybe she was human after all. Jodi could relate to her co-worker on that level since she'd suffered the pain of a break-up, too.

"Good." Keryn rapped her knuckles on the desktop, interrupting Jodi's mental wandering. "If you keep things on a professional level at all times then you'll work together just fine. And don't forget I'm right next door if you ever need help."

"Gotcha."

Jodi cleaned out the desk drawers the second Keryn left the room. She'd pitch the ketchup packets, but she wanted her pens, pencils and paperclips where she could grab them without a hassle. And she wanted her monitor and keyboard on the normal side of the desk. If she had her way, Brent would sit backwards, closer to the door.

After all, he always placed his keyboard in his lap and leaned back in his chair while working on the computer. She'd observed his posture from the corner of her eye from her cubicle across the way on numerous occasions. She'd also noticed how drop-dead sexy he looked with his tie askew and his shirt sleeves rolled up to his elbows and his long fingers combing through that thick mop of chestnut brown hair of his…

"Shit. I've gotta to stop thinking of him like he's some kind of a pin-up model. I'm worse than any male chauvinist. Maybe I should saw off a piece of my cubicle wall and nail it down the middle of the desktop? Sort of like those study carrels you find in the library…"

"What were you saying about libraries?" Brent entered the room, carrying a big box of office supplies and a few of the personal items he'd brought in recent days to decorate his cubicle. "I hope you don't mind, but I work better with some music blaring in the background."

Jodi grinned, quickly shutting the top desk drawer with her hip. "I don't mind. Just as long as you don't play country. I can't abide country music."

He plopped the box down in the desk chair opposite hers and laughed. "Great. There go all my Waylon Jennings and Willie Nelson mp3 files. I suppose alternative rock is okay with you?"

"It's fine."

She bit her lip. Now would be a good time to discuss their seating arrangements. "I'll let you play the country music crap if you let me have this side of the desk to work on."

He tilted his head and looked at her curiously. "Don't act so serious. I was kidding about Waylon and Willie. I only listen to them with my grandpa anymore. And Mr. J said he'd get us another desk."

"Another desk? In here? How will it fit?"

Brent slowly turned, visually scanning the room's meager dimensions. "Good question. Maybe we can find two smaller desks around here that no one's using to replace this one monster desk. That definitely would provide a more equitable set-up."

"Good idea. I think I know of some desks no one's claimed. I'll go ask now. The sooner we get Mr. J's permission to move the furniture, the better."

Jodi brushed past her officemate in her hurry to exit the room. At the touch of her shoulder to his, a shiver of awareness tingled down her arm and up her spine, zinged along her legs, curling at the end of her red-painted toenails. She jumped back, quickly averting her gaze from his handsome face mere inches from her own.

"I don't have the plague, Jodi," Brent said softly. "I took a bath this morning."

The mental image of Brent Davison in the shower—all six sexy feet of him lathered in slippery soap—made Jodi's knees instantly turn to Jell-O. She shook her head to clear her thoughts.

"Of course you did. I apologize. I've never really had to share close quarters with anyone except in college. Luckily for me, my roommate was a very kind and patient person. She only had to dump my clothes out of her drawers once to teach me how to stay in my own space."

He chuckled. "Only once? My roommate had to do it at least fifty times. Only child?"

"No, I have an older brother. Much older—like eight years. So, I guess I am an only child in a way.

You don't have any siblings?"

He shook his head. "Nope. Mom and Dad split up when I was five."

"Ouch." Jodi winced. "Sorry 'bout that. I was one of the few to live with both my birth parents in my kindergarten class....my grade school, middle school and high school class, too, for that matter. Our generation really got screwed by our screwed-up parents, didn't we?"

"Tell me about it."

What did Keryn tell her about keeping their conversation on a "professional level"? Already they were swapping stories about their childhoods. Next thing you know they'd be discussing what traits their ideal lover possessed... That was more than she could handle at this point. She had to nip this in the bud before it went any further.

"You'd have to ask my college roommate to expound further on that subject. She was the psych major. I was just a lowly business administration major. Now, if you'll excuse me."

Jodi dashed out of the office and down the hall, only slowing as she approached the cube farm and her former fellow phone handlers.

"Liking your new crib, girlfriend?" Raheesha called out over the top of the first cubicle.

"It'll do." Jodi shrugged. "At least it's got a window."

"Great. When you two get settled in, invite us all over for a housewarming, y'hear?"

Lotus scooted into the walkway from her cubicle. "Yes, let's all visit Brent and Jodi after lunch. Then we can ask Brent if he remembers our last names." She sat tall in her desk chair. "I know for a fact he knows mine."

Gabriela popped up like a prairie dog from her cubicle. "How could anyone forget 'Lotus Blossom'? You wear those hideous big floral patterns most of the time. It's a bit obvious."

Lotus smiled smugly and scooted back into her cube. "Yes, it is."

"Brent should know everyone's name by now," Gabriela continued. "He's been here a month. And I know he'll remember mine. I pointed it out to him on his desk."

"He's got your name carved on his desk?" Babs jumped up and leaned across the top of the wall she shared with Gabriela's cubicle. "Mr. J freaks if anyone defaces the furniture."

"No, no, no! I pointed out my name on his thesaurus. Get it?"

Babs shook her pigtails. "Your last name isn't *thesaurus*, Gabby."

Gabriela growled. "It's *Roget*—you know, like the name of the famous thesaurus." She rolled her eyes. "Honestly, Babs, honey. Were you ever awake in English class?"

"Nah. I slept through it most of the time since it was always after gym."

"Ladies—we have lines on hold," Melody shouted out from the reception area. "You'd better pick them up before Mr. J gets back from his trip to the bank."

Immediately the heads dropped below the cubicle walls and the conversation was at an end. Jodi made her way to the front of the suite to talk to Melody.

"Mr. J isn't here?"

"No, he stepped out for a moment to talk to some bankers." Melody began stapling big piles of papers together and sorting them into folders. "Something about this new project being one of the biggest investments he's ever made and needing help with cash flow."

Jodi leaned an elbow against the high counter of the receptionist's desk. "Cash flow problems? That doesn't sound good. I see a pink slip in my near future. Welcome to life and work in the twenty-first century."

"Relax." Melody stood and patted her on the shoulder. "You and Brent will work wonderfully together and everything will come out all right. I just know it."

"How do you know it?"

She shrugged. "I just do."

"Psychic, huh? So…what's that you're putting together?"

"Something for the investors' meeting tonight."

Jodi's eyes widened. "Investors' meeting?" She reached for one of the folders. "Let me see a copy of that prospectus real quick—"

"No, you don't." Melody swatted her hand away. "Mr. J. said this isn't to be read by anyone but the investors. Unless you're plunking the pocket change he's paying you back into the company you don't qualify."

"Ah, come on, Mel. I won't say anything to anyone. I just want to know what's going to—"

"No! And that's my final word."

Jodi took a step back. Melody looked as if her heart-shaped face would crack into a million pieces if she kept the unusually stern expression up for long.

"Wow. You've really changed—and I mean for the better. You project a lot more confidence nowadays, Mel. You're a completely different woman."

She smiled. "I am. I took what you all said about being a 'doormat' to heart. I've started reading books about assertiveness and self-confidence building. I'm tired of acting like a little girl in a world full of women. I'm growing up."

"Good for you." A sudden pain stabbed at Jodi's heart. She had to know. She took a deep breath.

"You're…you're not thinking of asking Brent out again, are you?"

"Maybe. I don't know."

Melody stacked the folders into a pile then slipped them into a box and stowed it under the counter. "That first bet we all made was really stupid. Sure, Brent is a looker and all, but he's not my type really. He's way too old for me."

"Too old?" Jodi laughed. "I think he's about twenty-seven. It's not like he's ninety-seven. You're twenty-one and don't seem to mind working with the rest of us so-called 'old folks'. Isn't Raheesha going on thirty-two?"

"Is she? She acts both younger and older than the rest of us at times. No, I guess you're right. Brent's not too old for me. He's just not my type. He's a bit too 'cerebral' for my tastes."

"You don't like them brainy, huh?"

"Brains are okay, but I like my guys to be more rugged, more outdoorsy and down-to-earth."

This was news. Melody had seldom opened up about what she looked for in a man. An image of shy Mel and a frequent office visitor sprang to mind. Why hadn't she put one and one together and come up with two before?

"Rugged you say? Outdoorsy like our Fed-Ex delivery guy Barry?"

"Barry?" Melody's voice slipped up an octave and her drab brown eyes burst into flames. She stood taller and smoothed the wrinkles out of her skirt. "Uh, you didn't happen to spot his truck out your window by chance, did you?"

"We're on the fifth floor, Mel. I can barely make out the people below."

"But a Fed-Ex truck... Well, it's so...so *big*."

"And tall, dark, hairy-chested and oh-so-muscular?"

Melody blushed. Jodi grinned. Her driving companion must really have a thing for the incredible hunk who delivered their packages. Barry was a nice guy, but he looked like a Neanderthal more than a model. Even Gabriela didn't think him worthy enough to flirt with him. But if Melody went for guys with sloping foreheads and massive biceps, who was she to tell her to stay away? It definitely would keep her from making any more moves on Brent.

And wasn't that exactly what she wanted?

Jodi backed away from the desk, hiding her jealousy behind her smile. "I'll keep a look out for

Barry and his big truck and let you know the moment I see him drive into the parking lot. All right?"

"Would you really? Gee, thanks. You're such a great friend, Jodi."

Yeah, right. So how come she didn't feel like one?

Jodi wandered to the back of the office suite to a dark corner that held two small tables that the company once used as typing desks. Maybe they could put their computers on these and forego the big desk? Some short, long-neglected filing cabinets stood nearby. Her ketchup packet collection would easily fit in one of them and Brent could use the other. Now all she had to do was to move her finds across the cube farm, down the hall and into their office.

"Need any help?"

The sound of Brent's sweet baritone shot a zap of electricity along her spine, increasing the tension building up between her legs. "Uh, yeah, sure. I thought we could use these old typing tables for the computers instead of sharing one big desk."

"Perfect. These look solidly built and they shouldn't be too difficult to move."

He stepped around her and easily lifted a table chest high. "Do you think you can handle the other one?"

Jodi screwed up her face and attempted to pick up the second table. It barely budged. "Um, I'll try dragging it instead. But don't we have to move that big desk out of the room first?"

"I did. It's standing on its side out in the hall. It might fit back in this corner after we clear it out. Those short cabinets behind you could be useful, too."

Like minds think alike…Jodi didn't want to dwell on what they had in common. They had a job to do, a project to work on. She took a deep breath and kept her head down so she wouldn't focus on Brent's tight buns ahead of her as she pushed the typing table toward their office.

"Wow, you look like you could use some help, Jojo," Lotus chimed in as they passed the break room. She motioned for Jodi to stop. "I'll take one end of the table and you take the other."

"Maybe we should ask Babs for some help? She's got the muscles."

"She does but she's already left for her noon-time basketball game."

With Lotus's help, the two managed to transport the table just seconds behind Brent's shapely backside.

"I think I'll put mine here." He placed his desk under the window. "I like natural lighting."

"That's fine. I don't when I'm on the computer." Jodi led Lotus over to the opposite corner and dropped her end first. "Thanks for your help, Lolo."

"Anytime, Jojo."

Brent sat on the edge of his table and crossed his arms. "Cute nicknames."

"Yeah, we use them now and again," Lotus explained, "but we really haven't come up with one for you, Brent. Any suggestions?"

"My friends in college called me 'Big B'."

Lotus laughed. "Your grade point average, right?"

"Maybe." His grinned broadened. "I suppose it could mean other things."

Jodi felt her cheeks warming. She had to change

the subject before her gaze was permanently glued to his crotch.

"Lolo, I really don't think we should confuse Brent with our nicknames when he hasn't really learned our real first and last names yet."

"I beg your pardon, ladies. I'm not a complete mental incompetent. I know everyone's name in this office."

Brent correctly listed everyone's full name until he came to Gabriela's.

"Gabriela's last name is…" He closed his eyes and took a deep breath. "No, don't tell me. She pointed something out to me to help me remember it. It has something to do with a reference book."

"Very good." Lotus nodded and rubbed her hands together gleefully. "Which one?"

"I know—Merriam-Webster's. Gabriela Webster."

Lotus collapsed in a fit of laughter. Jodi soon followed suit.

"What?" Brent stared, perplexed. "That wasn't it? I give up then. I know everyone's last name except hers."

"What's going on in here?" Keryn stood frowning, arms crossed, at the doorway.

Jodi slapped a hand over her mouth to stifle her giggles. It took several moments for her to calm down enough to be able to speak. "Um, nothing… Gabby just lost her bet."

Chapter Five

TO: ShaynaE@wazoo.com
FROM: jbaker@hit-on-us.com
SUBJECT: Call me an idiot

Shayna baby –

God, I'm so sorry to hear about you and Jamal splitting up. I didn't know things had gotten that harsh between you. You guys were always so lovey-dovey. I thought I'd be one of your bridesmaids before too long.

I don't know what to say. Just take care of yourself, girlfriend. Try not to let your bitterness at his betrayal skew the way you see all men. I know this for a fact.

You do get over the heartache. I didn't think I'd ever get over what's-his-face leaving me at the altar, but I have. "Time heals all wounds and wounds all heels," my grandma always told me. Jamal's going to be crying his eyes out longer than you when he wakes up and finally realizes he lost the best thing he ever had.

Okay, enough about that asshole. Let me cheer you up some with my most recent exploits into the realm of utter stupidity.

You know the way we're always making these stupid

bets in the office? Well, we don't actually make them in the office – we tend to make them on Ladies Night down at the Zodiac Café. But that's neither here nor there. Somehow, one of us gets some foolish thought in her head and it just seems to grow…exponentially. Times seven, you could say. I'm beginning to think that seven single women just shouldn't drink together. We get up to no good.

Lotus was having a grand time teasing Gabriela the other night about losing the latest bet. No, she wasn't too mean, but it was irritating to Gabby all the same. Gabby has enough pride to stuff a dead elephant for exhibition. She just couldn't stand the thought that Brent could remember everyone's last name except hers. I know she's always been the center of attention whenever she walks into a room full of men, so it really hurts to know that a straight male doesn't fall for her charms in twenty seconds flat.

How do I know Brent is straight? I…I really hate to snitch on anyone – especially myself – but I peeked into his filing cabinet drawer. It was by mistake, honestly. We'd just moved the two short filing cabinets into our joint office, and I was rearranging my office supplies from where Brent had emptied them in the corner before moving the big desk out of the room. I accidentally opened Brent's cabinet drawer and saw her. I mean you couldn't miss this photo – it's an eight by twelve in full color. She's beautiful. Perfect skin, perfect hair, perfect teeth…you name it. The woman is absolutely, positively drop-dead gorgeous. Brent told me he was an only child, so I have to assume she's his main squeeze and not his sister. And they're perfect for each other. Their children are going to be the most gorgeous, perfect-looking babies on the planet.

I'm getting off the focus of my story here, but you'll see how I'm a complete idiot when it comes to the next part.

So, we're all dancing, drinking and doing the usual Ladies' Night thing when Gabby gets it into her head that the bet she made is still on. She said she'd get Brent into her bed before week's end and there were still a couple of days to go. She had a little too much to drink by then so we all calmed her down and convinced her that it just isn't good company policy to sleep with a fellow employee. Eventually she agreed.

But that didn't stop Gabby from getting the girls to take her up on another version of the same bet…

*****

"We're supposed to test out our own theory of how to seduce a Martian? To see who can successfully seduce a guy the quickest?"

Lotus's pale blue eyes widened to the size of Frisbees. What little natural color she possessed leached from her fair skin. She took a big gulp of her mineral water, huddling further back into the booth.

"That's the bet, Lolo." Gabriela blew out a long trail of smoke and crushed out her cigarette. She rarely smoked except when she was drunk.

"Seduction is an art—not a science. How do we measure it?" They could always count on Keryn to point out the irrational side of any argument. "I mean do we all have to videotape ourselves in the sex act with a consenting male and make sure we have a date stamp on the tape to verify the exact time?"

"Video? I could do that," Babs said, nodding her head. After her second drink, Babs was bound to say—or do—just about anything with little goading. "So, each of us picks our own dude and we screw his little brains out and bring back proof we were successful in bagging him by the balls."

Gabriela chuckled. "Crudely put, Babs honey, but that's essentially it."

"How do you define *successful*?" Raheesha leaned her elbows on the table and stuck out her lower lip. "Successful to me means the guy is a keeper. He just doesn't walk out the door after he gets his rocks off. Successful means he wants to continue the relationship out of the sack as well as in it."

Keryn tapped her drink stirrer against her bottom lip. "Unless what Gabriela means by a *successful seduction* is that both parties experience a simultaneous orgasm, then I'm not sure how you could prove something like that except with Bab's video camera." She put down her drink stirrer and gave her best impression of a mad scientist. "Or by having a Masters and Johnson research assistant standing nearby with a clip board and electrodes."

Cringing, Melody slumped in her seat. "You guys are making me really uncomfortable. I'm not ready for that kind of relationship. I still live at home. And I promised my high school Bible study leader that I'd remain a virgin until I got married."

"Good for you." Raheesha put an arm around their youngest office mate and squeezed. "It's refreshing to hear someone has decent morals in this alley cat day and age."

Melody smiled up at her. "You go to church, Raheesha—are you still a virgin?"

The big woman sighed and shook her head. "No, I'm afraid not. I had that 'starter marriage' soon after I got out of high school. It only lasted the three years, but I've never been eager to repeat that disaster. And I hate to say it, but a lot of the guys I've dated in the last decade have been of the 'you'll sleep with me if you love me' persuasion. Dumb me fell for it many a time, too. But I know better now and have repented. I'm not in any hurry to experience another meaningless one night stand."

Lotus pointed a boney finger at Gabriela. "So, we can't say that *successful* means we have to sleep with our Martian. To seduce him, all we have to do is have him say he wants to sleep with us—we have to make him admit his undying love for us."

"No, no, no...You're getting it all wrong." Gabriela took another swig of her drink and fumbled for another cigarette. "We're betting who can seduce a Martian—a male, man, whatever. That means we lure him into our bed."

"Where's the love in that?" Melody pounded a fist on the table. The assertiveness training and self-help books seem to be working.

"There isn't any." Raheesha raised an eyebrow and leveled it at their instigator. "Gabby wouldn't know what love was if it hit her between the eyes and broadcast its message on every cable channel simultaneously."

Gabriela struck her lighter three times before it worked. "I would too."

"Enough already. This conversation is getting entirely out of hand." Jodi folded her arms across her chest and sighed loud and long. When would her crazy co-workers ever learn?

"Women do not have to stoop to the same level as men. We don't have to think of other human beings primarily as sex objects. We're all too mature here to be talking such foolishness."

Every eye at the table turned and stared at her. Jodi held her head high.

"I'm right, aren't I?"

Melody grinned. "Absolutely."

"I concur." Lotus opened her arms wide into big circle. "Let's create love and not war among the sexes. We should treat Martians the way we would like to be treated. Goddesses should not lower their standards and cheapen the act of love."

Raheesha chuckled and slapped her thigh. "Interesting way to put it, Flower Child, but I agree. Babs?"

Babs tapped her sneaker toe against the tile repeatedly. "Yeah, I guess so. My high school basketball coach always said, 'Fair play is the best way to play.' Seducing a man as part of a contest isn't exactly playing fair with him."

"Keryn?" Raheesha motioned to their tech head. "You got any words on the subject?"

"Sex is just a natural response to visual and genital

stimuli in my opinion. I mean it doesn't have to lead to *love and marriage and a baby carriage* if the two parties agree on the terms of the relationship up front. So, if Gabriela wants to start a contest to see who can get laid the fastest then she's free to do so." Keryn shrugged and threw up her hands. "Personally, however, I think acting in haste to snag a guy is a classic sign of insecurity."

"Insecurity?" Gabriela tried sitting up taller but tilted instead. There was a discernable wobble in her motions as she dumped cigarette ashes in Keryn's empty glass. "You're saying I don't think I have what it takes to attract and keep a guy's interest more than one night?"

Keryn scowled and leaned toward their drunken friend. "You tell me."

Jodi reached across and placed an arm between them. "Okay, time out girls. No more fighting in the locker room, or I'll have to report you to the principal."

A titter of laughter circled the table.

"Aw, come on. Let's dance some more." Babs jumped off her stool. "I've had my eye on this one real athletic-looking dude over in the opposite corner all night."

"I think he's got a date already," Melody observed. "They've been dancing together pretty much the entire time."

"Hey, two's company—but three's a helluva lot more fun!"

Gabriela threw back her head and snorted. "That's my Babs! You still on for the bet then, girlfriend?"

"Sure, why not?"

Jodi slapped her forehead in disgust. "Babs—don't. Gabby, don't egg her on. You know how Babs can't pass up a contest."

"Hey, I can't let one pass me by either," Gabriela drawled. She stubbed out her cigarette, slipped off her stool, yanked down her miniskirt and linked arms with her competitive co-worker. "Contests make life interesting. And if anybody could use interesting lives, it's the bored-out-of-their-gourds employees of Hit-On-Us dot com."

The two sauntered off toward the dance floor and within minutes, several hot bodies, their hips gyrating and swiveling to the music, surrounded each.

"They do look like they're having fun," Lotus remarked with a sad sigh. "Sex is a celebration of the life force, after all. It's just too bad that they both act so indiscriminate about partners at times."

Keryn put down her drink and squinted, peering into the darkly lit dance area. "Hmm…You want to join them, Lotus? I think Gabriela has a few extras she doesn't need. One guy appears to be wearing a *Greenpeace* T-shirt, sandals and cut-off khakis."

"Really?" Lotus stood and edged closer to the action. "I believe you're right, Keryn. And there's another Martian with a pocket protector and a pair of expensive leather loafers. A Bill Gates clone if I ever saw one."

"Expensive, you say? I'm in. Let's go."

Keryn and Lotus disappeared into the dancing crowd.

Jodi shook her head. "There's just no getting

through to some people, is there?"

"No, there isn't." Raheesha took a long sip of her drink. A thoughtful smile curled the corner of her lips. "But Flower Child is right in a way. Lovemaking is a good thing, and we don't have to ignore every homeboy we happen to meet. I've been needing a push to get back into the dating scene for some time now…Maybe Gabby's little contest is just the thing I need to light a fire under my buns."

"Raheesha! How can you say such a thing?" Melody's jaw practically scraped the tabletop. "I thought you didn't believe in one night stands anymore. I thought you believed in the sanctity of marriage."

"I thought so, too." Jodi screwed up her eyes and stared down her nose at her friend. "What changed your mind all of a sudden?"

"Nothing. I'm not going to pick up some fool in the bar tonight. I'm talking about a very nice man who has been sitting behind me in choir at church. He's been dropping subtle hints that he wants to take me out for the past couple of months, but I've just been putting him off. It's not really fair to him, is it?"

"Maybe he's a first class creep. You don't have to go out with a creep," Melody advised. "Use your assertiveness skills to tell him where to get off. Protect your self-identity and individuality from being assimilated."

"Uh-huh." Raheesha rolled her eyes. "Just what kind of books you been reading lately, girlfriend?"

Jodi grinned sheepishly. "Too many self-helps. It's my fault—I suggested a few titles to her. I think she's gone overboard."

"No, they were all good books, Jojo. You should re-read them. You need to know where to set your boundaries when it comes to sharing an office with Brent."

"Boundaries? You mean Jojo needs to build the Berlin Wall between her desk and Brent's desk or something?"

"Well, not exactly. I think it's more a matter of—"

"Okay, that's it on that subject." Jodi put her glass down hard on the table to make her point. "Brent Davison is not a topic for discussion—especially around Gabby and the 'Grab Ass Squad' out there on the dance floor."

Jodi's two co-workers stopped in mid-sentence and stared at her.

"Whatever you say, girlfriend." Raheesha took a sip of her drink and narrowed her eyes, watching Jodi closely. "But maybe you need a fire lit under your curvy backside, too. Or else you're going to lose out to somebody else."

"I'm not interested in Brent anymore," Melody confessed. "He's just not 'rugged' enough for me."

"Rugged?" Raheesha laughed. "You wanna land yourself a lumberjack, is that it?"

Melody blushed. "A semi-pro weight-lifter will do."

"Barry lifts weight competitively?" Jodi arched an eyebrow. "That explains all that brawn...How did you discover that golden nugget about his hobby?"

"I asked him. I just flat out asked him while he was delivering packages the other day. He told me he had a meet next Saturday and that I was welcome to come and watch. I think I will."

The smug look on Melody's heart-shaped face said it all.

"Our little girl is all grown up!" Raheesha beamed a smile and clapped her hands.

"Yes, she is—at last." Jodi gave Melody a squeeze. "I'm so proud of you, Mel. It's about time you trusted your instincts and got out more. You can't live at home the rest of your life."

"Why not? I like my bedroom, and my mom's an excellent cook."

"On second thought, perhaps our little girl isn't quite there yet," Raheesha muttered. She finished her drink and turned the conversation over to Jodi.

"So, Jojo, you're the only one in the office not chasing after a Martian. You gonna be our control again?"

"I don't want to have anything to do with this latest madness, thank you very much. I think Gabby is dead wrong."

"But what's wrong with going after that *special someone* who might just turn out to be Mr. Right someday?" Melody asked.

I've been down that path before...Jodi cringed inwardly. She realized now there wasn't a Mr. Right for every woman in the universe, and she'd finally made peace with herself on that subject. Still, it wouldn't be very nice of her to dash sweet Melody's naïve hope by letting her in on the awful truth about life and men.

"Why, of course I believe there's a Mr. Right out

there for me. I just don't have any special someone lined up at the moment. And, with this new project Mr. J has me working on, I won't have too many more girls' nights out to spend scoping out Bill Gates clones and tree-huggers in the Zodiac Cafe."

Raheesha raised an eyebrow. "Are you certain there isn't someone in particular you'd be interested in pursuing?"

Jodi shook her head and motioned with her eyes toward Melody. "No, there isn't," she said through gritted teeth. "And I'd like you to remember that, Rae."

The older woman raised her hands in surrender. "All right, just asking."

The dancers returned at that point to retrieve their purses.

"We're off to Harrison's place," Gabriela announced, casually flinging an arm around a tall, dark, handsome and well-dressed office jockey. Keryn and Lotus stood beside their dance partners and grinned as well.

"We'll meet you ladies outside," the obvious leader of the pack said. "Come on guys."

Gabriela blew her date a kiss as they departed. Even Keryn smiled at her man.

"Harry's invited us to check out his swimming pool and Jacuzzi," Lotus chimed in. "It's going to be a blast. You guys wanna come along?"

"No thank you," Jodi replied for her companions sitting at the table. "Where does this Harrison live just in case you don't show up for work tomorrow and the police need us to identify the bodies?"

Keryn nonchalantly tossed her bangs out of her face. "Oh, don't be so dramatic. Harrison Platte comes from one of the richest and most well respected families in town. In fact, that's his stretch limo pulling up out front right now to give us a lift."

Melody jumped up and did a double take. "Wow. I guess he doesn't live in Maryland Heights then."

"No shit, Sherlock." Gabriela flung her purse over her shoulder. "He lives in a mansion in Huntleigh Hills. Ta-ta for now, ladies."

Laughing, the group made its way toward the front exit.

"Where's Babs?" Raheesha called out. "Isn't she going with you?"

Lotus scooted back toward the table and lowered her voice. "No, Babs has already left with that couple out the side door. I guess three is more fun than two."

Turning, she ran to keep up with her ride. "I'll tell you all about Harrison's hot tub tomorrow."

"Dang. Babs is a right wild thing. I didn't know the girl was so freaky. I didn't know Flower Child was that adventuresome, either." Raheesha sighed. "I guess it's high time we called it a night."

"Yeah, I don't want to have dark circles under my eyes when I go see Barry lift weights." Melody collected her personal effects. "Ready to go, Jojo?"

Jodi nodded. "I'm more than ready to get out of here."

*****

...So you see, Shayna, we've fallen back into the same

old pattern of who can out do whom in the "Seduce a Martian" department. Raheesha is expecting me to make a move on Brent. I can't. I just can't.

But I'm happy for Melody and Raheesha. It seems they both have nice guys lined up to date. I hope it works out well for them.

And who knows? Maybe Gabby, Lotus and Keryn will hit it off with these rich dudes and things will work out happily ever after for them as well.

I don't know about Babs, though. I think she has a future in porn films if she doesn't make it into the WNBA.

Take care, girlfriend. If you need to talk, you know my cell number.
Jodi

PS I know what you're thinking right at this moment…I lived with you for four years…I know your thought processes better than you do. You're thinking Brent is just the guy I need to make me forget about what's-his-face. Too late. I've forgotten him already. I'm just lusting over Brent's hot bod. I don't want or need a serious relationship with any male at the moment. And I particularly don't want to screw up my chance to impress the boss by screwing around with my co-worker.

PPS When's your next break? Maybe you should come over and stay at my place. I'll introduce you to Brent.

You two might hit it off. ☺

Chapter Six

TO: MrBoJangles@crapster.net
FROM: bdavison@hit-on-us.com
SUBJECT: Tight squeeze

Congrats on the big deal, dude!

They've finally rewarded your talent. How did that record exec know you were playing in that hole-in-the-wall bar that night? His car broke down in the middle of nowhere? Not likely. I don't believe in coincidences. Someone tipped him off. Good thing, too.

So, you'll be moving down to Nashville to start recording soon. Don't forget your ol' drinking buddies when you write your album dedication. We knew you when – and we'll spill our guts to the tabloid press for the big bucks if you ever get on our bad sides.

RFLMAO! Remember I took a photo of you and that Delta Zeta doing the nasty on top of the washing machine when you thought everyone had gone out for the night? Classic! Can't wait to sell it to the Enquirer.

Oh, all right. I lied. I threw the photo out…But only after I scanned it in the computer and posted it at the Naughty Girls of Spring Break web site. She was already on there, you know. Several times.

To bring you up to speed on life on the cubicle farm, I'm no longer working in a cube. I'm now sharing an office down the hall with Jodi, my former cube neighbor. Yes, she's the curvy one with curly hair. We have a window, door, four walls, everything. Except space. We have almost no legroom. You know how I like to stretch out when I'm working on the computer? It's just not possible these days…

*****

"Watch out!"

Too late. Jodi backed into the room, arms filled to capacity and catapulted across Brent's outstretched legs. Papers went flying, hands waved wildly to regain lost balance, and her skull seemed headed straight for a nasty crack on the edge of the desk…until a strong arm reached out to block her fall, that is.

"Gotcha."

Brent's face went from normal to pale to bright red all within the span of two seconds. Jodi blinked hard and gazed up at her rescuer–from his lap. She'd never seen Brent from this angle. The curve of his chin wasn't as angular as she had thought it before. His face seemed a lot more accessible, less remote. She found herself staring deeply into his beautiful wide-open brown eyes.

She could tell her fall really shook him up.

"Are you sure you're all right?" His eyes raked over her body, scanning for any sign of injuries, his grip on her never lessening for a moment. "You didn't hit your head on anything or suffer whiplash?"

"No. I'm fine. Just a little winded, that's all." Jodi tried to extricate herself from her office mate's strong grip, but he appeared to have turned into stone. "I'm okay, Brent. You can let go of me now. I promise I won't fall again."

"Oh." He let his arms drop to his sides. "I'm so sorry for tripping you like that. I like to stretch out when I work on the computer. I forgot how tight this space is we share."

Jodi stood and brushed her hands on her slacks and straightened her V-neck top from where it had fallen off her shoulder. It was her favorite outfit, and she was glad she hadn't gushed bright red blood all over the gray pinstripes of her pants or her silky knit sweater.

"Yeah, it's a tight squeeze in here," she said. "But if you'll keep your feet closer to the window and away from the doorway, we should be okay."

"Will do." He stood and began collecting the scattered papers.

"I can do that. You get back to work on that new web site design. I promise I won't interrupt you again."

He continued with the clean up. "No, it's the least I can do since my number thirteens tripped you up. I'm glad you didn't hurt yourself."

"So am I." Jodi smiled. Where had this sensitive, caring side of Brent Davison been hiding himself all this time? Maybe his girlfriend's photo in the filing drawer brought out the best in him. "With all this paperwork stacking up, I don't have time to be out injured. I need to plow through all of this before next week's deadline."

Brent finished gathering up the spilled documents and stacked them neatly on his desk before handing them to her.

"Why, thank you. If I can ever return the favor, just let me know."

"Uh, you can actually." He cleared his throat and averted his gaze. "Could you stop wearing that perfume please?"

"Perfume?" Jodi wriggled her nose and sniffed. "Oh, you mean my cologne. I'm sorry. Are you allergic to it? Working in such close quarters, I bet it is irritating. I didn't realize. I'll go wash it off right now where I applied it."

He reached out and lightly touched her shoulder. She stopped and looked at him.

"No, that's not it. It's fine. It's a lovely fragrance. It just...reminds me of someone else whenever I smell that scent. And I'd rather not be reminded of her."

Someone else as in ex-girlfriend? Jodi thought, biting her lip. That would explain why the picture sat in the drawer and not on his desk. He was nursing a hurt like she one she'd nursed this past year.

Shit! What a stupid thing to do—wearing a cologne that makes your co-worker feel crappy by reminding him of how he was dumped. What a thoughtless thing to do. How she wished a great big hole would appear in the middle of the room and swallow her up at that very moment.

"Gosh, Brent, I deeply and sincerely apologize. I promise I'll never wear it again to the office. I certainly didn't mean to upset you."

"Upset me?" The old, gruff Brent seemed to emerge from his sensitive-guy cocoon right before her very eyes. "Upset *me*?"

He threw himself back into his desk chair and swung his keyboard into his lap. "I'm not upset. I'm trying to concentrate here. How can a man expect to concentrate on an important assignment when you're jiggling that cute ass of yours around practically in his face? It's like an episode of *Girls Gone Wild* in here."

Jodi's jaw dropped to the floor. She slammed the stack of papers down hard on her desktop and stood legs apart, hands on her hips.

"Excuse *me*? When have I ever bared my breasts for your personal viewing pleasure?"

"You know what I mean." He sounded irritated. He parked his keyboard on his table, fighting to keep his eyes away from her figure. "You all do it nowadays—dress inappropriately. That's what my grandfather calls it."

"Inappropriately?"

She charged toward him and grabbed him by the chin. "Look at me. *Look* at me. How is my outfit *inappropriate* by any standard, Mr. *-don't-always-wear-a-tie* Davison?"

Brent swallowed hard. Twice. The fight seemed to go right out of him. An inscrutable look of desire crept into his eyes.

"Uh…you look nice today. Nice sweater color—green goes well with your eyes."

Jodi squeezed his chin for good measure. "Damn right it does. Emerald is a very flattering color on me. And I'm not *jiggling* anything at anyone on purpose. I can't help it that I'm not a size six like Gabriela or Melody. God made some us actually look like women. I won't apologize for being full-figured."

"You're not fat."

"I said *full-figured* not *fat*. I know I'm not anorexic, but I'm not Oprah-sized, either. So, cut the male chauvinist crap and stop judging women by their outer appearance. We prefer you treat us the same as you would any male colleague."

With that, she dropped her hold on his chin and spun around. Suddenly Brent caught her by the hand and spun her back around. She plopped butt first into his lap. He reached out and quietly pushed the door shut with his foot.

"I don't judge by outward appearances," he said in a low whisper, his lips mere inches from her own, "but I can't help but feel attracted to a beautiful woman sitting less than two feet away from me day after day. I'm human, you know. And a guy. We tend to think with the lower half of our bodies at times, and you really have my lower half working overtime. I'm finding it hard to concentrate on my work because all I can think about when you're in here with your cologne and your curves is how delicious you'd look after a long night's lovemaking session."

Jodi felt her breath catch. Did Brent say what she just thought he said? Did he just tell her that he'd been secretly lusting after her all the while she'd been doing the same? Maybe Raheesha was right. Maybe it was time for her to spill her guts and confess her attraction to him.

What could it hurt? They were both adults. They

both obviously knew how to keep a secret. And maybe if they acted on their libidinous impulses and got them out of their systems, they'd both be able to concentrate better on their work assignments in the future?

"Brent...are you saying you're attracted to me?"

"What do you think?" His lips danced along her temple as his hands moved across her hips and cupped her backside.

She took a shaky breath and closed her eyes. "I think you are." She took another breath for courage. "I'm attracted to you, too."

His feather-light kisses sent shivers coursing through her frame. "Really?"

"But we've got to keep this a secret. If it gets out, the whole office will be buzzing about it. And I don't know what Mr. J would do."

He began playfully nibbling on her earlobe and the curve of her neck. "Probably nothing."

She moaned softly. "How can we be sure?"

"We can't. But he didn't get on all your cases when you all were trying to seduce me before."

Jodi's eye flew open wide. "What do you mean?"

Brent laughed. "That first week or so after I arrived? Remember? Everyone in the cube farm was going after me like I was the last piece of meat on the planet and you all were a pack of starving carnivores. Except you, now that I think about it. Why was that?"

"I...I was playing hard to get."

The lie sounded weak to Jodi's ears. How could she tell him it was because she felt attracted to him from the moment she laid eyes on him? How could she tell him that she worked hard not to gain his attention because of this very thing happening? How could she tell him that she'd had her fill of Mr. Right after the getting-left-at-the-altar affair? That she'd just wanted someone to hold her, love her, and not use her for his own selfish purposes? Could Brent's intentions mirror hers?

"Naughty girl. You wanted me to chase after you. Is that it? Is that why you've kept me in suspense until now?"

"Uh-huh." Jodi sighed. Her hands roved across his strong, broad shoulders and caressed his cheeks. She longed to have his lips possess hers.

"So…what do you do after you're caught?"

She shrugged. "Accept my punishment for trying to run away like a good little girl?"

He raised an eyebrow. "Good answer. You're saying you're up for a little playtime after hours with no strings attached. Right?"

"Right." Jodi shifted her weight and brought her lips in line with his. If a guy could enjoy unfettered, non-committed sex, then why couldn't she?

She cupped a hand around his face and brought his mouth closer to hers. "Shall we seal the deal with a kiss?"

His reply came with his lips. Jodi felt her heart hammering in her ears as his mouth greedily took possession of hers. She opened her lips and their tongues met, deepening the kiss. She pressed her breasts closer to his chest and tilting her head back to allow his sensual assault to intensify. She felt his erection stiffen against her belly as she twined her fingers into his hair. She sighed. Brent really was attracted to her...No doubt about it.

Time stood still for a moment. Then reality brought them both back to their senses.

"Keryn, come here. My machine just flashed the blue screen of death." Melody's soprano voice pierced through the smoky haze of Jodi's attraction. She sprang from Brent's lap as the sound of the conversation right next door grew more excited. Keryn worked to extract information from their panicked receptionist.

"You weren't attempting another one of your famous short cut maneuvers in Outlook, were you?" came the bored tone of their tech head.

Brent raised an eyebrow. "I see what you mean about keeping this to ourselves. Wanna meet somewhere after work?"

Jodi's breathing came in ragged gasps. "Um, tonight is Ladies Night down at the Zodiac Café. The rest of the office will be there—except Mr. J. We'd have this place to ourselves after five p.m."

"Is that all that's wrong?" Melody gave a loud sigh of relief. "I was sure I'd broken it for good this time. Gee, it's almost four-thirty. Wonder why Jodi and Brent's door is closed?"

Jodi dashed to her chair and immediately began to flip through the documents on her desk. Brent returned to his keyboard. Two seconds later came the expected knock.

"Come in," Jodi said as calmly as she could manage with her pulse racing off the scale.

Melody popped her head through the crack. "You two are awfully quiet. Working hard in here?"

"Very hard," Brent muttered without lifting his focus from his computer screen. "Close the door on the way out, will you? It keeps the noise pollution levels down to a minimum."

"Oh…I see." Melody slowly shook her head. "Yeah, this is a noisy office at times. I'll let you two hardworking fast-trackers be."

She turned to go then quickly spun back around. "Jodi, are you planning on going to Ladies Night tonight?"

"Not tonight. I have a lot of contracts to vet for Mr. J, so I'll be working late. Maybe next time. Sorry."

"That's okay. I understand. Do you want me to come back upstairs after a while and give you a ride home?"

Damn. She'd forgotten she'd ridden with Melody today since her car was still acting up...besides with the price of gasoline these days, car-pooling wasn't so bad. Until tonight.

"No problem—I'll give Jodi a ride home," Brent said nonchalantly. "I've got some extra work tonight, too."

"Okay." Melody flashed them both a half-smile. "See you both tomorrow then?"

"See you tomorrow." Jodi let out a long sigh of relief as the door clicked closed. "Shit."

Brent looked up from his screen. "You think she's going to tell the rest of the inmates that we're getting it on after hours?"

Jodi bit the top of her pen. "No, not really. Melody's too polite and too naïve to think anything at this point. I'm worried about Keryn. She may have overheard our little conversation earlier. She'd tell everyone. She'd probably sneak the entire bar up here to catch us in the act if she thought it was worth a giggle."

"Then we'll go someplace else."

"Yes, but we're supposed to be working overtime on this project, remember?"

He shrugged. "We'll tell them tomorrow that we both decided to work at home since it's quieter there."

"Yeah, that's an idea. I can easily take these contracts home. It won't take me more than an hour to shuffle through them. I only told Mr. J it would take longer just in case they turned out to be a real mess, but I can already tell they're not that bad."

"And I've got a better computer set up at my place. I'll just email a couple of files to my private e-mail and take it from there."

"Sounds like a plan."

Jodi frowned. All of a sudden, something didn't feel right. This office romance—correction, sexual escapade with no strings attached—wasn't going to work.

"Brent, I..."

"You're not getting cold feet about tonight are you?"

His face had lost its hard edge again. He looked like a little boy lost. Her heart flip-flopped at the thought of disappointing him. Even if it was just casual sex to him, Jodi hated the idea that her rejection would hurt him like the bimbo in the photo hurt him. The perfect-looking bitch must have hurt him bad, too. The heartache in his eyes was unmistakable.

She opened her mouth and surprised herself at what she said next.

"Brent, why don't we go to my apartment tonight? I live alone and my neighbors mind their own business. Nobody can rat on us there."

*****

...Bo, I wanted to tell you that I've given your suggestion about finding me a "bedroom buddy" a lot of thought, but I'm not sure I can go through with it. You were the brother who could sleep with one girl on Friday night, two more on Saturday and three others on Sunday – then call his girlfriend back home on Monday and tell her he'd been faithful to her all through the semester.

I'm just a wuss when it comes to lying to women. I admit I want to get Ms. Jodi Curvy-Ass in the sack, but I don't know if I can have just a casual relationship with her. Sure, if she makes the first move and is agreeable, I'll jump on the bandwagon and go with the flow. I'm just not sure I can do it all on my own.

How will I know if she's hot to trot? Yeah, I'm as smart as a sack of rocks at times, but I can tell when a chick is coming on to me. So far, Jodi hasn't. She hasn't gotten near me. But if she ever touches me – deliberately touches me to get my attention – then I'll know.

I keep thinking of how disappointed Helena would be if she knew I get a massive boner whenever my co-worker walks into the room. Stupid, I know, but I can't help it.

I'm all too human – and something or someone's bound to give eventually.

Keep us in the loop, Mr. Overnight Sensation…
B

Chapter Seven

There's a man in my house, Jodi thought, biting her lower lip as she switched on the foyer lights for the two of them to enter. *I've never brought a guy home to my place before. What's-his-face and I always did it in the dorms or in the back seat of his car or under the bleachers or whatever. This is my first true wild fling.*

Her heart thrummed a rapid tempo in her ears. Her palms turned a moldy basement kind of damp. She felt like dying on the spot.

"Nice place you have here." Brent followed her inside and shut the door behind him.

Jodi tossed her purse and jacket onto the high counter that separated the small kitchenette from the rest of the so-called "great room" and hung her keys on the rack beside the counter. " As you can tell it's not a very big place, but I had some money saved up for grad school and since I didn't use it right away, I splurged on this lease. Want a Coke or something?"

"Sure. Coke's fine."

As she fished two soda cans from the fridge, Brent doffed his leather bomber-styled jacket and scanned the living area. Jodi cringed as he took in the not-too-worn, powder blue, second-hand sofa, matching side chair and oak coffee table. A couple of framed watercolors and a pastel drawing some friend gave her for graduation were the closest things she had to true art. The board and brick shelving that housed her books, her modest CD/DVD collection and her small combo TV were a dead giveaway that she wasn't exactly rolling in dough.

"Hey, I use the same designer." He pointed to her homemade shelves as he sat on the sofa. "I like your décor."

"I call it *early college graduate* myself." Jodi handed him his soda then nervously took a seat in the chair opposite her guest. "I can swing the rent, but I can't swing buying new furniture. Oh well. It's probably for the best."

"For the best?"

"Uh, when I go back to grad school. I'll have to sell or give away most of my furniture if I land a fully-furnished place."

He raised an eyebrow. "You're planning on going to grad school soon?"

She shrugged. "Maybe. It depends on my finances. I need to save up a little more and get a decent car. Unlike yours, mine's a total junker."

Jodi took a sip of her drink and sank further into her chair. You have a cool set of wheels, Mr. Davison. I've always wanted a sports car."

"Thanks. I'll be paying on it for the next century, though. It sort of precludes me from any further educational instruction right now."

"Heck, you're not using all those diplomas hanging on your side of the office now as it is. Why bother cluttering up the walls some more?"

"True enough." He took a long gulp of soda. "You want to order pizza?"

Jodi blinked. It was a little after six o'clock, and

she did feel sort of hungry underneath all those kamikaze butterflies dive-bombing around in her stomach. But was this the way wild romantic evenings were supposed to start?

"Pizza's okay. I'm big on Chinese. We have a take-out place just down the block. Best Chinese food in the greater St. Louis area—or at least that's what their advertising says. And they take post-dated checks, too."

He chuckled. "Great. That option certainly helps come that last week before payday."

"No kidding." She stood. "Let me show you the menu. It's right here on the fridge door. They have specials on certain nights of the week where you can get two-for-one, too. Maybe tonight's special is something we both like."

To her surprise it was.

"You call it in, and I'll pay for it," Brent offered. "It's the least I can do..." His voice trailed off awkwardly.

Jodi furrowed her brow as she picked up the phone. Was he making a veiled reference that he'd pay for dinner in exchange for free sex? She didn't like that idea at all—not at all.

"You don't have to pay for dinner, Brent. We can split the bill in half. Fair is fair. You're not putting me out any by coming here."

He slapped himself on the forehead. "Shit, I didn't mean to imply I was paying for the use of your place in lieu of getting a motel room. I just didn't want to put you out since we're hanging out here."

"Quit while you're ahead," she warned him,

making a cutting motion toward her throat as she punched in the phone number. "Hi, Yu Li? Yes, it's Jodi over in the apartments. I want the number six dinner special for two. Does that come with both a free order of Crab Rangoon and the egg rolls? Terrific. Yes, I'll just come over and pick it up. You guys know me so well. See you in ten. Bye."

She replaced the phone receiver, picked up her purse and jacket and walked over to the door.

Brent rose. "You don't have to walk—I'll drive. It's not good to go out after dark."

"It's hardly dark—and there are plenty of street lights. And it really isn't necessary. The restaurant is just a few steps away, and I could use the fresh air. Why don't you set the table or something?"

"Set the table?"

"Or not... I'll be just a moment. Put your feet up, relax." *I sure wish I could,* Jodi thought, slipping out the door before he could protest.

*****

God, I can't do this. I've never felt comfortable around women. Only Helena made me feel relaxed. Only her.

Brent crumpled his empty Coke can and tossed it into a blue plastic container in the kitchen marked *recyclables* before he began pacing Jodi's small apartment. He felt like an idiot. What the hell was wrong with him? He wanted to jump on her bones—and she was agreeable. Or did he just imagine that she kissed him back like nobody's business in the office? She sure couldn't miss his enthusiasm... His pants got so tight his voice must have shot up at least two full octaves.

Damn! Why did his head and his heart have to crawl into bed alongside his cock?

Too late now. They'd both confessed their attraction and willingness to act on it. To back out now because of his nagging conscience would make him look like a total and utter fool. Jodi would spread the word around the office that he was all talk and no action. That vampire Gabriela would certainly gloat then. She'd been pissed when he ignored her none-too-subtle seduction attempts. She'd get back at him if she had any good dirt to fling.

Besides—why should he disappoint Jodi?

Jodi obviously felt as nervous as he did. There were no indications of her having any lovers before in her home. No photos on the walls or shelves. He took a quick look around. No men's clothing articles hanging in her closest. No old razor or aftershave sitting on the bathroom counter. She really did live alone. He wondered why.

She was young, intelligent and attractive. Surely, she'd dated some in high school and college. He didn't think she was a virgin, but he really didn't have a clue.

He was about to plop back down onto the sofa when a book on her shelf caught his eye. A yearbook. Those could be telling. He removed it from the shelf, sat down, and began turning pages. It was from her last year in college. An envelope hidden inside slipped out and fell to the floor. Picking it up, he recognized the familiar envelope of an invitation. Probably a graduation announcement.

Brent opened the envelope and removed the card. This graduation announcement looked different—very different. In fact, it wasn't a graduation announcement at all.

Mr. and Mrs. Tobias K. Baker
&
Mr. and Mrs. Cameron J. Sears
request your presence at the wedding of their children
Joanna Lynnette Baker
&
Cade William Sears
at
St. Joseph's Catholic Church
June 10, 2005
7 pm
Reception following

Jodi had been engaged? He had no clue. She'd never talked about it. No one in the office had ever said a word, either. She didn't sport a big circular dent around her ring finger suggesting they'd actually tied the knot, and then separated. One of them must have bailed after they'd printed the announcements.

It would explain her standoffishness when they first met. She had been nursing a broken heart like he had. And she was a private person like he was. She didn't want people feeling sorry for her being jilted any more than he wanted people feeling sorry for him about Helena.

He carefully slid the wedding announcement back into its envelope, put it back on the page where he found it and nestled the yearbook on the shelf. He'd respect Jodi's privacy about her love life.

Five minutes later, she returned with their food.

"The wok was hot tonight and Yu Li threw in some cashew chicken as well." Jodi placed the bag on her small dining table and started unpacking the cartons. "They were all out of those packets of spicy Chinese mustard for the egg rolls. I hope that's okay."

"No problem. I eat them straight up."

"Me, too. Let's dig in."

Her pleasant personality seemed to have returned after her short outing. She made small talk and attacked her food with gusto.

"Mmm...I haven't had Chinese for a couple of weeks. Thanks for the excuse for ordering out. I definitely need to go grocery shopping this weekend."

He grinned. "Is that how you spend your weekends? Grocery shopping?"

"Oh, yeah. I'm a regular hellion on the weekends. Grocery shopping, laundry washing, car oil-changes, the like. I'm just one wild party animal if you can't tell already."

"The huge piles of beer cans, the handcuffs and the underwear hanging from the track lighting gave you away."

"Really? I wondered where my thongs had all gone to. I suppose I should be more careful before I kick them off in a fit of ecstasy."

They both laughed then continued eating for several moments, their eyes focused on their plates and not each other.

"Brent, I have a confession." Jodi put down her fork and looked straight at him. "I'm not really all that comfortable with the casual sex thing."

He breathed a sigh of relief. "I have to admit I'm

not all that comfortable with it, either."

"Really? Whew." She smiled and wiped imaginary beads of sweat off her forehead. "That's a relief. Then what the heck are we doing here?"

"Eating Chinese food?"

They laughed again and finished their dinner with comfortable small talk.

At last, Jodi put her napkin down beside her plate. "Seriously, though. I feel like I've been leading you on, Brent, and that's wrong of me. I want to apologize. I will invest in a whole new office wardrobe—complete with burlap bags if it will make things easier for you."

"Holy shit, no. Never cover that beautiful body of yours. It would be a sin."

Her big hazel eyes glistened with unshed tears. Her full bottom lip trembled.

"You think I have a beautiful body?"

She sounded doubtful, unsure of her own desirability, her own worth as a woman. It had to be that idiot who left her at the altar. The jerk had wounded her soul. She felt vulnerable like he felt whenever Helena had made a casual comment about his lack of dressing skills or his unkempt hairstyle.

She needed his approval—not his rejection.

Brent rose from his seat and pulled her into his arms. He kissed and caressed her face as she sat in his lap, stroking her back while she rubbed herself against his stiffening erection, fanning the flames of passion between them.

"You are beautiful, Jodi," he whispered into her hair. "Don't let anyone ever convince you otherwise."

"You're not bad-looking yourself," she murmured,

returning his magical kisses with some inventive lip caresses of her own. "I thought we said we both weren't good at this casual sex business."

"Who said anything about casual?"

And then before Brent fully realized what he was doing, he swept Jodi up into his arms and carried her into the bedroom.

*****

What was she doing? What was she feeling? She'd never felt anything like this...so good, so very good.

All Jodi's resolve to end this farce between them dissolved as Brent pulled her into his arms and claimed her lips with his own. She was his now—to have and to hold and to break and to mold and to form in whatever fashion he liked. Despite the fact she had quit believing in finding "Mr. Right" ever again, could it be he was here in her bedroom ready to love her body and soul? She never wanted to leave home—or this bed.

Brent placed her gently on the quilt before lying beside her. He pulled her into his arms, and they both kicked off their shoes. His kisses zinged like tiny jolts of electricity, trailing from her forehead to her nose to her chin to the base of her throat to her heart. She reached for his shirt buttons and quickly removed his dress shirt, baring his nicely defined pecs and firm abs. He smelled of musky aftershave and honest sweat. His scent was all male.

"Hmm...nice," she said, her fingers roving freely across his chest, curling his hairs around her fingers. "You work out a lot?"

"I help my grandfather out with home repairs. It keeps me in shape. Speaking of shape," he lowered his lips to the pebbled peaks pointing through the thin cloth of her knit top, "you've got quite a shape yourself."

"Thank you." Arching her back, Jodi thrust her breasts toward his talented lips. Her moans came long and low as he nibbled. "Oh, Brent…I don't want you to stop, but let me take this hot thing off."

She sat up and quickly removed her sweater and reached for her bra hook.

"Allow me." He undid her black lacy restraint and freed her aching nipples eager for his attention. His mouth latched onto one strawberry-colored circle and slowly suckled while his deft fingers teased the other to an erect point.

Jodi bucked against him in delight. She was about to come with just the touch of his lips and tongue on her breasts. The pleasure practically overwhelmed her as his free hand delved between her thighs and massaged her wet mound through her clothing.

"You've got to get me out of these pants…" She gasped and twisted against the pressure of his palm. "I want to feel you inside me, Brent. I have to feel you deep inside me. I want you now. Please."

He raised his head slowly and chuckled. "Slow down, we'll get there. You're not about to come on the spot, are you?"

She ground her hips against his hand and groaned. "Yes, I am. I'm sorry…it's been so long. I can't help myself."

"No need for an apology. I won't let you suffer."

Grinning, he quickly helped her slide off her pants and panties. She reached for his zipper but he swatted her hand away.

"There's time for that later. Right now, let me concentrate on helping you out of your *predicament*."

Brent moved down on the bed until his mouth nestled firmly between her legs. Slowly his tongue danced along her sensitive nub, laving and sucking until Jodi screamed out in pure ecstasy. Wrapping herself about him, she let the waves of her climax rolled over and over again until she lay limp against the bed, his willing love slave.

He pulled back and smiled. "Hmm, what a tasty dessert you make. Do you think you can handle me now?"

"Handle…maybe," she babbled incoherently. "Uh, there's protection in the top drawer of my dresser there. Next to my thongs."

"Good place for them." He crossed to the dresser and opened the drawer. "Wow…so many colors." He lifted out a matching bra and panty set along with a purple condom. "Zebra and tiger striped, too. Too bad, you can't wear these bras in public. It would certainly spice up the workplace."

She laughed and rolled to her side. "How do you know I haven't already worn them to the office?"

He grinned and placed them back in the drawer. "You're right. I don't. I'd bet a million dollars you have worn them. My thong indicator certainly throbbed on your short skirt and tight top days."

"I'll never tell." She rose to her feet. "Here. Allow me to release your thong indicator before he completely breaks your pants zipper."

Jodi slowly lowered his zipper, keeping her eyes focused on Brent's face. Even while enjoying himself he kept a part of his true nature hidden. What exactly was behind that wounded soul mirrored in the depths of his gold-flecked brown eyes? Why did his smile waver a little whenever she turned her head? Had his perfect lover ridiculed his performance in the bedroom? Had she run off with another man?

If that were the case, she'd make extra certain that Brent Davison never felt unwanted again.

"My, my... You wear some colorful undies, too." She lowered his slacks to the floor and helped him step out of them. "I like a business man in banana colored briefs."

"What can I say? They were on sale and they were all out of the Hawaiian print boxers."

"Yum. Time for me to up my fruit intake." Jodi knelt before him and kissed his growing erection through the thin material. His sighs and moans serenaded her ego better than any love song could. "Yes, it's time for the banana to come out of his basket."

He helped her slide his sticky shorts down, fully revealing a long, thick penis standing at full attention.

"It's just like eating dessert." She kissed, nibbled and tasted her way up and down his firm shaft, around the base and back again to the quivering top.

"You don't have to—" Jodi silenced him by taking his full length into her mouth. "Aaah... Yes—yes."

He melted in her capable hands and lips. She stroked and tongued him until she tasted his saltiness and felt his knees trembling with his pending explosion.

"Oh, God, Jodi, you'd better stop now. I'm a bit rusty. I'll never pull out in time, and I don't want to hurt you."

Hurt her? He thought he'd hurt her by coming in her mouth? Maybe Ms. Perfect wasn't so damn perfect after all.

"You won't," she promised, taking his length into her throat deeper still. She stroked and squeezed until he came, crying out her name. Gently she led him to the edge of the bed and lay down beside him.

"There, there," she soothed, tenderly massaging his arms and shoulders. "I didn't suck your entire brains out, did I?"

"It sure feels like it." He chuckled. "I didn't know anyone could be so talented in the bedroom. Jodi Baker—you've missed your calling."

She kissed his cheek. "My calling? Are you saying you think I ought to walk the streets at night or work in adult films?"

"Not work in adult films—*star* in adult films."

She laughed and spanked him on the bottom. "I don't know about that. I'm not exactly a size six. I doubt they'd hire someone who wasn't the size of a model."

"Wouldn't know. I've led a sheltered life."

She stared at him through slanted eyes. "Really? I find that hard to believe from a guy who can lick me into shape in moments flat."

"Oh, okay, I'll admit I've seen a couple—maybe a half dozen or so."

Jodi rolled her eyes. "You beat me. I've seen approximately two. But I read a lot of erotic fiction—it gives you ideas, you know."

"Thank heavens for good literature." He pulled her lips to his and kissed her. "I'm just sorry we didn't get a chance to use this." He held up the condom.

"Who says we can't? You don't have to be anywhere tonight at a particular time, do you?"

Brent frowned. "No, not really. But I usually arrive home by now and my grandfather will be starting to wonder about me. He might call the cops to come looking for me and track me down."

He lived with his grandfather? Brent didn't just work on his grandfather's house alongside him? This was interesting information.

"Is he an invalid?"

"No, not really. He's in excellent shape—better shape than me. He's just lonely. It's been a period of adjustment for him, and I'm trying to help out."

Jodi spotted the distant look growing in her lover's eyes. "He's widowed?"

He nodded. "Yes, that's one reason why I moved in with him…to help him fix up his old Victorian in Maplewood. He figures he'll fix it up and sell it for big bucks. I'm sort of hoping he'll hold onto it. Lots of good memories of my grandmother there."

"I can imagine. I bet it's a lovely home, too. Maplewood is a cute older suburb. Big oaks in the yard and a front porch and everything?" Brent nodded. She reached over and caressed his cheek. "I'd love to see it sometime."

"You would?" He raised an eyebrow. "You're

into old houses?"

She smiled. "Yep. And antiques—I just love old things. They're different and unique. They don't make things like they used to, do they?"

And they don't make sensitive, caring guys like you anymore, either, Jodi thought. Where had Brent Davison been hiding out all her life? She wanted to know more.

"No, they don't make houses like my grandparents' home," he said, interrupting her reverie. "That's why I want to keep it in the family."

"Can you buy it from him?"

He shook his head. "I don't have the money. Gramps will probably get a huge offer on it after we're done renovating. I can't deny him the big sale since he could use the money to retire on. He wants to go live with his brother in Florida."

"Maybe you can talk him into renting it to you? That would give him a steady stream of income and keep it in the family."

Brent stroked his chin. "Hmm...that's an idea. But I'd never be able to pay the heating bills by myself. I'd need a roommate."

A roommate? Jodi felt a tingle of anticipation tickling down her spine. "How much?"

He frowned. "Come again?"

"I hope so." She giggled. "I mean how much would a roommate have to pay you in rent?"

"More than this apartment I'm afraid." Jodi told him her rent. Brent whistled. "Oh...kay, you probably could swing it if you can afford this place."

"I can't really afford it, but I've signed the contract and I have three months to go on the lease. Living in a house sounds infinitely better than staying in this shoe box."

"You'd have much more room. It has three bedrooms and two baths plus a full kitchen and dining room."

"Sounds lovely. But who really needs more than one bedroom?" Jodi pulled him into her arms and pressed her curves against his taut muscles. "I'm thinking we only need one bed."

They kissed. The kiss deepened and Brent's hands roamed across her back and hips until they cupped her buttocks firmly. She rocked her pelvis against his growing erection and sighed as his kisses trailed down her neck, pooling about her breasts.

"Don't you want to call Gramps?" she said breathlessly.

"Later. First, there's something very important I've been meaning to do all evening."

"Hmm...What's that?"

He rolled on top of her and handed her the condom wrapper. "I want to screw your brains out."

Jodi smiled and quickly undid the wrapper. Together they unrolled the protection over his erection. She spread her legs wide, sighing as he filled her core with every inch of his manhood.

"Oh, God...Oh...Brent."

"I'm not hurting you, am I? "

"Not at all." She arched her back and allowed him deeper access. Why was he always afraid of hurting her? "And no, you're not hurting me at all. You feel...perfect."

He responded with a slow, deep thrust followed

by several quick, hard ones.

"Yes, that's it," she encouraged him. Somehow, she knew he needed to be convinced he was a worthy partner in the bedroom. "You're fantastic. Go as hard and as deep and as long as you want. I won't last long if you do."

"Neither will I. I'm out of practice."

Jodi moaned. "Hmm…Good. We can help each other get fit then. I'm all for physical fitness, aren't you?"

He grinned and pulled her legs up over his shoulders. "Of course."

She met each of his thrusts with a determined tilt of her hips. Faster and faster and harder and harder until stars swirled and colors flashed across her eyes. The intensity of her orgasm took her by surprise as every neuron in her body fired at once and sent her catapulting over the edge. Brent's loud sighs and moans drowned out her cries as he threw back his head, his release shuddering throughout his taut frame.

As peace descended on them, Jodi giggled. "That's one down—ten more to go."

Chuckling, he collapsed onto the sheets beside her. "I thought we were trying to get toned up—not go down in the Guinness Book of World Records as first rate sex fiends."

"Hey, if it helps whip us into shape why shouldn't we go for it? I believe I have a few more condoms in my drawer. If you're ready, willing and able to go again then…"

Brent drew her into his arms and kissed her

soundly. "I'm more than willing, but I admit I am a bit tired. And I do need to report in so Gramps doesn't worry needlessly."

Slowly he disengaged himself from her grasp and searched for his pants. He retrieved his cell phone from his pocket and hit speed dial.

Jodi propped herself up on an elbow and tried not to act too interested as she observed her lover speaking with his grandfather. But damn it—she *was* interested. Brent had revealed very little about himself to her. And she was dying to know more about the wonderful sex god she had just entertained in her boudoir.

Oh, all right—she'd admit it. She hadn't exactly been forthcoming about her past, either, but it wasn't a secret. Everyone in the office knew the jerk left her at the altar. Surely, Brent had heard all the gory details by now. Maybe Brent had only gone to bed with her out of pity. Did he pity her for not being able to keep a man's attention long enough to make it to the "happily ever after" ending? Did he just want a roommate to replace his grandfather?

"I'll be home shortly, Gramps. Glad to know the game on TV kept you entertained and that you didn't even miss me. Bye for now."

He clicked the phone shut and turned to her. "He didn't even realize I was late. Shows you how little I mean to him."

That's a joke, right? Jodi couldn't be too sure. It sure sounded like a sarcastic remark, but if there was anything she'd picked up about Brent, it was that he hid his hurts underneath a veneer of dry humor and sarcasm.

"Oh, I bet he worried a little," she began slowly, "but the game got his attention and he focused all his energy into cheering on his team. Who was he rooting for, by the way? I didn't think the Cardinals were playing tonight."

"They're not. He's rooting for the Cubs."

Her eyes widened. "A Chicago Cubs fan here in St. Louis?"

Brent nodded. "I know. Horrifying to think, isn't it? I'm beginning to wonder if my Uncle Bill's influence is greater than I thought. When Gramps moves in with him in Florida, they'll both be at spring training and cheering on the Cubbies during the grapefruit league season. He's already put a Chicago sticker on his car bumper."

"Oh, my. Well, you can always tell the neighbors he's growing a bit senile in his old age. They'll forgive him."

"I already have. Some kid on the block was about to cover his bumper with a Cardinals logo when Gramps ran out the front door and caught him. What else could I say?"

"Nothing really." She watched sadly as he gathered up his garments. "Can I get you anything else to eat or drink?"

He finished buttoning his shirt before bending down to kiss her. "Just you. I could eat you up every day of the week. But I have to go now. Remember, we both have homework to do."

"I hadn't forgotten." Jodi rose and crossed over to her bathroom, trying her best to ignore his gaze. She pulled her thick, white chenille robe around her, protecting her emotional nakedness from further assaults of reality. "It's back to the grind for us after a wonderful dinner and…entertainment."

He slipped into his shoes and fished a comb from his back pocket. "Shall we make plans for tomorrow night?"

A sudden chill filled her every cell. She was an adult; Brent was an adult. They'd both acted straightforward in what they wanted from the other. There was no reason for them to deny the pleasure of each other's company as long as they kept their affair discreet. There was no telling what the other inmates of the cube farm would make of it if they knew little Miss Jodi Baker, jilted bride, was getting it on with their resident token male.

Still, his apparent casualness—particularly after he'd said earlier this wasn't "casual sex"—left her feeling lost and abandoned.

"I'd say we could meet at your place, but I don't think Gramps would appreciate it. Right?"

Brent nodded. "Yeah, he's a bit old-fashioned. He believes in marriage first and carnal relations second. I'd rather not upset him considering…because he's a…"

The words trailed off. Suddenly Jodi experienced a premonition…It was almost as though Brent was about to say he was the one widowed and not Gramps.

Chapter Eight

TO: ShaynaE@wazoo.com
FROM: jbaker@hit-on-us.com
SUBJECT: Have I done it again?

Well, well…

You certainly experienced a short grieving period over losing what's-his-face Jamal. But your departmental mentor? Girlfriend, really! Isn't he a bit old for you, Shay? I mean he has to be at least thirty-five…at least. Yeah, I hear ya – age doesn't matter when you both communicate on the same plane. Just please, please don't tell me he's married.

I know I'm one to talk. I always said that I wouldn't fall into another "just sleeping with you" type of relationship and I have. But, yes, the sex is sooooooooooooooooo damn good! ☺

Details? Heck, I'm not a guy. I'm not spelling out every deliciously dirty little secret for your evil mind. Suffice it to say, Brent can rock my world in just about every position in the Kama Sutra and then some. How do I know? Let's just say we've both been working together on our "fitness program" and we've discovered the perfect answer to late night ice cream binges that is much kinder on your waistline. ☺

I hope that doesn't give you any ideas…Like I need to give you any ideas when it comes to pleasing guys in the sack! LOL

But back to the real purpose of this email. I'm worried. I'm worried I've done it again to myself. I'm worried I'm getting just a tad too emotionally involved with one Brent Davison, and it's affecting my better judgment. I'm starting to dream about white dresses and bridesmaids and flower girls and rose petals and a chamber quartet playing Here Comes the Bride. You know what happened the last time I had those dreams…I dreamed myself right out of a relationship.

No, don't say it wasn't my fault. It was partly my fault. I rushed Cade to the altar just a little too fast. If I had been patient, I would be Mrs. Cade Sears today instead of Jodi Baker, career woman and total sex slave to one very hot body…

You know, that really doesn't sound too bad after all. ☺

Okay, let me catch you up to date about what's happening in the office this week with our Successfully Seduce Your Martian contest. You could say e=Everyone has found her match. Everyone except maybe Babs. Her match is more like a threesome.

*****

"You're moving in with a couple?" Melody shrieked. The break room echoed her sentiments for several moments before anyone dared to open her mouth.

Keryn put down her yogurt container and spoon. "I think that's exactly what Babs is saying, Mel. At least your rent payments will be less. Right, Babs?"

"Yep. And Dino's given me a free pass to use the gym he manages for my workouts. That saves me hundreds a year right there. Plus, Shasta cuts my hair and does my nails for free." Babs wiggled her fingers in front of Jodi's face. "You like?"

Jodi put down her sandwich. "Nice work. I like the racing stripes."

Melody snorted. "But really."

Jodi smiled. The idea was a bit unconventional, but then again, Babs was an unconventional person. Her new living arrangement made sense in a very unconventional way. But, still, she didn't like seeing Melody so upset.

"It's all right, Mel," Jodi whispered in her ear. "Babs will see the error of her ways before too long. She's a big girl and has to make her own life decisions."

"I wish Raheesha wasn't out sick," Melody said with a sigh. Rae can set people straight. She's very good at that."

"Straight?" Keryn raised an eyebrow. "I doubt Raheesha can set Babs straight if Babs is bisexual. Right, Babs?"

Babs shrugged and took a bite of her apple, chewed it thoughtfully and swallowed. "Yeah, I guess. But I don't think I'm bisexual anymore. I prefer Shasta over Dino any day of the week."

Melody's face paled. Jodi put an arm around her shoulder to prevent her from falling out of her chair. "Is that so?" Jodi asked, trying to keep the conversation on a lighter note. "Dino is a pack rat or something?"

"Now that you mention it, he is. He's a first class slob. Poor Shasta has to do all the housecleaning. If she didn't have me to help her out she'd..."

Babs's brow furrowed. "Hey...wait a minute. That's all I seem to do whenever I'm with Shasta—clean up around the house. You don't think she's leading me on just to get me to move in with them and become a live-in maid, do you?"

"Sounds like a distinct possibility," Keryn agreed. "What is Shasta and Dino's relationship like? I mean do they hang out with you or with each other more when you're not out clubbing?"

"They hang out together more than they do with me." Babs's puzzled look became angrier by the second. "I'm beginning to think they don't love me after all."

Melody rolled her eyes. "How could they? They love each other. That's what being a couple means. One plus one doesn't equal three."

Jodi stared at her younger co-worker. For being so naïve, Melody demonstrated some rather deep insights on occasion.

After lunch, Jodi returned to her office and the mile-high stack of papers she was processing for Mr. J. But Melody's thought stayed with her all through the afternoon. *One plus one doesn't equal three.* When it came to her relationship with Brent, one plus one didn't even equal two...somehow, things never seemed to add up emotionally between them.

She'd finally confessed her engagement and how close she'd been to saying "I do" before the jerk called it off. That revelation didn't seem to phase Brent one bit. However, he didn't reciprocate with a confidence. He never told her about his past relationships. He never told her who the name of the perfect woman in the photograph was. He never told her what that old relationship was like and how it ended.

Of course, after spying that wounded look in his eyes, she'd never even dared to ask.

A knock at their office door startled Jodi out of her troubling musings.

"Jojo, can you check this over for me? With Raheesha absent today, I'm feeling a bit lost at the lead position."

"Sure thing, Lotus. Come on in."

Jodi scanned the document and pointed out two small errors. For her first day subbing as the lead, Lotus was doing an excellent job.

"I sure hope Rae feels better soon," Lotus confessed. "She sounds so froggy on the phone, though. Since she's got quite a bit of sick leave accrued, I doubt she's going to be in until next week."

"That's too bad. But just think—you're gaining valuable work experience."

"Really?" Lotus sighed. "That's one way of looking at it. But I don't think I can keep up the strenuous pace much longer."

Jodi gave her co-worker a quick squeeze. "Oh, Lolo. Have more confidence in yourself and your abilities. You're doing great. Tell me, how are you and

Mr. Maxwell getting along these days?"

Lotus's perpetually pale cheeks turned bright pink. "Max and I get along great. We're going to a rally this weekend to help save virgin forest stands in Mark Twain National Forest."

"Sounds exciting. Do you get to hug each other while you hug the trees?"

Lotus blushed again. "Uh-huh. That's part of the fun. Afterward, when we have all these loose cords lying around we…"

"I'm trying to think here," Brent interrupted. "Take the conversation outside."

"Oh, so sorry."

Lotus quickly gathered up her papers and exited. Jodi mouthed, "Don't mind him," but she could tell Brent's boorishness had hurt the gentle hippy's feelings.

"You owe Lotus an apology," Jodi said through clenched teeth. "Your rudeness was uncalled for."

"My rudeness? If you let her go on, she'll talk your ear off about saving the whales, the seals, the penguins *and* the Continental Building. The woman is addicted to supporting causes."

"And what's wrong with that? At least she's not afraid to put her beliefs into action."

Brent sighed and twisted away from her in his seat. "Meaning?"

"Meaning? It means Lotus possesses some backbone. Not many people do."

"Backbone? Standing up for sea mammals isn't exactly the world's most important issue when we've got suicide bombers lurking around every corner."

"What's fighting terrorism got to do with having the courage of your convictions? Honestly, Brent you don't get it, do you?"

"Yeah, right." He snorted. "Like I'm the one who doesn't get it."

"Enough already. Let's end this discussion, okay?"

He refused to take the hint. "How about Gabriela?"

Jodi furrowed her brow. "What about her?"

He continued to tap away on his keyboard. "I have to admit it surprised me to hear she's still seeing that millionaire. That takes backbone. I'm actually beginning to believe Ms. Roget has fallen in love for the first time in her life. She's stopped dressing like a tramp and cut back on the make-up. She doesn't drool over every guy who walks past her cubicle. It's quite refreshing."

"Argh!" Jodi screamed, slamming her cabinet drawer for emphasis. "Quit with the male superiority complex stuff. You feel offended since she's stopped coming on to you. Admit it. You miss all the attention you got here in your early days, and you're jealous Lotus and Gabriela have found some measure of happiness."

"No way. I'm glad no one tries to put the moves on me anymore. I need to get this stupid project done for Mr. J by his ridiculous deadline."

A low knocking at the door made them both jump in their desk chairs.

"Do you need more time, Brent?" Mr. Johansson asked. "If so, I can give you a few extra days but that's about it. We need to take this project to the backers before next Tuesday."

Brent slapped his forehead in disgust and tried to talk, but the words wouldn't come.

"We'll make it by the original deadline." Jodi did her cheerful best to fill in the dead air. "I'll even help Brent on his project if he tells me what to do."

The balding boss beamed a smile at her. "Why thank you, Jodi. You always go the extra mile. I see only good things in your future with that go-getter attitude." He frowned at Brent. "I'll let you two get back to work now." He quietly closed the door.

A long, relieved sigh escaped Jodi's lips. "Whew. That was close. You almost got yourself thrown out on your ear, Brent."

"Mr. J wouldn't can me for saying something was ridiculous—would he?"

"Oh, yes he would. You didn't see him fire Frankie. And Frankie's only crime was dressing up like a woman and singing to customers over the phone. If Mr. J has the balls to throw out the world's greatest Cher impersonator for acting stupid late one afternoon before Ladies Night at the café, then he'd gladly toss you out for your impudent remarks."

Brent ran a lanky hand through his mop of hair. "Gee, thanks for telling me now."

Another knock at their office door cut into their conversation.

"I couldn't help hearing…you need help with your project?" Keryn stood tall in the doorway. "I've done some programming before. I could help."

"Really?" Brent closed out the file he was working

on and opened another. "Can you help me with this?"

"Probably." Keryn approached his desk and gazed into the monitor. "That doesn't look too hard. Email me what you want me to look at, and I'll take a stab at it."

"Well, the files that really need work are on my home computer. I'll have to send them to you from there. Unless you want to come over and take a look at them."

Jodi felt her heart pounding in her ears. How dare he! They'd been sleeping together for several weeks and Brent hadn't even invited her home to meet Gramps in person. Brent must be ashamed of her—ashamed of their relationship.

And he was ready to move on with Keryn!

"I thought you were going to help me with these flow charts tonight," Jodi said through gritted teeth.

He gave her a blank expression then said slowly, "Oh, yeah…right you are. I'll email the files to you, Keryn, if that's okay."

She shrugged. "Either way is okay with me. I can ask Pointdexter his opinion if you like."

"I thought his name was Peter." Jodi scratched her head. For all her competitiveness, Keryn had kept her relationship with the Bill Gates clone very quiet. "You're still seeing him since that night you all went over to the millionaire's mansion?"

"Yeah. Off and on. I find him…interesting. And funny at times. We have a lot in common."

Jodi blinked. Keryn Wiseman had found a kindred soul? If anyone on the planet seemed destined for eternal singlehood, she had thought it would be

Keryn.

A chill zinged down her spine. Maybe of all the single women in the office Jodi Baker was predestined to remain a spinster.

"That's great you two laugh together," Brent said. "It's always good to have something in common other than just sexual attraction."

Sexual attraction? Was that all she and Brent had? Was that all they meant to each other? Jodi felt a burning lump of regret forming in her throat. She tried to swallow it, but it wouldn't go down.

After Keryn went back to her office, the silence remained as thick and dense as an autumn's fog rolling in from the Missouri. Brent continued tapping away on his keyboard with the occasional moan or gripe. Jodi mechanically forced her way through her paperwork, but her mind couldn't focus on the task at hand. Finally, at four o'clock she called it quits.

"I can't read any more of this stuff." She put down her pen and reached for her purse. "I'm calling it a day."

He put down the keyboard and turned to face her. "Didn't you catch a ride with Melody to the office?"

"Yeah, I did. Oh, well…I'll just go down to the plaza and hang out in front of one of the bars until she's ready to leave."

"If you want, I can knock off early, too."

Jodi rose to gather her jacket off the back of her chair and her lunch box from on top of her file cabinet. "No, I don't want you to fall behind. You go ahead and keep working as long as you like. I'll tell Mel I'll wait for her downstairs."

A pause, then softly, "You want me to come over later?"

She turned her face away from him. "You can…if you feel we have anything in common."

His response was swift and immediate. He kicked the door closed and pulled her into his arms. "What's that supposed to mean? Are you thinking I'm only attracted to you for your body?"

"Ridiculous as it seems, the thought had occurred to me."

"You have a great mind and a great personality, too." He kissed her forehead.

"Thanks. I should feel pleased it's not only my boudoir talents that fascinate you. Somehow I don't."

He frowned. "You don't?"

Should she come out and say what was on her mind? She bit her lower lip and summoned her courage. He would either make her happy with what he said next, or he would dump her ass first onto the carpet.

"How come you've never invited me over to your home and introduced me to your grandfather?"

"Say wha…?"

Brent appeared thoroughly perplexed for a full ten seconds before the mental light bulb switched on. "Oh, you thought I was introducing Keryn to Gramps. Well, I wasn't. Gramps isn't even in town this week. He left last week to go down to Florida to visit Uncle Bill on his birthday."

"Oh." It was all Jodi could think of saying at that bit of news.

"You can meet him when he gets back. We should

have all the plasterwork completed by then. The house is practically uninhabitable with all the renovations going on at once. I really wished Gramps could have stayed put until things were more orderly."

"So the only reason you haven't shown me your home and introduced me to your grandfather is because your place is total disaster area?"

He nodded. "Yep, that's pretty much it."

Jodi relaxed. "Sorry. I'm sorry I assumed it was because of other reasons."

"Like we don't have anything in common besides great sex?"

She grinned. "Well, besides the fact we both adore Chinese take-out food and religiously watch *Futurama* re-runs, what do we have in common besides sex—and work?"

"We both think we're not living up to our potential. We both like the Cardinals over the Cubs. We both like how convenient it is to have parents retired and living out of state."

"That's not whole lot to have in common." Jodi pulled his lips closer to her own and kissed him soundly before pulling away. "Maybe it's better if all we do have in common is great sex and Chinese take-away."

"I've never taken you on a date, have I?" Brent asked matter-of-factly. "I apologize. I rushed you into an intimate relationship and never considered your feelings. You want to go to the movies?"

She shrugged. "Maybe. What's on?"

"I have no idea, but I can bring up the Wehrenberg Theaters web site, and we can check what's playing over at Ronnie's Cine."

"Okay." Jodi stood up and allowed him use of his hands. "Hmm...Nothing much. I wonder when that new Orlando Bloom flick is coming out."

He pointed to the screen. "What do you mean there's nothing much? I see about five action movies running. You like Jackie Chan?" Jodi screwed up her face and stuck out her tongue. "Okay, then how about Bruce Willis? I hear in his latest they blow up at least two hundred cars, planes and other forms of transportation."

"Goody. Sounds terribly environmentally incorrect."

"Of course." Brent caught Jodi's eyes focusing on the title of the film below it. "Oh, no...We can't see a chick flick."

She placed her hands on her hips and broadened her stance. "And pray tell, why not?"

"I don't know. We just can't. They're so...boring."

"Boring? How can anyone who thinks beating up people and blowing up things is okay say that a movie in which human relationships are explored realistically on screen is boring?" She folded her arms across her cleavage. "We have nothing in common—cinematically, at least."

"Obviously." He tapped in a few keystrokes and brought up another web site. "How about we just go out to eat tonight? You like Japanese?"

"Just as long as they cook it, I'm game."

"I'm with you—no sushi. But I know a great Japanese steakhouse on Olive." He typed in a few more words. "There. I made us reservations at seven."

"That's not that far away from here. It's hardly worth the commute down I-270 and back. I might as well stay here and work some more on these documents."

Jodi put her lunch box, purse and jacket down on the cabinet and picked up her pen again. They worked in amiable silence until five fifteen when the office cleared out.

"You two don't burn the midnight oil too much," Mr. Johansson warned. "I don't want you burning out before you help me make the presentation to the investors."

"We won't," Jodi assured him. "Besides, we both expect to receive several weeks' vacation to make up for the overtime hours we're putting in."

"Oh?" The balding man's eyebrows shot up a foot. He thoughtfully stroked his chin. "Well, all right. I guess that's acceptable. Fill out a time sheet and we'll call it even."

"Thanks, Mr. J."

"Smart move," Brent said as the sound of the front door closing behind their boss echoed into their office. "But that's what I've come to expect from one very smart and very sexy lady."

He put down his keyboard and came over to her sitting at the desk. Slowly he massaged her neck and shoulders.

"Mmm…Feels good. Don't stop."

He lowered his lips to her ear and whispered, "I wasn't planning to."

His hands kneaded her muscles like putty. Jodi

felt the tension of the day melt away under his tender touch. From her neck to her shoulder blades, he rubbed, occasionally dipping to cradle a breast in his firm grasp.

"Is that what you call a Swedish massage?"

Brent chuckled as he slowly traced the outlines of her areola beneath the thin material of her cotton v-neck shirt. "No, but this is." He tweaked the nipple beginning to bud. "Nice, but you have a pair." He tweaked the other.

She leaned back against his torso and sighed. "Aren't I lucky? But please, continue Mr. Swedish massage. What else can you *relax* for me?"

"Is it relaxation or exhilaration you want?" His hands delved beneath the V of her shirt and caressed her breasts again while the bulge in his pants moved up and down her spine. "I think it's the second option, don't you?"

"Hmm…Yeah, that sounds nice. But you forget we're at the office. We've never done it here. What if somebody come back to the office? They could catch us in the act."

"Really?" He rubbed his erection against her back with more enthusiasm. "Then we'll have to make it a quickie…A get-down-and-dirty fast one right here on the desk. Are you game?"

Jodi gulped. She felt sorely tempted. She'd always wanted to make love somewhere exotic or erotic or at least some locale that wasn't everyday mundane. Her apartment at least was private. She alone held the key. But at the office? Well, probably nobody would return except Mr. J if he needed something for his upcoming presentation and that didn't seem likely.

"Close the door," she commanded. "Lock it."

Brent did as she instructed, then turned around and began unbuttoning his shirt. Jodi kicked off her shoes and yanked her top over her head. She flung it to the floor then began to work on her skirt zipper. It wouldn't budge.

"Damn! It's stuck. Can you help?"

He stepped out of his shoes and trousers and kicked to the side. "I'll try." He tugged hard at the pull. "Shit. It's caught in the material."

"Oh, crud. I like this skirt, too. I don't want to rip it."

"We won't." He pushed the material up above her hips and then slid a finger under her thong elastic. "After all, this is a quickie, remember?"

She smiled. "Right."

He lowered her panties to the floor and allowed her to kick them away. His fingers delved between her parted thighs, massaging her throbbing mound. Jodi drew him into her arms and their lips met, tongues touching and tasting in a dance of boundless desire.

"We've got to get you out of those things," she murmured at last. The overpowering smell of his sex made her mouth water. "Shall I do the honors?"

"Be my guest."

She tugged his briefs down and was shocked at the enormity of his erection. She wrapped an eager hand around the base and began to stroke it. His groan sent a tremor of expectation zinging through her body.

"My, my, Mr. Davison. You must have been feeling excited all day."

"I can't help it. You're sitting within arm's reach of me and looking so damn hot in that tight skirt and clingy top. You really know how to make a guy sweat, Jodi Baker."

His affirmation of her sexiness did more to make her juices flow than did his talented touch on her body. "Thanks. Grab my purse off the cabinet there. I've got a condom secreted in the inner pocket."

Brent retrieved the protection then lifted her up and placed her buttocks on the edge of her desk.

"The papers!" she cried, moving them to her chair. "I don't want to mess up all these documents. What would Mr. J and the investors think?"

"They'd think you had a very good time vetting them." His grin resembled the devil's own. He arched an eyebrow. "Lean back a little and let me show you what I think."

Jodi did exactly what Brent told her. Brent quickly sheathed his erection and pulled her hips closer to the edge. With one hard thrust, he drove into her and set the stars before her eyes spinning off into space.

"You okay?" he asked, freeing her breasts from her bra cups. She nodded. "Good. Put your arms on my shoulders, hook your legs around my back and hold on."

Each plunge came harder and faster than the last. Jodi tilted her head back and allowed the hairpins to fall from her unruly mop. An animal cry tore from her throat and reverberated through the empty office suite as Brent continued his amorous assault unabated.

As she fell back to her elbows, he lowered his lips to her breast and suckled. She moaned. His hands fondled her buttocks and helped her tilt her hips in time with each thrust. The symphony of pounding, fondling, suckling and groaning threatened to overwhelm her. She tensed and he eased his pounding.

"You're holding back. Don't, Jodi. Let go and enjoy the moment."

She panted. "I'm still worried someone will catch us."

He chuckled. "Then show them the real woman you are. Show them you know how to have a good time that doesn't involve a battery operated device."

Who needs a vibrator when I have a lover like Brent Davison?

"All right. Do me so hard I scream and break every single window in this building."

Brent accepted her challenge with unbridled enthusiasm. He corkscrewed his hips as he plunged himself ever deeper inside her. Jodi shrieked repeatedly at the pleasure-pain, pleading with him to go faster, harder, ever deeper…

Before either knew what was happening, their massive shared climax crashed over them like a tidal wave on a hurricane-swept coastline. Drenched in sweat they embraced.

"You want to lie down on the carpet?" he asked, carefully withdrawing.

"Uh-huh. I wanna take a shower, too. I can't walk into a restaurant smelling like a hooker, can I?"

He grinned and helped her down from the desk.

"Why the hell not? I find it a turn on."

"You would." She laughed. "Okay, but I have to wash my face and fix my make-up first."

"Skip the blush—you won't need it." He pulled her down to the floor with him.

"Yeah, I bet my face is beet red. Rats… I just realized I left my cover stick at home. You didn't leave any noticeable marks did you?"

"Want me to go over you with my tongue and make sure?"

"Sure. Just call me the appetizer. Can I have you for dessert?"

"Sounds like a plan." He trailed kisses down her neck and across her breasts and stomach. "Yum. I definitely could eat you all up."

Jodi groaned as he sank his face between her thighs and began tonguing her again. The man was insatiable. Thank heaven he was all hers.

Chapter Nine

TO: MrBoJangles@crapster.net
FROM: bdavison@hit-on-us.com
SUBJECT: White lies turn into snowballs

Hey, Big Shot!

I heard from our mutual acquaintance Bob "the Blunderer" Bormon that you were already advertising for a tour band. That's fantastic. Do you think you'll be playing in St. Louis anytime soon? It's where so many new bands in the Midwest start out and make it big. You could play the Pageant. I'd get front center seats comp, right? That would be awesome.

I'm so proud of you, bro. I wish I could say the same about myself.

Before you wonder, Jodi's fine… Yes, she's really fine like I told you. The woman can make love better than any woman on the planet. But I'm getting cold feet here. She's starting to ask little nosy questions about my past. I just want us to be friends—well, a little more than friends, but you know what I mean. But somehow, it's difficult to divorce one's heart from one's head.

I told her the reason why she couldn't meet Gramps was that the house was a total pigsty. That was true for the first couple of weeks of our relationship, but I can't honestly say that now. Gramps finished the wall work and painted the place in about three days with very little help from yours truly. Yeah, I feel bad about that, too. I was hanging at Jodi's – watching her TV, eating her food, enjoying her bed. I told Gramps I didn't come home right away after work because I was working overtime on a big project for the boss. And that's true – I am, but I'm not quite working as many hours as I led Gramps to believe.

But I'm lying to the two people who are closest to me in the world, and it's starting to make me feel mega-guilty. Help.

Do I continue lying to Gramps about having a girlfriend? I'm not sure. I don't think he'd mind – actually, I think he'd feel relieved. He's been watching me like a hawk, especially on anniversaries of important dates Helena and I shared. He'd probably frown at the fact that Jodi and I are a little more "friendly" than two people who really don't know each other should be, but he'd get over it. In fact, he'd be asking me when he should expect great-grandkids and the whole wedding thing…Oh shit. Maybe I do need to keep Jodi a secret a while longer.

Do I continue lying to Jodi about the house? I know Gramps is proud of it and wants to show it off, but I don't think he'd want to rent it to me with Jodi as my roommate. And the photos of Helena…They're still all over the bookshelves. I don't have the heart to remove them, and I can tell Gramps likes them there.

He was so happy when Helena and I were engaged. She reminded him so much of my grandmother. And he was as devastated as I was when I got that call…

I don't know what I would have done if Gramps hadn't been there for me.My parents are more like crap stuck on the bottom of your shoe in their homes in Arizona. They couldn't wait to fly back to their respective homes after the funeral. It's like they have a whole other life out west now and no time for those of us who remain in the hometown. Well, to hell with them! I got through grad school on my own and I'm making it on my own now. Who needs shitheads like that hanging around screwing up the place?

Sorry about that. Their actions still royally piss me off—or lack of actions, that is. What can I say?

But I still think I need to come clean with both Gramps and Jodi. Jodi will never understand about Helena…or why I can't let another woman take her place.

It just wouldn't be right. And it wouldn't be fair to Jodi, either.

Lay it on me "Dr. Phil". I could use some of your words of wisdom. You always were the "touchy-feely" one of the frat. Don't disappoint me now.
B

*****

Just when Jodi thought she had him figured out, Brent Davison did something totally out of character.

Their date to the Japanese steakhouse turned out to be quite enjoyable. They conversed on subjects that didn't revolve around work, sexual positions or Cartoon Network's *Adult Swim* animations. They relaxed and had fun just being themselves. Jodi felt proud to be sitting next to the most handsome and witty man in the restaurant all evening. For a moment, she could almost convince herself this was the real thing—that she could risk her heart being hurt again.

Still, there was something missing in some of Brent's responses.

"You've never told me what high school you attended," Jodi had asked between sips of her drink. Brent had ordered a Japanese beer and she had indulged in a piña colada. "For being a native St. Louisan that's pretty unusual, you know."

"Yeah, it is. I always thought that habit was annoying. My parents always asked other adults what high school they attended. It seems so snobbish, like you're trying to peg a person into what neighborhood and social status they grew up. I don't think any other city in America places so much emphasis on where you attended high school as St. Louis does."

"So you went to Maplewood High then?"

"Heck no! I attended CBC."

She whistled. "Uh, yeah. So who's talking about being a snob now? A poor boy from Maplewood goes to the most expensive boys' school in town."

"Hey, my grandparents wanted me to go there. They helped my parents with the tuition. You're one to speak. Didn't you go to Lindbergh?"

Jodi fiddled with her drink straw. "Well, yes. But it's a public school, and we didn't live in a mansion if that's what you're getting at. We lived off Baptist Church Road. That's hardly the Country Club area.

He nodded his agreement then finished his beer. The waitress placed their first course of a small salad marinated in what Jodi could only describe as "Japanese Thousand Island dressing" in front of them. She felt ravenous from their recent lovemaking session and devoured her salad in seconds flat. Hunger pangs sated, she decided to probe further into Brent's upbringing.

"What was it like attending an all boys' Catholic high school? Boring? Fascinating? How did you guys find dates for your dances?"

"We didn't. They found us. The Catholic girls' schools arranged their schedule so we could attend each others' socials."

A distant look crossed his features. His gaze suddenly left her face and focused on something in the long distant past. Jodi knew he was thinking of the woman in the photograph. *Ms. Perfect* had accompanied him to a social function—and probably more than one.

"Did you have a steady date?"

"Let's change the subject, okay?" He sipped the clear broth the waitress set before them. "I hate rehashing ancient history. Let's enjoy our food."

Jodi took the hint. How could she miss it? His rigid posture and frowning brow practically screamed *Don't poke your nose into my past.* She scooped up a spoon of soup and blew on the hot liquid. Fine, she'd do as she was told--for now.

The animated hijinks of the family of six seated at the teppanyaki table beside them filled the lull in their own conversation. Soon their chef appeared to cook their orders. His entertaining antics of flipping Ginzu knives and spinning raw eggs on the hot cooking surface soon distracted Jodi from prying further into Brent's history.

The following Saturday they went to the movies.

"Are you sure you want to see this with me?" she had asked as they stood in line for popcorn. "This isn't exactly an action flick. It's about a woman who thinks she'll never date again. It has a large ensemble cast of talkative girlfriends and eventually her long lost love returns, too. And everyone lives happily ever after without once blowing up a car or a building."

"Yeah, sounds good."

Jodi blinked and stared at him a full twenty seconds. "You feel okay?"

"I'm fine. Maybe we can take in that other movie you pointed out on the billboard next weekend."

"Okay..." Something definitely wasn't right. The man who hated chick flicks wanted to take her to not one, but two movies. Overwhelmed by Brent's generosity, she couldn't help but suspect that he was only being nice to her in order to soften a future blow.

Their late afternoon Sunday stroll through Laumeier Sculpture Park further reinforced her fears.

"I can't believe you grew up in St. Louis County and never visited the sculpture park before." Jodi couldn't contain her laughter as they made their way in and out of the giant wooden artwork she'd knick-named "The Log Pyramid".

"Hey, I grew up in Maplewood. Sunset Hills very well could have been in another time zone for all I knew."

"Yeah, it's gotta be what—a whole seven or eight miles away? You'd drive that far into the city for a baseball game, wouldn't you?"

"Of course. But that's a sport, not an outdoor art exhibition area. Anyone in their right mind would drive that far for a sporting event. I'm not too sure about people who'd drive that far to see odd shapes made out of wood and metal. Something's definitely wrong with them upstairs." He laughed. "Nah, I'm kidding. I'm just more into classic art than abstract stuff."

"Still, you have to admit it's a lovely place."

He stopped and stared at her for a long moment. "Yes, it's beautiful. It's nice to know that something around here still has trees and hills and hasn't been totally flattened and transformed into a strip mall."

"Don't hold your breath. Land is at a premium out here. They may yet turn this place into a golf course or retirement complex."

"Probably."

Brent turned away and headed down the path. Jodi followed in silence until they reached the short glass and steel footbridge that spanned a small ravine. Something was definitely going on. She could sense it. Beneath that gorgeous mane of thick, brown hair lay an enigmatic mind that hid secrets better than she had ever hidden her stash of Halloween candy from her pushy big brother.

"Spill it, Davison. What's up?"

He walked halfway across the footbridge before replying. "I don't know what you're getting at. Nothing's up."

"You forget I share an office with you—and occasionally a bed." She slowly walked toward him. "I can tell you're feeling out of sorts. You're being too nice to me."

"Who says a guy can't be nice to a girl without having some kind of guilt issue, huh?"

That was a new one. *Guilt?* What was Brent feeling guilty about? The wife he left behind at grad school? Jodi took another step toward him and paused.

"Being nice to a lover doesn't have to be an admission of guilt, but now that you mention it…What are you feeling guilty about, Brent?"

The hurt look overpowered his previous nonchalance. It appeared that he was no longer able to restrain whatever dark secrets he'd been keeping from her. He turned his face away.

"I don't. I just don't like myself very much at the moment. I don't like how I've treated you. I want to make amends."

"Make amends?" Jodi frowned. "Are you saying you feel sorry you've slept with me?"

"No, that's not it at all. Stop putting words in my mouth."

Brent hiked down the path toward the next sculpture. She quickly followed, grabbing him on the shoulder and forcing him to stop and look at her.

"What the hell do you mean then? I don't need yours—or any man's—pity. I can take care of myself."

"Of course you can."

"Good. I'm glad we agree on something." Brent continued to frown. She had to know what was going on inside that puny male brain of his. Men were such irrational creatures at times.

"What's eating you alive about how you've treated me? You've acted fair overall. You aren't the most romantic man in the world, but lately…lately, you've gone out of your way to be agreeable. Is this what guilt does to you?"

He nodded and began walking again. "Yeah, that's it. You want me to go back to simply showing up at your place ready to jump your bones without slipping in a kind word edgewise?"

"Well, no. I rather like your nice persona here. It's what I've always suspected about you. Underneath that gruff exterior is a teddy bear of a guy. Why don't you let your sensitive side come out to play more often?"

"I don't know." He shrugged. "It's just been difficult to let my façade drop since…"

His words trailed away, but instantly she knew how to fill in the blanks.

"Since she left you?"

Brent halted dead in his tracks. Deep, soul-wrenching pain emanated from his features, a face frozen with a grief unhealed and unspoken. Jodi's heart felt as if he'd ripped it in two. She gathered him into her arms and held him close, tenderly stroking his head.

"She didn't leave—at least, not in the usual sense of the word."

"You don't mean..." Jodi gulped. "Did...did she die?"

He nodded. Still, tears did not fall.

"Oh, Brent. I'm sorry. I didn't mean to bring such a painful subject up, but you've got to admit you can't keep something like this bottled up forever."

He pulled back and scanned her face, self-loathing coloring his every word.

"What do you know about forever, Jodi? Have you ever met someone and fell in love from that very first moment? Have you ever grown up side by side and planned your big wedding day repeatedly in infinite detail? Have you ever had to pick up a phone and hear a stranger say, 'I'm sorry to inform you, but your fiancé's plane crashed and there were no survivors'?"

Jodi sniffed. A steady stream of tears trickled down her cheeks. Brent's behavior made sense now. His filing cabinet drawer housed a photo of the world's most perfect woman—fixed perfectly in time. She'd never age and he'd never forget her. He had suffered the ultimate loss.

"No, I can't begin to fathom what you've been through. But is it fair to her memory to keep yourself from opening up and sharing your heart with others? Would she have wanted you to feel miserable and guilty?"

He wiped her cheeks dry with a finger and let out a deep sigh. "No, she wouldn't have wanted me to turn into a gloomy bastard. But I have."

"You don't have to be unhappy, Brent. You can choose to be happy again."

"I know. But I'll never really be the man I was before Helena got on that airplane."

Jodi smiled up at him. "I know, but you can become someone better—wiser and stronger for the experience."

"Better? Wiser?"

His cynical laugh sent a shiver of dread racing along her spine. She took a step backward, away from him.

"Yeah, right. I was scum of the earth before that plane crashed—and I'll remain a bottom-dweller until the day I die."

Jodi reached for his hand. "No, please don't say those things about yourself. You're not responsible for her death. It was an accident, right?"

"Responsible? Hell, I'm totally responsible. I'll never forgive myself for allowing Helena to go on a trip she shouldn't have gone on alone. I'll never forgive myself for being so wrapped up in my own life that I couldn't take a few days off to accompany her. I let her get on that airplane—I killed her. So I'll have to live with it—the guilt, the what-ifs, the whole stinking, unholy mess."

With those words echoing in her ears, Brent trudged away, leaving Jodi alone in the woods, quietly crying, in the rapidly approaching dusk.

Chapter Ten

TO: ShaynaE@wazoo.com
FROM: jbaker@hit-on-us.com
SUBJECT: My life is a soap opera

Hey, girlfriend –

Long time no hear. How's the "mentoring" coming along? ☺

Things aren't so hot here. I've always been suspicious that it's my big mouth that gets me into trouble and turns guys off, and now I know it. My very words are poison…My speech is more lethal than a thousand silver bullets or a stake in the heart.

I need to learn to keep my big yap shut. I won't go into details. It's enough to say my bed has a whole lot more space in it than last week.

Fortunately, my old cubicle is still open and Mr. J needs me to help fill in on the phones so I'm not cooped up with my ex-sex god for extended periods. Thank heavens for small mercies.

I'm actually subbing for Gabriela. First, it was Raheesha who got the royal crud throat and now it's Gabby. Lotus's natural herbs seem to be keeping her healthy. Babs sweats out her germs on the basketball court—and the bedroom, no doubt. Keryn and Mel both work away from the cube farm so they tend to stay healthier.

With any luck, I should have a fatal dose of the nasty bug soon enough. Bury me in that periwinkle skirt and blazer set I wore to graduation. It's a bit out of date, but it still looks good on me. I want people to say at my funeral, "She certainly knew what colors flattered her complexion the best. Too bad she never learned how to keep her fat mouth shut."

Enough of the soap opera already! Let me know if you can get away some weekend for a quick visit. I could stand a real flesh-and-blood shoulder to cry on. Cyber-shoulders just aren't quite as comforting.

Call me if you can't make it in person—

Jodi

*****

"Raheesha—it's great to have you back!" Melody ran from behind the receptionist's area and threw her arms around her co-worker. "Ooo, you feel a bit thinner but definitely healthier. Did you miss us?"

Rolling her eyes, Jodi tossed some outgoing mail on the counter. "Uh-huh. Who in their right mind would ever miss this place?"

"I think the fever cooked my brains so that would explain it if I did." Raheesha laughed and gave them both a one-arm squeeze. "But miss y'all? Yes and no. I did until..."

Melody's eyes widened. "Until?"

Raheesha bit her lower lip. "Well..."

"Aw, come on now. You've piqued our curiosity." Jodi lowered her voice and leaned forward. "You had a regular visitor during your convalescence—didn't you?"

"Exactly," she whispered back. "Remember that nice gentleman from my church choir I've been dating off and on? He came over to my place with a big pot of his mother's homemade chicken soup and nursed me back to health."

"How lovely!" Melody clapped her hands together. "Is he a medical professional?"

"Hardly. He's a funeral home director."

Melody frowned. "You mean he *buries* people for a living?"

"Six foot under or more, honey child. It's a very lucrative profession and not at all as I'd pictured it. TV and movies do not do the funeral business any favors. There are some very kind and compassionate folks involved in it. And they need lovin' too."

"Raheesha! You don't mean..."

Jodi grinned. "You guys are officially an item?"

The big woman smiled. She withdrew her left hand from her coat pocket and flashed a one-carat diamond solitaire under their noses for suitable admiration.

"Ahh..."

"You're engaged?" Melody blinked. "To a funeral director? That's...that's wonderful! Congratulations!"

The three hugged again and drooled over the flawless stone once more.

"Congrats, Rae." Jodi choked back a sob that seemed perpetually stuck in her throat this past week. "If anyone was going to show Gabby up on one of her stupid bets, I'm so glad it's you."

Raheesha narrowed her eyes. "Hell, I don't want to show Gabby up—I want to thank her for putting a fire under my butt. I'd been allowing my prejudices and misgivings to keep me from dating Darnell. Once I got to know him better, I realized how wrong my assumptions about him were. And I'm not letting this fish get away."

Melody raised her coffee mug. "Here's to fighting our prejudices. If I had allowed my fears of walking into smelly gyms with a bunch of sweaty weightlifters get in my way, Barry would have never invited me to his next meet."

"Good for you." Raheesha smiled. "You and Barry ever do anything but go to weightlifting meets?"

"Not really. He practically lives at the gym when he's not working. Sort of like Babs—they're addicted to exercise, I guess."

"Time for you to start a new hobby then, girlfriend. There are such things as lady weightlifters you know."

"I know, but I'm such a weakling. What if Barry laughs at me? I don't think I could take it."

"You don't have to take it—you can tell him to forget ever seeing you again if he's got that kind of attitude problem. And speaking of attitudes," Raheesha turned her focus on Jodi. "How goes sharing a cubbyhole with our gorgeous token male?"

Jodi tapped her pen on the countertop and shrugged. "I'm sitting in my old cube."

"Say what?"

Melody put a finger to her lips. "Jodi is filling in for Gabriela. We were awful short-handed for a couple of days with both of you out. I even took a few calls. Mr. J said I handled them quite well, too."

"Great, but it doesn't explain why our most talented employee isn't shacking up in her office with our token piece of male flesh."

"I work better alone." Jodi turned and headed toward the cube farm. "Relay my calls to my old desk, Mel, will ya?"

"Sure thing." The younger woman leaned toward Raheesha and lowered her voice. "Lover's tiff."

"Excuse me?" Jodi whirled around and stormed back to the front. "What did you just say?"

Melody blushed. "Uh, nothing."

"She said you and Brent had a lover's tiff." Raheesha squared her shoulders and placed her hands on her hips. "Wanna come clean?"

"No, I don't."

Jodi turned to walk off but spun back around before her co-workers got the wrong idea. "I meant since we're not seeing each other in the romantic sense there's nothing for us to have an argument over. Case closed."

"The more you try to explain it the more I know you're fibbing." Raheesha motioned to Jodi to follow her to the break room. "I need a cup of java to get my day going and so do you. Follow me."

Jodi obediently tailed her co-worker to the coffee pot. Raheesha poured them each a cup and then sat down at the table. She took a long sip of the fragrant brew before she spoke.

"So, you and Brent had a little misunderstanding. Is that correct?"

Jodi shrugged nonchalantly and slowly sipped her coffee. "We butt heads all the time. It's unavoidable when you're working on a project and come from such radically different viewpoints. He's much more IT oriented than I am, and he can't understand the importance of cost analysis and projecting income rates and—"

Raheesha put down her mug and ended the babbling with a cutthroat gesture. "Enough of the snow job, girlfriend. Tell me the real reason why the man ain't rockin' your world this week."

Suddenly all the hurts and disappointments of the last few days came crashing in on her. Jodi felt crushed by the weight of sadness upon her heart. What could it hurt to confess her feelings to a close friend?

"He's still in love with his late girlfriend."

"Late? You mean she's pregnant?"

Jodi shook her head and grimaced. "No, I mean she's not ever coming back."

"Oh…" Raheesha nodded solemnly. "I see. Yes, that's a problem all right. If she were alive, you could confront him about her faults. But no one outshines a dead loved one. You only remember their good points, never their bad ones."

"You learn that from Darnell the Undertaker?"

"Nah, I learned that on my own. I remember how my grandmother idolized my grandfather, but my mama and my aunts and uncles all recall how they argued all the time. After he died, he became a saint. No one living can compete with a saint."

"Tell me about it." Jodi sighed and slumped in her chair. "It doesn't hurt that she was the most dang beautiful bitch in the world, either. Sort of like Helen of Troy with a face that could launch a thousand ships." She absentmindedly twirled a frizzy lock around a finger. "No wonder he dumped me."

"Dumped you?" Raheesha narrowed her eyes. "You sure you didn't dump him?"

Jodi felt uncomfortable under her friend's searching gaze. "What do you mean?"

"Are you sure you didn't just let him walk away from you. Did you put up much of a fight?"

"A fight? For heaven's sake, Rae, the man's in love with his dead fiancée. He wasn't going to argue that point after he admitted it. It was hard enough for him to tell me in the first place."

"Yes, he's a proud guy. I could tell that the moment I spied him sauntering into the office. I wasn't sure what he was hiding behind those big, sad, chestnut-colored eyes of his." The older woman sighed. "But I'm sure glad it wasn't anything like he'd run over somebody while under the influence. Now, that would be something you couldn't get over ever in a million years. I think you've got a chance with it just being his first crush biting the big one."

Jodi finished her coffee and rose to place the mug in the sink. "It's more than a *first crush*, Rae. They had the church booked and the whole shebang. Just like what's-his-face and I did. Instead, the reason why his sweetheart didn't show up wasn't that she was a selfish jerk like my intended. She actually did show up at the church on their wedding day—except she was wearing her wedding dress while lying in a pine coffin."

Raheesha cringed. "Ooo. Is that for real?"

"I don't know...Okay, maybe I'm exaggerating about the dress. But they buried her on their planned wedding date. I went online and checked out the *Post-Dispatch* archives. I found their engagement announcement and her obituary. I read them both, and it was all so damn tragic I cried for over an hour."

Raheesha rose and put an arm around Jodi's shoulders. "Yep, that's the stuff tearjerkers are made of. Still, Brent found some reason to keep living otherwise he would have since joined her in the box. What is it? Does he give you any clues?"

"I'm not sure, but he's living with his grandfather and helps fix up the old house to sell it." Jodi wrinkled her nose in thought. "Maybe that *is* what keeps him going—his Gramps along with his memories of the world's most perfect woman."

"Could be. This *Gramps* person might be able to shed some insight into his inner-workings. You ever talk to him?"

Jodi shook her head. "Nah, Brent's never invited me over to his house. I think it's because he was ashamed of showing me off to anyone he really cares about. As long as I was a good time in bed and we had a place to meet, things went along okay. Only after I started prying into his past did things fall apart."

"Hmm...As long as you two could be 'friends' without the emotional commitment of being boyfriend-girlfriend you got along, right?"

"Yeah, that's about it. You and Mel are right about giving out the goods too early in a relationship. Why should a guy stick with you if he knows he can have his fun and walk away without a second thought?"

"It's water under the bridge, sugar." She gave Jodi another squeeze. "You gotta start from where you're at now. I think a visit to Gramps is in order, don't you?"

Jodi swallowed hard. It made sense. If she really wanted an answer to the question of why Brent had turned so cold then his grandfather probably was the only person in town who could tell her. But the idea of sneaking behind Brent's back made the kamikaze butterflies in her stomach start their dive-bombing runs all over again.

*****

The freshly painted white, modest-sized Victorian looked picture perfect bracketed by tall oaks and stately maples. The steep-pitched green slate roof and coordinating ivy vine pictured in the stain glass windows on either side of the sturdy carved cherry wood door only added to its unique by-gone charm. A covered porch with pine-green, straw-bottomed rocking chairs brought back to mind days gone by when people sat outside to keep cool in the summer. The multi-colored potted pansies and begonias in delft blue and white glazed pottery bowls on the steps added the perfect touch.

Here stood a true *home* and not just a *house,* Jodi decided as she drove slowly past her destination. Its exterior oozed warmth, love and acceptance. No wonder Brent didn't want his grandfather to sell it to strangers. Like many things in his life, it expressed sheer perfection.

She found a parking spot on the narrow street about a half block down. Good. If Brent came home unexpectedly, then he wouldn't spy her car and maybe she could slip out the back door and escape undetected. But why should he return home? It was his lunch hour and he was probably surfing the Internet while chowing down on a burger or some other greasy fast food sandwich. Jodi only hoped that Melody didn't spill the beans if Brent walked into the break room.

It had been difficult enough sneaking out of the office.

"Where you going?" Melody had asked as Jodi tiptoed past the receptionist area. "Got an appointment?"

"Uh, yeah. An appointment. That's why I drove in today. I have an appointment somewhere." She turned to exit the office, but her younger co-worker was persistent.

"I hope you don't have the crud throat like Rae and Gabby did."

"No, I'm not sick. I'm fine. It's my car. I'm going to have a professional look at it and see why the alternator's timing seems off. Some guy off Page Avenue's supposed to be an expert on old junkers like mine. I hope it won't take long. You'll cover for me, right?"

"Sure, Jojo. I know your car has been a royal pain lately. I'm sure Mr. J won't mind if you're a bit late coming back. You've worked so much overtime this month already."

"True enough. Bye, Mel."

Melody winked. "Brent not going with you?"

Jodi froze at the door. "Why would he be going with me?"

"Oh, I don't know. I thought maybe you two had kissed and made up and were meeting over at the Holiday Inn."

"I don't know what you're talking about."

"Here, I'll show you." Melody bent down and pulled out her wastepaper basket. She reached to the bottom and pulled out part of a torn condom wrapper.

"Where did you find that?" Jodi felt her eyes bulging out of their sockets. There could be only one place…

"I dropped some mail off on your desk the other morning and noticed something shiny in the corner beside your filing cabinet. I thought it was a candy wrapper that fell out of your trash so I bent down to retrieve it."

"Oh."

"Don't worry. I won't tell Mr. J. I won't tell anyone. I know you and Brent want to keep it a secret."

Jodi sighed. They did want to keep it a secret, but since their relationship was kaput what difference did it make now?

"Thanks," she said then exited the building.

After that awkward departure, nothing seemed too difficult. Jodi parked the car and strolled up the tree-lined sidewalk toward the beautifully restored house owned by Brent's grandfather. Melody probably had shown everyone in the break room the piece of condom wrapper by now. Brent would be livid. It didn't matter now. She was going to get answers to her questions.

Besides, things between her and Brent really couldn't get any worse at this point. Right? She timidly knocked on the door. No sound came from within. She knocked again. No answer.

What an idiot… What was she thinking? Gramps was probably out of town or at lunch with a friend. She'd wasted her hour driving from Westport to Maplewood and she felt rather silly for not attempting to call first to make sure he was home. She turned to go.

"Hello there. What can I do for you, young lady?"

In her mental dressing-down, she'd forgotten to walk off the porch. Jodi looked up slowly. A distinguished silver-haired man in his mid-seventies with a distinctive Ozark twang stood tall in the doorway.

Brent was the spitting image of his grandfather. My, the Davison men aged well. She gulped.

"Uh, hello. Mr. Davison?"

"Yep. That's me all right."

"Good. Um, my name is Jodi Baker. I work at Holliday's Internet Travel with Brent. I wanted to ask you a few questions."

"Come on inside then. It's a bit damp out there today. Fall is definitely in the air."

Jodi followed Gramps into his home and he led her to an overstuffed chair beside a delft blue-tiled fireplace with built-in bookshelves. Hummel figurines and hundreds of family photographs covered the shelves and side tables. A weathervane in the shape of a rooster decorated the wall opposite the bay window where a cane-backed rocking chair sat filled with calico-covered throw pillows. The living room possessed a true country feel.

Gramps sat opposite her on a red, white and blue quilt-covered sofa. "Now, what can I do you for today, Miss Baker?"

"I...I wanted to ask you about Brent, Mr. Davison—"

"Bert. Call me Bert. Better yet, Gramps. Everyone 'round these parts does."

"Okay, Gramps. I wanted to ask you a question..." Words failed her. She stared hopelessly at her hands. "I-I don't know what I'm doing here. Forgive me."

"You in love with my grandson?" He raised a bushy white eyebrow and smiled. "Don't be afraid to admit it. I won't bite your head off."

Jodi blinked hard and then suddenly burst into tears. "Oh, how do you know? Is it so obvious?" She frantically dabbed at the teardrops spilling down her cheeks with her fingertips. "I've never said it out loud to anybody."

"Least of all him... And I don't blame you a bit. He give you that line about how he can never love another woman because he killed his Helena."

She nodded and sniffed. "Uh-huh."

"Thought so." Gramps sighed and leaned back and crossed his legs. "Well, well. He hasn't changed much. And here he was fooling me into thinking I could get on with my life and move on down to live in Florida with my brother. Uh-uh. I don't think so."

"He told me he lived with you because you needed him, but I can see it's the other way around. He needs you."

The older man shrugged. "Not really. He needs to forgive himself and get on with his life, too. He could do that with the love of a good woman. Are you that woman?"

She hiccupped. "I…I don't know."

Gramps chuckled then got to his feet. "Let me get you a drink of water for them hiccups of yours. Come on in the kitchen. Don't mind the dust—we're remodeling."

Jodi smiled through her tears at the sight of Gramps' kitchen. The room had a country motif as well with an antique slate blue painted wooden table and chairs and sunflower wallpaper.

"I love your interior design," she said, accepting the glass of ice water. "Who's your decorator?"

"Brent picked out the paper and then matched the furniture colors and knick-knacks. Actually, it's just a slight update of his grandmother's tastes. We're from the country originally if you can't tell by my accent."

"I'd never have guessed." She placed the glass on the sunny yellow counter by the sink. "He said this place held a lot of memories of his grandmother."

"It does. And I hate the idea of leaving it, but I'm not getting any younger. If I'm going to sow my wild oats in my old age I need to get on down to Florida soon. Besides, the property taxes and heating costs are dreadful nowadays. St. Louis is getting too expensive to live in."

"So you're looking forward to retiring to sunny shores and soaking up the rays?"

"Oh, my, yes!" His chuckle reminded her of Brent's laugh. "But I'll stay here as long as my boy needs me. And it sounds like he still does. He's been trying to fool me lately, but I'm catching on now."

"What do you mean?"

"Let me show you something."

Jodi followed Gramps out to the living room and over to a bookcase. He reached up and retrieved a burnished-gold framed photo.

"See this photo montage of our family from a few years back? Notice something missing?"

She took a step forward and squinted. "Why...there's a blank spot. Why isn't it filled with a photograph?"

Gramps touched the side of his nose and then placed the photo on the shelf. "Helena's face is missing. You'll notice that in a few other frames up here. Brent has been trying to convince me that he doesn't think about her much anymore and that she's not important to him. But why would anyone remove the picture of someone who isn't important to him unless she was. Think about it."

Teardrops dotted Jodi's lashes. "Yes, it's sad. He doesn't want reminders of her constantly. He needs to come to peace with himself about her death."

"You know how she died?"

"In a plane crash?"

"Yep, that's the how, but do you know the why?"

Jodi shook her head. "Brent only said he felt responsible for letting her get on the plane by herself. He should have been with her."

"That's not really the truth of the matter." Gramps motioned for her to sit down. They assumed their previous seats. He leaned forward, elbows on knees and cleared his throat

"Brent couldn't have been with Helena on that flight since he didn't know she was flying in the first place."

Jodi's brows knitted together in thought. "He didn't know she was going on a trip?"

"No, he didn't until after the fact. She had given him some cock and bull story about driving over to see her cousin in Columbia to talk over the wedding plans, but she headed to the airport instead that day."

"Was she running away?"

"Nah, she wanted to get married." Gramps sighed and shrugged. "But she wanted a career, too. Helena had a great opportunity out west. So, she left to go on a job interview. She didn't want to upset Brent if she didn't get the job, but if she did...Well, it would have been settled at that point that they'd have to move."

Jodi frowned. "She knew Brent wouldn't want to leave town. She didn't want to make him mad before the wedding by telling him about her job interview. So she lied to him. Is that right?"

"Yep. That's about the size of it. Brent won't

admit it, but he's angry. Angry that Helena, who up until that time had shared everything with him, would keep her job interview a secret and then get herself killed in a plane crash."

"No wonder Brent doesn't want a serious relationship with me." Suddenly it all became clear to Jodi. "He believes it's impossible to trust a woman to keep her word on important matters. And he doesn't want to risk getting hurt again."

"Brains as well as beauty. You're a right smart young lady. Maybe you're the one to change his mind about the female gender." Gramps winked. "You willing to give it a try?"

Jodi returned his smile. "Yes. I have nothing to lose and everything to gain." *Including one smart and handsome potential grandfather-in-law.*

Chapter Eleven

TO: MrBoJangles@crapster.net
FROM: bdavison@hit-on-us.com
SUBJECT: Bogus Journey or Excellent Adventure?

Hey Bill S. Presley, Esquire!

Ted "Theodore" Logan here. Strange things are afoot at the Circle K…

I thought things were over between Jodi and me, but now I'm not so sure. Monday morning she started talking to me again —friendly— and she even invited me over to her place for dinner tonight. I'm thinking I'll even get some "dessert" if I'm reading her signals right.

It's like she's come to her senses and is okay with the fact that I'm not ever going to take the relationship a step further. Your advice to be straight with her really worked, bro. She seems cool with it. Thanks.

But women on the whole are a bunch of loonies in my opinion. On some days, total and bizarre unpredictability surrounds me. Get a load of this latest workplace drama…

*****

"Gabby – you're what?"

Babs booming voice reverberated throughout the cube farm. Heads popped up and poked around corners within nanoseconds of her outburst. Jodi, who had been walking between her shared office and her old cubicle to retrieve her favorite highlighter, stopped just short of Gabriela's cubicle.

"For God's sake, Babs, keep your volume down. I don't want the whole world to know the news yet."

"Know what?" Melody asked as she wandered into the back area, tossing mail on various desks. "What's the scoop?"

Gabriela still looked pale from her recent illness – a bit too pale Jodi thought. She didn't want to pry into her co-worker's personal life, but things were starting to add up.

First off, Gabriela had stopped regularly attending Ladies Night Out with the group at the Zodiac Café. No one saw her sipping anything alcoholic when she did go out with them.

Secondly, she had become less critical of others and more introspective as of late. She kept to herself many days and was often caught staring at a photo of Harrison Platte she kept beside her computer monitor.

And last, but far from least, rumor had it that Gabriela puked her guts up in the ladies room a few days after returning from her sick leave. When confronted, Gabriela denied everything and only said she still felt a bit under the weather.

Jodi took Melody by the arm and led her out of the cube farm. She motioned with a toss of her head for everyone to get back to business.

"Hey, I didn't find out the big news," Melody said, pouting. She sat down at the reception counter and starting logging in their morning package deliveries. "You think Mr. Millionaire popped the big question?"

"I hope so—for her sake."

A light bulb flickered on over their receptionist's head. "Oh? Oh...Poor Gabby. You mean she's...?"

Jodi put a finger to her lips. "We don't know that for certain. And it's up to Gabby to let us know if she is. Let's not spread idle gossip, shall we?"

"Of course. I doubt she wants Mr. J to know until she's showing. He's a bit old-fashioned—he may expect her to quit work before she's ready."

"Yeah, that's it. Keep your lip zipped. Hopefully it'll work out for the best."

"But will she even want to work after she becomes Mrs. Harrison Platte?" Melody wondered aloud.

"Who says he's asked her?"

Melody sighed. "Oh, but if she's already told him...Well, I can see why he hasn't if she hasn't told him yet. When she does, I'm sure he'll be thrilled."

"Positively floored is more likely."

Jodi grinned wanly and returned to her office. Melody was the eternal optimist of the office. The *Playboy Platte* showed no signs of settling down according to the society columns. More than likely Gabriela was looking forward to life as a struggling single mom.

Jodi entered her office and froze in place. Keryn and Brent sat side-by-side, practically head-to-head staring at his computer screen and mumbling. A sudden pang of jealousy stabbed at her. Nothing of a romantic nature was happening to make her feel the green-eyed monster's bite, but she couldn't help it. She bit her lip and turned to exit.

"See what I did here? And here? That's how you do it."

"Got it. Thanks Davison. I owe you one." Keryn stood to leave and caught sight of Jodi's back. "Hey, you want to hear some great gossip?"

She slowly turned around. "Gossip?"

"Gabriela's knocked up."

"Keryn! Don't say such things." Jodi lowered her voice to a whisper. "And it's none of our business if she is."

"She left the test kit out on the counter in the ladies room just about twenty minutes ago. If she didn't want people to know, she would have done it at home."

Jodi simply frowned. Words were inadequate to express her disgust.

"It's the millionaire's kid, too," Keryn continued. "She's really sweet on him. I don't think this was planned, either, although it could work to her advantage."

"That is so cold." Jodi walked past the techie and sat down at her desk. "Gabby is your friend and she could be in trouble. You make everything sound so…so mercenary."

"It's not mercenary to force Platte to pay child support if it is his kid," Brent said. "It's the law."

Jodi's eyes widened with surprise. Brent's reaction seemed the opposite of what she'd expected a guy to say. Deep down he truly was a caring person.

But like Gramps had said, Brent desperately needed to separate his sensitive inner self from his angry exterior.

"True enough," she said to them both in her most motherly sounding voice, "but it's up to Gabriela and Harrison to work things out. We need to keep our noses out of it until Gabby feels comfortable sharing information with us. Agreed?"

They both nodded.

"Good. Now go about your work, children and let Auntie Jodi finish hers."

"It's still great gossip," Keryn muttered. She winked at Brent and left the room, closing the door behind her.

An irritating buzzing sensation jabbed Jodi at the temples. There was nothing going on between Keryn and Brent—was there? She'd sat out front for a week and a half...Maybe something had occurred in the meantime. She had to find out.

"You still teaching Keryn how to debug programs?"

"Yep." Brent's keyboard sat firmly planted in his lap once more, using the extra chair Keryn had occupied as a footstool.

"Anything else?"

Brent shrugged. "I taught her a few programming tips. That's about it."

"I'm glad. It's great you're willing teach others. You're a very kind individual."

He continued tapping away. "If you say so. I'm surprised you aren't jealous."

Wow...He sure picked up on her feelings. She had promised herself never to lie to him like Helena had, so she had to come clean.

"I am jealous—a little. When I came in here and saw how close you two were sitting, I sort of freaked. But I got a handle on it."

No outward reaction other than his tapping slowed. Jodi continued.

"It's my own insecurity speaking. I feel jealous because I project my sense of inadequacy into situations. For the life of me, I can't figure out why a handsome guy like you could ever go for a boring person like me. Keryn is so tall, dresses sharp and is smart. How can I compete with that?"

His gaze left the screen and caressed her curves. A grin tugged at the corners of his full lips. "There's no competition. You win hands down."

She blushed. "Thanks."

"Am I still invited to dinner?" he asked.

"Uh-huh. I've…missed you."

"I've missed you, too." He scooted his chair toward hers and leaned close. "I've missed holding you in my arms."

"So have I. And I understand why it's hard for you to make a commitment now."

"You do?"

Jodi gulped. It was time to make good her confession. "Yes, I do. I chatted with Gramps over lunch the other day."

Brent scooted his chair back to his desk and picked up his keyboard. "I see."

"I won't lie to you. Your grandfather is the most charming gentleman I've ever met. And talk about handsome? Hmm…if you look half as good as he does at his age, you'll be fighting off retirees with a stick."

"So you're telling me you've got a thing for my granddad? Sheesh! You two making plans to run off together and live in Florida?"

"No, not at all. We just talked. He's worried about you. He said he appreciated how I was helping you learn to live life again to the fullest."

"Gramps said that?" Brent scratched his head. "You mean you told him we were sleeping together?"

Jodi scrunched up her nose. "Well…not in those words exactly. But he said he could tell some days after you'd been *working* long hours that you were much more mellow than usual. He thanked me for mellowing you out."

"Great. I guess it's better than mellowing out through drugs and booze."

"Exactly." She rose and gently put her hands on his shoulders, whispering in his ear, "It's good exercise, too."

He chuckled. "You saying I need to burn a few calories?"

"Hey, I'm not the one who likes to eat Big Macs." She patted his stomach. "Without a little exercise, those fast food burgers put on the pounds."

"I could always join Babs for some one-on-one on the basketball court sometime."

She laughed. "No, you won't. You despise basketball."

"You think you know me, don't you?"

Jodi stopped laughing and took a step back. "No, I don't. I want to, though. It's okay. You can trust me, Brent. You've trusted me so far—don't say you haven't."

He turned, observing her through narrowed eyes. She could tell he was thinking hard about what she just said.

"Yes, I have trusted you, Ms. Jodi Baker. Then again, we both don't want people talking about us in the office behind our backs. Our silence is mutually beneficial."

"If you can trust me to keep my mouth shut, you can trust me to tell you the truth, too. I promise—I won't ever withhold important information that concerns you."

"Like a job interview?" he said quietly. "Is that what Gramps told you Helena was going on?"

Jodi nodded.

"It wasn't quite that simple. Helena wouldn't have jumped on a plane to go for just a job interview. No, she wanted to break things off, to get her distance. Landing a job far away was the perfect excuse. She felt like we both needed to see more of the world—and date other people—before tying the knot. In short, she got cold feet."

Gramps had intimated that Helena hadn't been quite as enthusiastic as Brent was in planning their wedding at times, but that she had gone along to make Brent happy. They'd both been twenty-one at the time and had been dating seriously since high school. Jodi could understand Helena's desire to wait until they both finished graduate school or worked a few years before getting married.

She took a step toward him and held out her hands. "I'm sorry. Guys aren't the only ones who can abandon people at the altar. It works both ways. And just because Helena didn't think she was ready to get married right after college didn't mean she didn't love you."

Brent stared right through her as if she wasn't there. Had she gone too far?

"Maybe it was because Helena loved you that she wanted to wait a year or so until you both were gainfully employed," Jodi said, trying to bring his focus back to the present. "Lots of couples postpone their wedding until they feel more financially sound."

His frown told her she was on the right track. "What's with females and this need to set up house right out of the chute? We could have lived in a one-bedroom apartment for a few years, no big deal. We didn't need two incomes—I could have supported her just fine."

"But would *she* have wanted to live in a one-bedroom apartment? Didn't *she* have valid career plans of her own?"

He shrugged and turned back to his keyboard. "I suppose she did."

"Don't just say 'I suppose'—*convince* yourself that she did. Women make career plans the same as men. And just because they do it doesn't mean they're afraid to make a marriage commitment at the same time."

Jodi returned to her desk and plunged back into the pile of papers in her in basket. From the corner of her eye, she watched her lover's actions the remainder of the day.

Brent didn't act as if her words seriously upset him. Then again, his was a difficult face to read. His neutral "mad at the world" expression had changed a little during the course of their affair. Gramps was right. Mellowing was a good word for it. The mellowness seemed to have taken over Brent this time. He didn't seem angry. That had to be a good sign.

Jodi smiled to herself. What Brent needed was someone he trusted to confront his twisted thought processes. He needed someone he trusted to make him come to terms with Helena's fateful decision to get on that plane. And Gramps had planted the idea in her head when he asked her if she was the woman for the job.

"Gramps" Davison is a genius, Jodi thought. If she possessed half his brains, she'd straighten out Brent's thinking in no time.

Chapter Twelve

Brent followed Jodi's junker down Interstate 270 in late rush hour traffic, trying hard not to get cut off by the jerks merging onto the crowded roadway from Highway 40.

"Get off the road, moron," he shouted as an SUV swerved in front on him right as he was about to change lanes. Maybe going over to Jodi's tonight wasn't a good idea after all.

They'd eat take out and then he'd want to screw her brains out. She was like candy and ice cream and cookies and cake all rolled into one. He couldn't get enough of her sweetness, her goodness, her hot, tight…

A semi honked at him as he changed lanes. "Eat my dust," he muttered. "I signaled—did you?"

The stress of rush hour traffic didn't seem to dilute his desire. If anyone looked inside his car, they'd think he owned two gearshifts. He switched on the radio to distract his wandering thoughts.

"I've got to stop thinking with the lower half of my anatomy. I'm using Jodi to satisfy my carnal cravings. It's wrong. If I'm not going to make a commitment to any woman I have a sexual relationship with, then I should become a priest or something."

But celibacy held no real appeal for him. In fact, the idea of standing in front of a church only made him envision Jodi marching up the aisle in a long, white dress and delicate veil, holding a bouquet of lavender roses and baby's breath… And then he saw himself in a tux lifting her veil and tenderly kissing her soft, pink lips.

"Down boy. Where in the world did that image come from? I must have seen something like it in some magazine or on TV. I must have caught it on Lifetime while flipping channels to find Spike."

He quickly changed lanes again and followed Jodi's small car off the highway to the secondary roads. By the time they reached her apartment complex, he felt calm enough to exit his car without drawing undue attention to his zipper area.

"Man, it's a madhouse out there today." Jodi grabbed her purse and crawled out from behind the wheel. Brent followed close on her heels to her door. "Staying late at work has been a blessing in disguise. My new motto is, 'Stay late, stay alive—let the crazies drive home at five.'"

"My thoughts exactly. They should outlaw semis on the road between the hours of four and seven in my opinion."

Jodi rolled her eyes and nodded. "Uh-huh. I just think they need to outlaw them altogether. They always cut me off and they change lanes without signaling. I'm surprised they haven't crunched my rear end yet."

I'd love to crunch your shapely rear end, too, given the chance…

Brent mentally kicked himself as they entered the dark apartment. He couldn't keep his mind off sex—specifically, sex with his gorgeous co-worker.

"What's for dinner?" he asked as she walked into the kitchenette and began flipping on lights and opening cupboard doors.

"It's a surprise." She smiled and shooed him away. "Go sit down and relax. I'm making you a home-cooked dinner, and you're the guest."

He shuffled over to the sofa and plopped down on it. "Don't go to any trouble for me. You know how my tastes run to fast food and take out. I detest home-cooking."

"Yeah, right. Gramps told me how much you loved your grandma's chicken pot pie and her beef stew and even her version of toasted raviolis."

"He told you all that? I thought you said you spoke with him for less than an hour."

"I did…the first time. He called and we chatted a bit a few other times this past week, too."

"Gramps is your phone buddy?"

Brent frowned and rubbed his temples. Gramps kept few secrets. Obviously his and Jodi's relationship was one of them. For some reason, it bothered him. What other things had his grandfather forgotten to inform him about lately?

"I thought the only person Gramps ever called regularly was my Uncle Bill, his brother down in Florida. He usually emails my cousins and my parents."

Jodi pulled out a skillet from under the counter and poured some oil into the bottom then switched on the stove. "He likes to email me the occasional joke, too. What a sense of humor he has. He really cracks me up."

Gramps emailed Jodi on a regular basis as well? Brent ran a hand through his almost shoulder length mop and sighed. "The next thing you know you'll be telling me he's already visited your place."

"He has once." She turned to fill a large pot with water and then placed it on the stove before filling it with pasta. "He said he'd like to see the place where you'd been spending so much of your free time."

"Don't tell me. You showed him your bedroom, too."

Stirring the pot of noodles, she laughed. "Why, of course. This is a small apartment. But don't worry—I cleaned up before he came over. I hid the vibrator and condoms and stashed the fuzzy handcuffs under the mattress. I don't think he peeked into the closet, so he doesn't know about the leather harness and whip."

"Whip? You told him that? Wonderful." Brent couldn't help but feel that his secrets had been found out and exposed. He couldn't help it. Jodi had been his find and he didn't like the idea of sharing her with anyone else—including his grandfather.

"Don't be too hard on Gramps. He's looking out for you. And besides, his lady friend lives over near this area. He said it was no trouble at all to swing by here."

Lady friend? Brent stood and walked over the counter and sat on the bar stool in front of the stove. "What *lady friend* is that?"

Jodi scrunched her nose in that cute, sexy way she had and shrugged. "I don't recall her name exactly…Marge? Maggie? Marjorie? Yeah, that's right. Her name is Marjorie."

"Marjorie?" Brent's eyes narrowed. "Are you sure? That's the name of the lady who cuts his hair cheap."

"I'm about ninety percent sure. He referred to her as his little 'honey bun' in our conversation. She must be quite the looker. He claimed she was a knock out in her swimsuit, and said he couldn't wait to oil her up for some fun in the sun on Daytona Beach."

Gramps and another woman that wasn't his grandmother? Brent swallowed hard. It felt like someone had just kicked him below the belt and added a karate chop to the back his neck as well. Gramps had never even looked at another woman—or so Brent thought—since his grandmother died. *How could he?*

"You okay?" Jody put down her stirring fork and crossed over to him. She placed an arm around his shoulders. "You didn't know about Gramps' sweetheart, did you?"

He shook his head. Nothing came out when he tried to speak. She grabbed a glass from the drying rack and filled it up with ice water from the refrigerator.

"Here, drink this. It's okay. The shock will pass."

"Thanks," he managed at last. "What other important pieces of information did my grandfather tell you in less than a week's time that he's not told me in the last few years?"

Jodi placed an arm around him and drew him close. She kissed him tenderly on the forehead. "That's about it. They've been seeing each other for a while now. They met at the wake for a mutual friend and discovered they had a lot in common. Neither of them wanted to be lonely anymore or die before their time like their respective spouses. They wanted to live some more—love some more—enjoy life some more. And that's one reason Gramps wants to move down to Florida so much. Marjorie also has friends and relatives down there. Together they'd all have a wonderful support group and plenty of sunshine."

"Until the next hurricane blows in and wipes them off the map." Brent grimaced. "Shit. I know I shouldn't think that way. It's mean. Gramps deserves to be happy. I'm glad he's not lonely."

She kissed him again on the cheek. "Good. He's glad you're not lonely either. And he doesn't want to wait too much longer to get down to Florida. Your Uncle Bill recently met one of Marjorie's single cousins down there. I take it they're an item now."

"And all this time I was completely oblivious to it all."

Brent pulled away from her and crossed back to the sofa and sat down, his head dropping into his head. "I'm a complete idiot."

Jodi sat down beside him. "No, you're not. You've just been in your own little world for so long that you've not noticed other people changing and growing. Gramps still misses your grandmother, but he's also getting on with his life. He wants you to do the same."

"It's not that easy for me. Gramps and Grandma were married for forty-some years. They had a long time together. Helena and I never got that chance."

"Yes, you did. You had the chance to meet and fall in love. Even if it were only for one hour, it would have been worth all the grief it caused. Some people search all over and never find a special someone to love. Others are fortunate and find more than one."

She placed a comforting hand on his arm, her voice crackling with emotion. "You *can* make a decision to belong to the second group, Brent. I know it took some time, but I did it. I want you to join me. We both can learn to love and trust again."

He turned to her tear-streaked face and framed it in his hands. Her violet-blue eyes glistened with hope. Here was his chance out of hell.

"Help me, Jodi. I've lost my way. Can you take me with you?"

She nodded and pulled him into her embrace. Their lips met, two magnets that couldn't deny the forces of nature. Her mouth parted and their tongues danced the age-old duet of give and take, desire and fulfillment, longing and commitment.

Commitment. Was he ready? Was she ready? Was it even a question still? Hadn't they decided that question a while back when they first fell into each other's arms?

The kiss deepened. His hands caressed her curves, squeezing her backside. Dear God, how he wanted to mold his body to hers and melt within her.

Forget the food… Forget mere sex. He was starved for something deeper, broader, even more transcending than the physical act of intimacy.

"Let's make love," he whispered against her hair. "I can't wait until dessert."

She smiled. "All right. Let me turn off the stove first. I don't want to burn the place down. What would my landlord and the fire department think?"

He chuckled. "That we couldn't get enough of each other? That the flames outside couldn't compare to the ones inside?"

She quickly ran to the kitchen and put her dinner plans on stand-by then joined him at the bedroom door. Without a second's pause, he swung her up into his arms and carried her to the bed.

Their mouths met again as they fell onto the mattress. Brent kissed every inch of her face and neck, cherishing every special trait that made Jodi unique. This was the woman he wanted beside him—not some guilt-ridden ghost of a former love. He hushed her with his lips and began to undress her, glorying in her every freckle, dimple, nipple and curve with a feather-light kiss.

"Oh, Brent..." She sighed and arched her back as he slipped off her pants and kissed her lower abdomen, thighs and legs. "It's like I'm the only woman in the world and you're worshiping me."

"You are and I am." His lips lightly caressed her mound through the thin material of her panties. She moaned and wound a finger through his tresses. "You deserve to be treated like royalty for having put up with some of my self-centered stunts."

"Then your queen orders you to remove your garments so she can enjoy the view."

"Yes, your majesty."

He rolled away and stood before her. With his eyes never leaving her face he slowly undressed. A gasp of delight escaped her full, pink lips each time he unfastened a button. Her eyes glowed with desire and anticipation. She was practically drooling by the time he got to his belt.

"Want some help?" she offered.

"No, I can manage." He grinned and turned around. "You enjoy a slow striptease ,don't you?"

"Uh-huh. But I have to tell you I was the one yelling for those Chippendale dancers to get on with it when we all went to see them. Just ask any of the girls in the office. They thought I'd have a heart attack if those guys didn't get down to their g-strings within ten minutes."

"Sometimes it can be worth the wait." He slowly unhooked his belt and slid it from his waistband. "The looking can be as good as the getting."

She licked her lips and swallowed. "You know this from experience, right?"

"Exactly. You can't imagine what all I think when I'm sitting across from you at work. Every time you push your curls behind your ears while you're working on the computer—it drives me wild."

"So it *is* true." She laughed and pulled herself up on her elbows. "They say whenever a woman touches her hair it gives a guy a hard on, but I never believed it." She deliberately pushed her hair back behind her ears and wriggled an eyebrow. "Ahem."

"Believe it." He tugged his zipper down, revealing his erection straining against his briefs. "Does it make you feel powerful to know just thinking about you makes me as long and hard as a tent pole?"

"Yes…yes, it does." She slid her tongue in slow motion across her wet lips. "You wanna know what else makes me feel powerful?"

He stepped out of his trouser and kicked them away. "I can imagine. But I want to make love to you first. I'll let you have dessert after dinner, if that's okay with your majesty.

"Well, I'll give you permission to forgo it this time. I can't wait to feel you inside me, pounding me hard against the bed, screwing my brains out."

He placed a finger to her lips. "No, I'm not going to screw you. We're not two animals going at it in a zoo. We're making love. I want to make love to you from now on, Jodi. Not use you."

Crystal tears trickled from the corners of her closed eyes. "No guy has ever said anything like that to me before. I thought maybe love wasn't in their vocabulary when it came to sex."

He sat beside her, drew her into his arms and kissed away the tears. "Sometimes guys forget there's more to two people coming together than just the act itself. Sometimes it takes a beautiful woman to remind a guy that his heart has to be engaged for lovemaking to truly heal the spirit."

"Sexual healing. Hmm…I always loved that song by Marvin Gaye. I know I could use some healing, too."

His kiss was full of promise and awakening. Together they'd rebuild their broken hearts and smooth over their souls' rough spots. Their remaining clothing barriers fell away as they grabbed a condom to come together as one. Brent groaned with happiness, thrusting repeatedly into Jodi's heavenly body.

"Yes, harder and faster…please," she begged. "I

love it when you don't let up."

He gasped. Her tightness enveloped him completely. He felt like he would tumble over the edge at any moment.

"I only let up because you'll have me exploding into you too soon if I don't. You are so hot and moist… You're a love vise, squeezing me to completion before I know what's happening."

She arched her hips and invited him to plunge even deeper. "No problem. I'll be there with you before you know it. Just fill me, Brent. Fill me with your love."

There was no need for her to beg. He couldn't help himself if he tried. Her pelvis bucked against him as he drove his cock deeper and faster into her sweet confining core. The cry tore from her lips as the first shudder overcame her and threatened to pull him to the brink with it.

"Yes! I'm there…I'm there! Don't let up."

"Never," he whispered.

He grasped her buttocks and tilted her hips so he could plunge ever deeper. She gasped, moaned and shouted again as her second orgasm overwhelmed her.

"Oh… I must have died and gone to heaven," she said, panting. "Come join me, my angel."

Brent took a fortifying breath and continued his sensual offensive. Holding tightly onto her hips, he thrust harder and faster. With a triumphant cry, he released all his fears and self-incriminations. Bliss-filled trembling wracked both their frames as his seed burst forth, filling and completing his lover and himself. Two had become one.

*****

"You want thirds?" Jodi asked an hour later.

Brent raised an eyebrow and grinned. "Don't you ever get enough?"

"Oh—you." She whipped her dishcloth at his arm.

"Yow! Yes, I'll have another helping. You're a great cook. So how come we only ate take-out before?"

She ladled more fettuccine onto his plate, careful not drop any on his bare lap. Eating dinner in the nude was an interesting experience…Particularly since they interrupted courses with kissing and heavy petting.

"We ate take-out since you were buying. I'm on a very tight budget, you know. I told you that my lease expires in a few months, and I probably won't be able to sign another one."

He dug into his food and quickly swallowed, wiping his mouth with a napkin. "That's okay. The neighbors will probably be grateful that you're moving after that last go round. I never knew you could scream that long or that loud."

Jodi giggled. "Neither did I. Wanna see if I can break my own record?"

"Let me clear my plate first." His chuckle was low and throaty. "I need the energy."

You most certainly do, Jodi thought as she watched him eat his third helping of fettuccine Alfredo and fifth helping of toasted raviolis with gusto. Gramps had said Italian was Brent's favorite type of food. He wasn't kidding. But her hint about her apartment lease expiring didn't bring about the response she'd expected. Time to put Gramps' Plan B into action?

She scooted her chair closer and fingered a lock of his chestnut-colored hair. "We could always go to your place and visit if my neighbors ever act bothered by our wild lovemaking."

"My house?" Brent frowned. "I don't care if Gramps is swinging single, he isn't going to want to hear us knocking the headboard against the wall all night long."

"Well, he won't be there forever. He's making plans even as we speak to move his personal effects down to your uncle's place. You're going to have to pay the bills yourself unless he lands a buyer right off the bat."

"Gramps has listed the house with a real estate agency already?"

Jodi nodded. The hurt and confused look on Brent's face brought tears to her eyes. Gramps had told her that he wanted his grandson to either move out or make up his mind about the house and soon. Gramps was putting the "For Sale" sign up next weekend, in time for the parade of homebuyers who regularly checked out the Sunday afternoon Open Houses.

She laid her head on his shoulder and hugged. "Don't worry. You can always move in here with me. It'll be a tight squeeze, but you seem to enjoy it."

"Yes, I enjoy how tight you are but I think we'd drive each other insane in this little place. Besides, didn't you tell me how you'd love to live in a remodeled Victorian?"

Jodi's head popped up. "I did. I'd love it. You

want me to be your roommate?"

He smirked. "Roommate? That's a euphemistic way of putting it."

"But I would be. I'd pay my share of the rent and utilities. I'd clean up after myself and help around the house. I don't expect to only be your love slave."

"Love slave…I like the sound of that." He pulled her into his lap and wrapped his arms around her. "Since you and Gramps seem to have taken care of everything I might as well let you move in as soon as he moves out."

"What do you mean Gramps and I have taken care of everything? I didn't do a thing. I simply showed up on your doorstop one day and had a chat with him because I was concerned about you."

Brent began nibbling her neck and earlobes. "Uh-huh. You concerned about me now?"

His hand dropped to her curly mound and began to massage her sensitive nub. His lips moved down her throat to her cleavage and caught a nipple between his lips.

"Yes…I'm very concerned." She moaned and arched her back, allowing him greater access. "I'm concerned you're acting out of character, Mr. Davison."

"How's that?" His tongue twirled about her pebbled peak and his finger slipped into her. "Is it out of character for me to want to take you right here on your dining table? You're wet enough already at just the thought of it, aren't you?"

Jodi moaned, felt her juices flowing at the mere mention of his desire. "Okay, I'll take that back. If you liked doing me on a hard desk at work, then doing me on the table between courses wouldn't be a totally new idea for you."

He pushed the plates to the side, stood and positioned her on the edge of the small round table. "Is it hard on your back when I ram into you on this kind of surface?"

"Kind of." She grinned and leaned back on her elbows. "But I forget the pain after a while."

"Well then…Allow me to do something not quite as bruising on that cute, round tailbone of yours. It's time for dessert."

Before she knew what was happening he sandwiched his face between her thighs. Jodi cried out then moaned as Brent's tongue turned her into Jell-O with its exquisite touch. She rocked her hips against his chin and idly fondled her breasts.

"Oooo, there. You hit the spot. Oh, God, I don't think I'll last much longer if you slip your finger inside me."

He rose up momentarily and wriggled an eyebrow. "You mean like this?"

She squealed with delight as he thrust not one but two long fingers into her. He frantically stroked her G-spot while simultaneously licking her into a frenzy of sensation. True to her word, she soon started to buck and bounce across the table, sending empty plates and forks clattering to the floor. Inner shudder after tremble after quiver overpowered her until she screamed and howled louder and longer than ever before.

"Oh, oh, *oh*! You have to stop. They'll call the

cops on us."

He casually withdrew his tongue but kept his fingers busy inside her. "I can think of worse things to be arrested for than simply disturbing the peace."

Jodi panted. "How about contributing to the delinquency of a minor then? There are children in this apartment complex."

"You're right. I wouldn't want anyone to accuse me of anything like that. Should I stop?" He slowly removed his fingers and scooped her off the table, carrying her to the couch.

"We made a mess of my dining area," she giggled. "I hope I can get the food stains out of the carpet."

"Food stains?" He stood tall above her as she sprawled across the sofa, dizzy with bliss. "They'll come out. How about this couch? Do you own it?"

She nodded slowly. "Uh-huh. Why do you ask?"

He grinned and knelt on the edge near her face. "You haven't had your dessert yet."

Jodi licked her lips and turned to face his red staff standing rigidly at attention. "Wowee. My screaming is quite a turn on, isn't it?"

"So are you and I haven't had enough of you yet."

Before she could say a word, he plunged his tongue between her legs, cradling her buttocks in his hands while lowering his erection to her eager lips. She took him into her mouth and twirled her tongue around and around his sensitive shaft until she generated a groan of desire from deep within him.

"Hmm…You're going to get more than your fair share of dessert I'm thinking." She laved his balls with her tongue and slowly stroked his shaft before sliding him back between her lips. "If I come too hard, don't be afraid to pull me out and let me come on your breasts. I don't want you to choke."

"Always the gentleman," Jodi said, laughing. No wonder she couldn't imagine making love to another human being ever again. Sexy Brent Davison had spoiled her forever.

She sighed and swallowed him as deep as she could, arching her mound toward his talented tongue. The fog of ecstasy soon enveloped her as his expert attentions brought her close to the brink once more. Her mouth instinctively tightened about his rigid staff. He groaned loudly. She felt the pulse of his impending explosion against her lips. She sucked him deeper as orgasm erupted, allowing him to pull back and shoot some of his hot seed across her body.

"Ooo!" She rubbed his sticky surprise around and around her tingling nipples, immediately eliciting a star-spinning, mind-numbing explosion of her own.

"We'll have to move my couch over to your place," she said sleepily a few minutes later as they shifted positions. She laid her head against his chest and sighed.

"Why is that?" He nuzzled her neck and shoulders, snuggling closer.

"'Cause I don't want to get any stains on that lovely piece of furniture currently sitting in your living room. I'd hate explaining to any visitors what happened to it."

Chapter Thirteen

TO: ShaynaE@wazoo.com
FROM: jbaker@hit-on-us.com
SUBJECT: Love and a job promotion

Hey girlfriend!

You're looking at the newest sales manager at Holliday's Internet Travel Online US!

Working long hours and sucking up to Mr. J has finally paid off. The presentation we gave (Mr. J, Brent and me) to the investors this past week did the trick. We got the loans, we got the plans and now all we have to do is bring in the customers. So, Mr. J bumped me up a notch and named me regional sales manager. I even get to help hire some more staff members.☺

Brent also got a promotion. He's now something like a "manager in charge of technical applications." He acts like he could care less, but he took the pay increase without a fuss. Not that either of us are making much more money than before, but at least our current titles look good on a resume.

I'm still planning to move in with Brent at the end of this month. Brent's grandfather–Gramps–has started sending some of his things down to Florida. He and Marjorie are looking at renting a condo close to his brother's place. The photos of the retirement community are gorgeous. Golf courses and bike trails and beaches. Gramps says we can come down and vacation there anytime we want. I can't wait! ☺

Things are definitely looking up here…and that's why it hurts me to hear you're feeling blue again. I hate people who say "I told you so" but I did kind of warn you about the dangers of dating a married man.

I know, I know…He's more of an "in-the-midst-of-a-divorce-and-twenty-years-older-than-you-are" man and not quite married, but the effect on your relationship is the same. He still has feelings for his wife and kids. There's nothing you can do to change that. The only thing I've learned with Brent is that you never quite get over someone you loved deeply. Sure, the feelings fade with time, but they are still there, lurking beneath the surface. Eventually, you put them into perspective, but you never stop loving that person.

(And that's exactly why I know I never really loved Cade. I can't even remember what the jerk looks like anymore. It helps that I tossed all his photos out a while back.)

But we really have to quit whining. Our problems are a nothing compared to Gabriela's. Even I have to admire how she's handling things. Maybe some of that arrogance pays off in the end.

Gotta go now – the girls and I are going to Ladies Night to celebrate my promotion tonight and because it's been a while. You take care and lay off the married guys, okay?

Jodi

*****

"What do you mean you don't want to marry him?"

The others more or less echoed Melody's shocked surprise, Jodi noticed, not so much in words as in posture. Raheesha sighed. Lotus shook her head. Keryn arched a finely plucked eyebrow. Babs shrugged.

Gabriela took a long sip of her ginger ale and put down her glass. "That's what I said. I don't care if Harrison Platte asks me or not. I'm not marrying the man simply because I'm carrying his child."

"But Gabby, you've got to think of the baby." Lotus smiled kindly in her earth mother way. "He or she will need food, clothing, health insurance. Even, I, as an herbalist, know you can't risk living in this day and age without a good health insurance policy."

"That's rich coming from an anti-establishment pseudo-hippie," Keryn quipped. Lotus scowled back at her. "Hey, no offense meant. And you're right on the money—Gabriela's kid deserves the best. Its papa can afford to give it the best out of his pocket change. She shouldn't have to struggle to support this kid on her own."

The murmur circling the table concurred. Jodi knew it wasn't her place, but she just had to know.

"Have you even told Harrison about the baby

yet?"

All eyes rested on Gabriela who colored under their heated glances. She squirmed in her seat and frowned.

"You haven't told him—have you?" Babs interjected. She threw down her drink stirrer and swore under her breath. "I know you haven't. You're too stubborn to admit that you haven't."

Gabriela angled her body away slightly and raised her chin, looking down her nose at them all in her familiar style. "So what if I haven't told Harry I'm pregnant yet? The way gossip travels around this town, he'll know by the ten o'clock news."

Melody's eyes were larger than an anime character's. "Don't you want him to hear the news first from you?"

Jodi patted her younger co-worker's hand. It was obvious how much Melody wanted to throw a baby shower for their office mate. Every event that they could celebrate—from birthdays to good job performance reviews—deserved a home-baked and frosted cake courtesy of Melody's mother.

Raheesha, who had sat quietly amid the fracas, put her drink down and voiced the question they'd all been thinking. "You're not planning on getting rid of this baby—are you?"

Melody turned pale. Lotus cringed. Even laid-back Babs and cool Keryn looked disturbed. Jodi placed an arm around both Melody and Lotus and they leaned on each other for support.

Gabriela leveled a hard gaze across the table at Raheesha. "What if I am? It's my body and I can do with it whatever I please."

Raheesha looked her straight in the eye and leaned forward. "Or you can give it up for adoption like your mother did. Give this child a chance, Gabby. Aren't you glad your mother gave you a chance?"

Suddenly the damn broke. Tears poured down Gabriela's cheeks. For once, she appeared mindless of ruining her mascara. She collapsed into Bab's arms, accepting the gentle pats and embraces of her equally moist-eyed friends.

"Oh, God! I love him so much and he barely knows I exist. What am I going to do, you guys? What am I going to do?"

The group hug lasted for several minutes before several male club patrons stopped and asked if they could be of any assistance. Jodi mouthed, *Boyfriend trouble.* They took the subtle hint and blended back into the crowd.

"Let's get out of here." Jodi blew her nose. "This is no place to talk."

"I agree," Keryn said, gathering up Gabriela's purse as well as her own. "We can go over to my apartment. I don't live that far from here."

Jodi commuted with Melody that morning and was glad not to have to drive the short distance over to Keryn's place off Dorsett Road. She sniffed and blew her nose again.

"Funny how we've worked together for several years and never visited each other's homes before." Jodi could tell Melody was doing her best to make light of the situation, but the gravity of the circumstances weighed heavily on their conversation. "Maybe I should invite everyone over to my house for our holiday office party?"

"That would be nice. I think everyone else lives in an apartment and wouldn't have room to handle a big party with dates and spouses and all."

"Only Mr. J has a spouse—so far. But I expect Raheesha and Darnell will marry soon enough. She keeps saying she's not getting any younger."

None of us is, Jodi thought sadly. Sniffling, she blew her nose again. "You could throw a big bridal shower for Rae. That would be nice."

Melody sighed then turned the corner, following Keryn's car into the apartment complex parking lot. "Throwing a baby shower is nice, too." She pulled into an empty spot and switched off the engine. "Did you know Gabby was adopted?"

Jodi shook her head. "No, I didn't. I guess Raheesha was the only person she ever told. I don't think Babs knew and their cubicles have been side-by-side since day one."

"Explains a lot."

"How does it explain anything?"

Melody shrugged. "I don't know...I've always wondered why Gabby has always acted like she was dying for attention—any attention. It explains why she always dressed up and acted like everyone had to look at her. Men, women, children, whoever...she seems to eat up attention."

"I think it's called abandonment issues. She wants people to love and adore her to make up for feeling abandoned as a child." *Poor Gabriela...and I've been so mean to her at times because her attitude drove me up the wall. I should have realized she needed a friend–not a critic.*

A rap on the passenger window caused Jodi to jump practically out of her skin.

"You getting out or you going to stay in there and yak all night?" Raheesha asked. Lotus stood beside her wrapped in her wool poncho, acting even more spaced out than usual. Maybe she was meditating. Thank goodness she had accepted a ride from Raheesha.

"We're coming." Melody unbuckled her seatbelt and motioned for Jodi to do the same. "Did Babs drive Gabby?"

Keryn strolled over to the gathering. "Yeah. Here they are now."

Babs sporty four-wheel drive mini-SUV fit her personality to a tee, Jodi observed. It wasn't the best vehicle for transporting a pregnant woman in heels, however, as demonstrated by Gabriela's trouble climbing down from its high step.

"Follow me." Keryn led the assembly along a narrow walkway to a first floor townhouse with tastefully potted plants standing on the stoop.

"Nice ferns," Melody said. "You grow them yourself?"

Keryn nodded then opened the door. "You don't think a computer nerd has a green thumb? You'd be surprised."

Lotus clapped her hands as they entered Keryn's tastefully decorated living area. "Wow, look at these plants. You really did keep all the ones Pete gave you."

"You're still seeing Peter?" Gabriela asked between sniffles. She sat in a low black leather rocker in front of the gaming console.

Babs flopped down on the carpet beside her cubicle neighbor. "I thought you and Pointdexter had parted ways a while back, Keryn."

"We've been seeing each other off and on," Keryn said matter-of-factly. She parked herself in a small recliner opposite the futon. "Besides, Peter's stepbrother Max is dating Lotus, so we've done a little double dating. No big deal."

Lotus grinned as she fingered a plant leaf. "You lie. You told Pete that if the plants he gave you all turned brown it meant you two were never meant to be. And just look."

Jodi plopped on the low, futon sofa beside Melody and Raheesha and admired the variety of plant life. "Is Peter a botanist? I thought he was into computers?"

Keryn shrugged. "He is, but he rents a house with Max who's an organic chemistry grad student. You should see all the things growing around their place, some of which aren't exactly legal."

"You mean…marijuana?" Melody whispered.

Lotus giggled. "Among other things. I can't begin to tell you what all they have. I'm not sure Max even knows. Most of the plants are part of his doctoral thesis. He's searching for a cure for cancer."

"Has he found the cure for a broken heart by chance?" Gabriela moaned and began crying again. Babs handed her a tissue. "I'm sorry. It's the hormones. They make me feel weepy even when I feel okay."

Tears became contagious as they passed the tissue box around the room. Even Keryn got in a good nose blow or two, Jodi noticed. Their hostess wasn't completely immune from human emotion. But she worked hard to put up a good front like Gabriela.

"What are you crying for, Jojo?" Raheesha elbowed her gently. "You've done bagged yourself a Martian. Brent's stopped running from you, hasn't he?"

Jodi wiped her tears dry with the back of her hand. "Well, yeah, but…hey, girlfriend! You're the one with the rock on your finger. Are those tears of joy?"

They all laughed and dabbed their eyes.

Melody put her handkerchief aside and smiled. "Yeah, and I've got my ruggedly handsome Barry. I shouldn't be crying. Lolo has her Maxwell, and they're so perfect together. Keryn has her Peter off and on. And Gabby has her baby to love. We all should be happy."

"But it's still sad." Jodi allowed a long sigh to escape. "Sad to think it takes a crisis for people's facades to drop and you see them as they truly are." She turned to Gabriela. "I never knew you were adopted, Gabby."

"I don't generally go around telling everybody. But Rae asked me once about why I seemed so down around Mother's Day and I told her. She's been a good friend and kept it a secret—until now." She stuck out her tongue at Raheesha.

Raheesha returned the gesture. "I love you, too, girlfriend."

The room broke into peels of laughter.

"Hey, it's okay," Gabriela said as their giggles subsided. "It's not where you come from but where you are going that matters."

"Very wise words." Lotus sat cross-legged beside her. "Where do you and the baby want to go?"

Babs sat up and re-entered the conversation with a vengeance. "I know where I want to send that Harrison Platte—straight to hell. If he ever crosses your path and upsets you again I swear I'll pulverize his ass into powder and stick it in a pipe and smoke it."

Gabriela patted her shoulder. "That's sweet of you, Babs honey, but if you ground the guy up how will he pay child support?"

"Now you're thinking." Keryn pulled newspaper off the end table. "Let me see…There's an article here in the business section." She turned pages until she found it.

"Ah-ha! I was right. The fool's family is worth several hundred million according this reporter. Platte can afford to keep you and the kid in style. You'll never have to work ever again—unless you want to, that is."

"But you'd rather marry him, wouldn't you, Gabby?" Melody said softly. "You said you loved him. Maybe he loves you, too?"

"I wish he did…" Gabriela's voice trailed away.

"Are you sure Harrison doesn't care for you just a little?" Jodi's hopeful smile echoed all of their desires. "You guys have been seeing each other for a while now."

Gabriela shook her head and sighed. "No, I'm fairly sure he doesn't care one bit for me. I was a pleasant diversion and nothing more. He's married to his sports cars and his family's business. He told me he doesn't have time for a wife or girlfriend. I was a series of convenient one night stands."

Raheesha *tsk*ed. "It's like my mama always said, 'Once they gets the milk for free, they ain't wantin' to buy the whole cow.'"

"My mom says the same thing," Melody said, frowning. "Not in quite those terms, but it's pretty close."

"You gotta be careful not to lose your heart to one of those 'free milk only' men," Raheesha continued. "They'll milk you for what you're worth then walk off without a second glance backwards."

"But Gabby…I thought you said you were on the Pill." Babs scratched her head; a puzzled gleam danced in her dark eyes. "How did you wind up pregnant?"

Gabriela leaned forward and everyone did likewise. "You all remember the flu bug going around? I went on antibiotics for it. The doctor told me that the drug interactions can alter the Pill's effectiveness, but I was too busy to listen. And I was stupid enough not to insist on Harry using a condom once or twice."

"Oooo, always a big mistake." Babs grimaced. "You shouldn't risk the chance of getting an STD even if you're on the Pill."

"I know. But I assumed Harry loved me at that point in our relationship. It was only later that I found out what a great actor he is…Did you know he actually took acting lessons from a respected Broadway drama coach as part of his sales experience?"

Melody's jaw dropped. "Whoa! He's an actor as

well as a successful businessman…Double threat there."

Keryn folded the paper and put it aside. "No wonder the family's worth millions. They've charmed their competitors right out of business through several generations according to this article. Harrison Platte comes from a long and illustrious line of con men."

"Con man or not, you've still got to tell him, honey child." Raheesha reached for Gabriela's hand and squeezed it tight. "A baby ain't a toy poodle. A child deserves to know who his or her daddy is—even if that daddy is a complete asshole."

"Rae!" Jodi gasped. Melody shut her eyes and threw her hands over her ears. "I've never heard you swear like that. We've got an impressionable young lady here."

"Sorry about that. Sometimes curse words seem to sum up a person just right."

Babs grinned. "You get no complaints from me. You pegged the dude—asshole, first rate. Asshole con man who'll say anything to get laid."

"But Platte has one saving trait that you all haven't taken into account," Keryn said. All eyes—including Melody's—turned to stare at her.

"One saving trait? What on earth is that?" Jodi crossed her eyes. "He's still breathing?"

"Exactly. He's alive and he's a businessman. He lives to better his family's business and he'll do anything to protect it."

"So?" Gabriela sighed. "That's why he wouldn't even think of marrying me—I'm not a big enough *catch* or high enough on the social ladder to help his family's business. I'm a big, fat nobody."

"But having his baby would bring about the type of publicity that he and his family wouldn't appreciate. It wouldn't help their business." Keryn rose and crossed to the front door, double-checking that it was shut tight. "The Platte family would want you to keep quiet."

Babs sprang to her feet. "You mean, they'll try to bump her off? Hell, we need to call the cops right now."

The room buzzed with gasps and groans of fear and surprise.

Keryn frowned. "No, no, no…You're not following me. I sincerely doubt the Plattes would hire a hit man. Think of their reputation—they do."

"That's a relief." Lotus slumped and sighed. "And you're right, Keryn, about how they see their reputation. The Plattes only humor Max and Pete because they're cousins. They tend to ignore them when they're socializing in the upper circles since Max and Pete's family isn't quite as well-to-do."

"Right. There's the saving trait. They will talk turkey when it comes to child support to keep you from talking to the media."

Keryn sat down beside Gabriela. "You have the advantage, Gabriela. Get a blood test and get Harrison Platte to take one, too. The evidence will work in your favor. Just wait and see. And if he still gives you trouble, have a paternity test done after the baby is born. You'll have undisputable proof the baby is his."

The remaining portion of their evening revolved around discussing baby names and the most preferred maternity wards in the metropolitan area.

"I don't know. Money can't buy you love," Melody said as she and Jodi walked toward her car. "And I can tell Gabby would rather have a whole lot of love than a whole lot of money. She'd preferred that Harrison Platte helped her raise their child over bribing her to keep quiet about it."

Jodi swallowed hard. The ache in her heart could not be denied. She'd feel the same way. She'd preferred love to money, too. What woman wouldn't?

Melody was right. For being so young and naïve, it was amazing how right the girl was at times.

Chapter Fourteen

TO: MrBoJangles@crapster.net
FROM: bdavison@hit-on-us.com
SUBJECT: Warning: women's moods are contagious!

Yo, Bo-man,

You'd better not be playing Ike Turner…'cause you know how it's going to turn out if you do. Bad for you and good for her. Besides haven't you warned me before about being careful while mixing business with pleasure? I thought you wanted to be the lead in your band – your songs, your words, your voice. So what if you don't have a strong singing voice? Neither do Eric Clapton or Mick Jagger and they've done all right for themselves. So what if she's a knock out and can dance? I thought you said you were in the business to make music – not music videos.

Just be careful your relationship with this woman doesn't piss off the rest of your backup singers. You did watch the movie What's Love Got to Do With It, right? If you haven't, do yourself a favor and go rent a copy tonight.

Yes, I admit I'm overly cautious. It's just that working around so many females has given me some keen insights into how their convoluted minds work. In short, they don't. They don't think through things at all. They simply react to whatever crisis is current and follow each other around like lemmings to a cliff.

No, they're not all pregnant—just the one is. And she's handling things well considering all the stress she's under. However, the rest of the office is freaking out because the rich dude that got her in the family way doesn't want to do right by her.

No, I'm not stepping up to take his place. But if you ask me, he really is a first rate sleaze. Harrison Platte is his name and his family is worth mega-millions. So, you can see why they don't want their little boy marrying a poor working girl without a title or connections. Plus he's a spineless bastard who won't go against his parents. Cinderella won't land her Prince Charming in this fairy tale. It's really sad.

Shit! I'm beginning to sound like a woman. Jodi is moving in this weekend. The chance to regain my male thinking patterns could be lost forever. I'll be permanently in touch with my feminine side. Shit.

Stop laughing. This is serious stuff here. Great… I sound just like one of them, don't I?
B

*****

"Looking good, Gramps. Wherever did you find that Hawaiian print shirt? You need earplugs just to look at it."

Jodi teased his grandfather and the comments

cycled back and forth until they both were hooting and hollering like a couple of uncouth Hoosiers. Brent continued lugging boxes out of the back end of the rental van, up the front steps and into the house. The least she could do was open the door for him.

"Oh, I'm sorry, Brent."

Finally she stopped flirting and came to his assistance. She swung open the door for him and followed him inside and up the staircase. "Do you think we'll be able to fit all my things in the guest bedroom?"

He grunted as he made the landing turn. "If not, we can put things in the attic. Gramps moved a lot of stuff out that was his and Granny's. There should be about three square feet cleared for storage."

"That doesn't sound like much space." She pushed open the bedroom door for him. He stacked the box on top of the first row of boxes he'd already hauled inside. "Where is my bedroom suite going to go?"

Brent dusted off his hands on the back of his jeans. "Since the bed frame is taken apart, it shouldn't take up that much room up in the attic. Your mattress we could plop on top of this old bed in here for now. The dresser and vanity we could try to fit into my old bedroom since Gramp's room will be mine from now on, and I'm moving my stuff in there."

Grinning, she sidled up to him and rubbed his aching shoulders. "Yes, I agree. As landlord you should get the biggest bedroom."

"Not that Gramps believes for one moment I'll be sleeping alone in that big old bed ."

"I don't think sleeping will be what we'll be doing." She kissed him on the cheek and massaged his back vigorously. "In fact, I doubt we'll sleep at all some nights."

"Tonight I most certainly will—especially since it appears I'm carrying all your junk inside by myself." He groaned then yawned. "I'll be exhausted."

"Sorry. But you said not to let Gramps do any heavy lifting. I was doing my best to distract him."

Brent turned to look at her and raised an eyebrow. "Distracting him? Yeah, that top you're wearing certainly is a distraction. You think it could be cut any lower?"

Jodi looked down at the deep vee of her powder blue, wrap-around style shirt and blushed. "It could, but then I'd be falling out of it. I didn't think you wanted Gramps *that* distracted."

Without warning, Brent pulled her into his arms and kissed her. His hands cupped her breasts then roved across her backside as her lips parted and allowed his tongue deeper access. His briefs suddenly felt like they were ten sizes too small.

"Hmm…Wanna try out this old mattress before we pile another one on top?"

"It's tempting, but what will Gramps think? In fact, we'd better go back out front before he decides to start moving the heavy things by himself."

Sighing, he let her go then followed her back downstairs. Sure enough, Gramps was already dragging two of Jodi's dining chairs up the front steps.

"Gramps, stop right this instant. What did I tell you about moving heavy items?"

He halted, panting. "But they ain't heavy. They're just kitchen chairs. Not heavy at all."

"Allow me to take one," Jodi suggested removing one from the elderly man's grasp. "Where are we putting them, Brent?"

"Let's stow your dining set in the basement for now. We can use the table to fold laundry on."

Jodi pouted. "Laundry? But I paid good money for this set. I practically didn't eat for a week because of how much it cost. I'd rather my personal sacrifice didn't get all moldy down in your basement."

Gramps reached the top step of porch and put down the chair, leaning heavily against it. "It is a shame to hide Jodi's nice furniture. I suppose I can take the kitchen set down to Florida with me. Marjorie's only got a tiny chrome dinette table and two chairs and we could put that on our covered patio."

Granny's table...in Florida? Brent felt a twinge of sadness stabbing at his heart. It was bad enough Gramps was taking the sofa and easy chair from the front room and the old oak roll top where Granny used to sit and type her original recipes on an old manual typewriter. Now Gramps wanted to remove some of the last vestiges of Granny's presence from the kitchen as well?

"It's too big." Brent frowned. "You'll never be able to fit Granny's table into your condo. Besides, isn't Marjorie moving all her furniture? You didn't buy a big house—you'll end up selling things that won't fit."

"Well, it is *my* table, Brent," Gramps said emphasizing his ownership. "I bought it about thirty years ago because the other decrepit piece of junk we had in there was literally falling apart. Your grandmother put up just as much fuss as you're doing now over trading out tables. Must be hereditary."

Jodi bit her lower lip and took a step toward Brent. "I don't really mind storing my table and chairs in the basement. You don't have to take the kitchen table yet, Gramps."

"Times change and we have to move on." Gramps leveled a hard gaze at his grandson. "A person isn't only remembered by worldly possessions. And your Granny didn't care one whit about that kitchen set."

"Take it then," Brent muttered. "We don't need it. We'll use Jodi's."

"Good. Glad you see things my way for once."

Gramps winked at Jodi. "You can store your table and chairs in the garage out back until the big moving truck gets here tomorrow." He lowered his voice, closely watching Brent's rigid posture. "The moving guys are loading up Marjorie's stuff now."

Jodi returned Gramps' smile, but inwardly she grimaced. Brent's mechanical movements as he traipsed back and forth from the van to the house possessed a definite note of sadness. As the screen door slammed behind Brent she leaned closer to Gramps.

"Yes, I know about the van. Marjorie said on the phone that you two had set a date for the big day, too."

"Yep. We're going to tie the knot on New Years Eve. That way you and Brent and Marjorie's kids can all get off work and come down and celebrate a little fun in the sun."

"I'd like that, but I'm not sure if Brent will. He'll probably want to stay in St. Louis for the holiday."

"It figures. He's a traditionalist. Never one to try new things if he wasn't the person suggesting them. Well, he's gotta learn to give and take. I've given all this time and now it's my turn to take charge of my own happiness. Marjorie and I are getting married during the holidays and that's that."

Gramps slapped his knee and stood up. "Let me show you where to put these chairs."

Jodi followed him around to the back of the house to a one car detached garage painted white to match the house in front. Gramps put down the chair and swung open the green door, revealing a storage shed bursting at the seams with memorabilia.

"Wow…Whose bicycles and skateboards are all these? Brent's?"

"Some of them are—and some of them are mine."

Gramps snaked a path through the shiny metallic clutter. The sparkle in his eyes told Jodi that he'd miss his old workshop once he settled in Florida. Jodi doubted Marjorie would allow him to grease bike chains and tighten bolts in their brand new condo.

"I love things with wheels. I used to fix up old bikes to give to charities and to kids at the Boy's Club." He attempted to ring a rusty bell on an equally rusted handlebar to no avail. "Oh well…It's mostly junk."

"I don't think so." She put down the kitchen chair and picked up a half-built girl's bicycle with a banana seat. "I always wanted a bike like this so I could ride a friend on the back."

"I'm sorry I can't help you there. My eyes and

fingers don't cooperate as well as they used to. I had to give up rebuilding bikes. I was hoping Brent would take the hint and start working on some of these vehicles himself. Guess not."

She put the girl's bicycle down and approached him, patting him gently on the arm. "Don't be too hard on Brent, Gramps. He's more gifted in the computer field than the mechanical. I'm afraid most of our generation is. But we can learn. Maybe you can teach me a few tricks."

He grinned. "Maybe. It would be nice to think all these bikes could have homes again."

Gramps happily occupied himself sorting through various tools and nuts and bolts and old chains in need of a gear wheel. Jodi went in search of Brent to see how the unloading was coming along. She found him sprawled on the front steps, trying to catch his breath. She sat down beside him and nestled his head in her lap.

"I'm almost done moving the boxes and little things," he said, closing his eyes in the Indian summer sunshine. "You'll have to help me with the mattress, sofa and kitchen table—unless we can track down Melody's boyfriend again."

"Is there a gym near here? That's probably where we can find them. Or did Mel say they were going to some kind of weightlifter's meet this afternoon? I can't remember now."

"Neither can I. All I can remember is how he showed off for her by picking up your headboard with one hand. Such a jock. A big muscle-bound, puny-brained jock."

"Yes, isn't he?" She sighed dreamily. His eyes flew open. He glared at her.

"Hey, I only looked. I didn't touch," she reminded him.

"But you thought about it, right?" Brent sat up. "Why are women always lusting after Chippendale dancers and lumberjacks? Why can't they love a guy for his mind?"

Jodi's jaw dropped open in shock. "But I..." The grin tugging at the corner of his full mouth gave him away. "Why, you... You're just teasing me."

He caught her about the waist and drew her tight against his chest. Her hands entwined themselves in his thick hair and brought him closer. He claimed her lips, parting them with his tongue. She sighed against his kiss.

"Ahem. You two better move that van before too long."

They released each other as Brent's grandfather's words brought them back to reality.

"We know, Gramps. We were just discussing how to go about unloading the heavy stuff without Melody's brawny friend Barry to assist us."

"Really now," Gramps said, scratching his chin, a playful glimmer in his eye. "It looked like you were trying to make a different sort of move on Jodi instead of moving her furniture into the house. What will the neighbors think?"

Brent smiled and stood, helping Jodi to her feet. "Like you've ever cared about what neighbors thought. You've outlived and outlasted them all, Old Man. Maybe I will in time, too."

"That you might. That you very well might."

Brent turned to Jodi and motioned with his eyebrows. "There are a couple of boxes yet to carry in. Then we'll tackle the bulky stuff and get to bed early after Gramps goes over to check on Marjorie, okay?"

She winked. "Sounds like a plan."

Gramps approached her. "Can I borrow your main squeeze for a moment? I wanna show her something out back. It'll just take a second."

"All right. But don't tire her out lifting bike parts. She's got to help move that sofa and table."

Jodi followed Gramps around the house to the garage. "Now what's this you want to show me?" She halted dead in her tracks and gasped as she spied his surprise. "Oh, my…How adorable!"

She knelt down to admire the antique tricycle up close. Its navy paint had faded to a watery blue, but the silver chrome of its fenders, handlebars and bells shone brightly in the dappled sunshine peaking through the trees.

"Was this Brent's tricycle?"

Gramps nodded. "Yep, and it was his father's as well. Sort of a family tradition you could say. I want you to keep it here. Don't misplace it neither—you may have use for it someday."

"Oh, Gramps…" Jodi felt a sob welling up deep within her. She swallowed hard, pushing the tears back. "We'll cherish it always."

The older man winked and kissed her cheek. "I know you will."

She watched Gramps go back into the shed to resurrect more memories then turned back toward the house. Where had that sudden sense of melancholy come from? She had never realized how much she wanted a child until just now. Was it because of Gabriela's growing-ever-more-obvious pregnancy? Or was it because she could think of no other man she wanted to father her children more than Brent Davison?

"What did Gramps want to show you?" he asked as she met him at the van.

Jodi shook her head to clear the cobwebs. "Something from your childhood…Your tricycle."

"My blue trikey?" Brent laughed then hopped up into the back of the van and began to push the kitchen table toward the ramp. "I haven't seen ol' trikey in years. He was my trusty companion in all my backyard adventures. He belonged to my dad, too."

"That's what Gramps said. He wants us to keep it safe. It belongs in the family."

Brent frowned. "Grab that side of the table and lift it slightly there—good."

Jodi did as she was told. "Tell me more about trikey."

"That's it. Walk it slowly down the ramp," he instructed. "We'll get it to the back and store it in the garage. Tomorrow we'll borrow one of Marjories' movers to help us get it into the kitchen."

"Good." She sucked up a big lungful of air, slowly waddling around the house with her end of the table. Still, she was curious as to why Brent had changed the subject so abruptly.

"You understand why Gramps wants us to keep your tricycle, don't you?"

"You're dropping your side. Watch it."

Jodi summoned all her strength and lifted her end of the table a quarter inch.

"A little higher," he ordered. "A little more."

She sighed and put down her end, glaring at him.

"Okay that'll do." He gently lowered his end to the ground.

"We're only halfway there, Brent. Give me a moment and I'll get my breath back. In the meantime, you can stop pretending you didn't hear me. You know very well why Gramps wants you to preserve your tricycle."

He shrugged. "He wants his great-grandchildren to ride it, of course."

She smiled. "So, you're telling me you understand what he's implying?"

"That he'll have great-grandchildren?" Brent's eyes widened slightly. "But that doesn't mean I have to have children."

"Doesn't it? Aren't you an only child?"

"Yes, but Marjorie has kids and grandkids. He could want us to keep it for one of their kids."

"Right..." Jodi rolled her eyes and tried lifting her end of the table once more. It barely budged. "And I'm a professional weight lifter."

"Can I help lift your side, Jodi?" Gramps came from around the back and grabbed her end of the table, raising it easily from the ground. "Pick up your end Brent and let's move this thing before that rain cloud overhead dumps on us."

"What rain cloud?" Brent looked up. A plop of rain fell straight into his eye. "Oh. That one." He lifted his end of the table and they quickly made their way to the garage.

"I'll get an umbrella," Jodi said, dodging raindrops as she bolted toward the back door. Once inside the kitchen the heavens opened up, releasing a deluge of epic proportions where moments earlier there was sunshine and light.

"That's life for you." She sighed, hoping the sudden appearance of storm clouds on a sunny day weren't a bad omen.

Chapter Fifteen

TO: ShaynaE@wazoo.com
FROM: jbaker@hit-on-us.com
SUBJECT: I got the baby shower, wedding shower, overworked blues

Hellooooo... Anybody home? What's up with you?

Long time no hear. Last time that happened you'd switched boyfriends. Do I hear the sound of a breaking heart coming from your neck of the woods? Or is that the sound of the cogs and gears spinning in your head while you work hard on your dissertation?

I got to work early today because of the paper piling up in my in basket. It looks like one leg of the Gateway Arch. I kid you not... If I had known a promotion and a slight pay raise meant I'd be drowning in paperwork, I would have said "no way" and hopped on the next plane for the coast.

Big news in the office this week: We're throwing Gabriela a surprise baby shower. It's not for a while yet, but we're all in the "secret planning phase" at the moment. Melody's mom makes the big sheet cake—that's a given. Raheesha is going to make some of those scrumptious muffins she's known for and Babs is in charge of the punch. (Babs is also in charge of the punch for Raheesha's wedding shower, but that's not very far into the planning stages yet since they've not set a firm nuptial date. I wonder if it's Darnell or Rae who is dragging a foot?)

We warned Babs it's got to be a no alcohol punch since Gabriela is pregnant, but I'm not sure the message is getting through to her. She's acting very weird lately – even more so than usual. She's moved out of her threesome situation and is looking for another roommate. You can imagine how hard it is to afford to rent a decent apartment on the slave wages we make around here. I think Babs is hinting for Gabriela to move in with her. That way Gabby will be able to save some money that she'll need for daycare expenses.

It's a generous offer, but I'm not sure Gabriela will go for it. She's very independent…and being pregnant only brings out her bossy side. No word from Harrison Platte about paying child support, either. She acts like she could care less, but I can tell she's deeply hurt by his blatant disregard.

How do I know? I caught Gabby staring at a snapshot of them together one day while walking past her cube. No, I didn't barge in there and tell her to rip it up – Babs would definitely do something like that if she'd caught Gabby pining after the jerk. I acted cool. I didn't invade her privacy.

After all, I sympathize with her totally since I was jerked around by what's-his-face. At least Gabriela didn't run out and buy an expensive wedding gown, rent a reception hall and pick out a china pattern like yours truly. I feel like a total idiot when I look back at myself during that period. Oh, well…We live and learn.

Not much else to say at this point. Brent and I are traveling along two parallel tracks it seems. If we didn't live together we wouldn't see each other some days. They cleaned out an old walk-in closet in the back and turned it into another office for him. He doesn't seem to mind that it doesn't have a window since he's working on a computer most of the time. Personally, a room that small without a window would make me claustrophobic.

The sex is still great—when we aren't both dead tired from overwork. (I'm beginning to understand why my parents fought more after Dad was promoted. It's hard to feel in the mood when you've got a huge deadline hanging over your head and you're physically exhausted.) We sound like my parents discussing bills and talking about improving the house. It's really freaky. Almost like we've fallen into an episode of the Twilight Zone or something.

In reality, this living together business isn't all it's cracked up to be. I was hoping for a deeper relationship to develop. I've discovered if you don't have a piece of paper saying you're committed to the other person, there's not much incentive to work on developing that relationship. Raheesha, Melody—and even my parents—have the right idea.

Whoa. Sorry to get so philosophical here.

There's some kind of commotion coming from the break room. I can hear it all the way down the hall here. I'd better check it out. I'll call you tonight if I don't hear back from you via email in a reasonable amount of time – say a couple of hours? You know how impatient I can be. ☺

Take care, girlfriend,
Jodi

*****

"Oh, my gosh!" Jodi heard Melody's squeal the second she stepped out of her office. "Lolo, you did, didn't you? You and Max? I'm so happy for you two."

"What's all the fuss?" Raheesha demanded upon entering the break room. "Oh, my…That's wonderful, Flower Child. Congratulations. You done beat Darnell and me."

"Lotus beat you and Darnell doing what exactly?" Jodi rushed into the room. Melody tugged Lotus's hand away from Raheesha's nose and toward Jodi's, waggling it about for the blushing bride.

"See?" Melody smile split her face in two. "It's a wedding band. They're married."

Jodi's heart skipped a beat. Another office mate had taken the plunge into the matrimonial pool. "Why, I didn't even know you and Max were engaged. Congratulations."

"Thanks." Lotus blushed again.

Keryn entered the break room and headed straight to the refrigerator to retrieve one of her energy drinks.

She turned around and cracked it open then sipped slowly.

"What's up?" she asked after a moment. "More baby shower planning?"

"No, we're admiring Lotus's wedding band," Melody informed her. She tugged Lotus's hand closer to Keryn. "See?"

"Nice. When did this happen? Over the weekend?"

"Yeah. You could say it was a spur of the moment thing."

Lotus slipped her hand from Melody's and sat down at the table. Everyone else followed suit.

"Max and I attended a retreat about saving the rainforests where we met this very nice lady who marries people and we thought, 'Let's do it.' So we did."

Raheesha's eyes narrowed. "Is this lady an ordained minister or something?"

Lotus shrugged. "Not exactly. She's a priestess for a local neo-pagan group. She's got a paper from the state that says she's allowed to perform wedding ceremonies, and we got the marriage license from the courthouse. It's legal."

"It counts as long as you got the marriage license filled out properly," Keryn said. "Well, your story clears up a mystery for me. You guys didn't stop to call and tell Peter what you were up to, did you?"

"No, we didn't. I guess in all the excitement we sort of forgot." Lotus bit her lip. "Is he angry with Max?"

Keryn rolled her eyes and put down her drink.

"Angry? No. He came by my place Sunday night worried out of his mind. He thought his stepbrother had been kidnapped by eco-terrorists or something when Max didn't come home after his weekend retreat like he said he would."

"Poor Pete!" Melody cried. "Did you comfort him, Keryn?"

"Uh, yeah…I *comforted* him all right." Keryn smiled then turned to frown at Lotus. "You forget that Max and Pointdexter are related to the Plattes. Paranoia and fear of kidnapping are rampant phobias among the ultra-rich. You scared him good."

Lotus's head dropped into her hands. "Oh, dear. We didn't mean to scare Pete. Max stayed at my place since it was closer and we wanted to…to have a little more privacy."

"Is that where you two plan on living?" Raheesha asked. "How is Max, the plant man, going to fit all his plants into your dinky little apartment?"

"We haven't thought it out that far yet. We both want to move a little ways out into the country." Lotus bit a nail. "Hmm…I suppose for now we could live at Max's house until we've saved up enough for a down payment on a small farm."

Melody's eyes widened. "But what about Pete? Where will he live?"

"The house has three bedrooms. Pete can stay put."

Jodi shook her head. "I'm not so sure a single guy would really want to live with a newlywed couple. Besides, doesn't Pete have a say in this? Isn't his name on the lease or the deed?"

"No, Max's great-aunt left the house to him in her will because he always admired her garden." Lotus sighed dreamily. "And what a garden... I'll always have happy memories of it."

Keryn snorted. "Yeah, you should since you two seem to enjoy rolling in the hay out back often enough."

"What? You mean they did *it* outside in the grass?" Melody shuddered. "What about the neighbors?"

"What about poor Peter?" Jodi reminded them. "He's essentially homeless."

"No, he's not," Lotus corrected her. "He can stay. After all, when Pete needed a place to live Max was more than happy to let him move in. Max won't throw his stepbrother out on the streets."

"That's mighty nice of him considering it was Peter who wired the place up for Max's computers to maintain the temperature and moisture controls on his greenhouse in the first place." Keryn rose from the table and tossed her drink can into the recycle bin. "But if push comes to shove, Pointdexter can move in with me."

"You'd offer Pete the option of moving into your place?" Raheesha arched a finely plucked eyebrow. "Impressive. I always took you to be pretty much the loner type, Keryn."

"I am." She turned her face away from the group. "But I don't mind helping out a friend when he's down."

They all stared in shocked silence a full minute after Keryn strolled out the door.

"Wow. I thought I'd never see the day," Raheesha said, chuckling.

Lotus smiled. "Yes, it is sort of magical."

"Magical?" Jodi shook her head. "Uh-uh. It's more like a miracle if you ask me."

Melody frowned. "What is? What are you guys talking about?"

Lotus reached over to pat Melody's hand. "Keryn is in love."

"You really think so? It's difficult to tell with her." Melody shrugged. "I don't know. I like to tease her about Peter, but she always maintains they're just friends with nothing but computers in common."

"There are worse things to have in common." Jodi grinned. She thought of how she and Brent both enjoyed computer gaming. Their friendly rivalry sometimes lent itself to making outrageous bets on who could score the highest points on a particular level. Strip poker had nothing on strip *Half-Life*.

Melody sniggered. "Their kids will be first rate computer nerds."

"Nothing wrong with that, honey child. At least they'll be assured of landing a job." Raheesha stood. "And if we all don't get back to what we're supposed to be doing, we won't have ours much longer."

As Jodi drifted back to her office she daydreamed of raising a herd of computer nerds with Brent. After all, Gramps had wanted them to make good use of the family tricycle. It seemed a sin not to carry on the tradition.

A knock on her half open door at lunchtime brought her back to reality.

"Can we talk?" Brent entered the room briskly. He tapped his fingers annoyingly against the edge of her desk.

"Sure." Jodi sat up straighter, shaking the nostalgic fog from her brain. The anxious glint in his eyes and the frown instantly made her take notice. "What's up?"

"Mr. Johansson wants me to go on a trip out of town."

"Where to? To that software trade show conference in Reno he was talking about yesterday?"

"Yeah." Brent turned away from the desk and leaned an arm against the wall. "I won't go, though."

Jodi frowned. "It's a free trip to a big tourist attraction where you can meet others in the field. Hotel and food paid for and everything. You'd be nuts to turn this opportunity down."

He took a deep breath. "I don't fly."

Helena...So the fear went even deeper than putting someone else on an airplane. Jodi sprang to her feet and placed an arm around his shoulders.

"It's okay." She tenderly kissed his cheek. "I understand. But you can't live in the twenty-first century without stepping onto a plane. You could have a job some day where your boss will expect you to travel constantly. What will you do then?"

"Take Amtrak or Greyhound. Drive there myself. But I won't get on an airplane."

Jodi sighed. His stubborn streak showed no signs of weakening. "What about hypnotism?"

"Hypnotism? How in the world can hypnotism get me to Reno?"

"It can't—but it can help. You know, have a hypnotist help you with your flying jitters. If they can help people stop smoking or lose weight then they could certainly help you with getting on a plane."

His eyes narrowed suspiciously. "The next thing you'll be saying is to drink like a fish before boarding so I'm so wasted and won't even care where I am."

"That works, too. At least it does for me," Jodi had to admit. "It's probably the number one reason why so many people drink so much in airports. That, and alcoholism."

Brent turned and headed for the door. "Thanks for your support."

Support? What was he going on about now?

"You're welcome—I think."

"You don't. Think, that is. You don't think how hard it is for me to even get near an airplane. You don't think how it could cost me my job—and my family's home."

"Brent, I—"

Too late. He darted down the hall. Jodi peeked around the corner and watched as Brent knocked and entered Mr. Johansson's office.

*****

TO: MrBoJangles@crapster.net
FROM: bdavison@hit-on-us.com
SUBJECT: my ass is covered

Newsflash: I still have my job. I can pay the bills on the family homestead. Hallelujah.

I freaked for about a total of fifteen minutes yesterday, but it's worked out for the best. Mr. J isn't such a bad guy after all. He said he understood about my being hesitant to get on an airplane and that if I couldn't get a train ticket to Reno, he'd find someone else to cover the trade show for Hit-On-Us. What a relief.

I bet you're happy you don't have any problems with flying. Where did you go last month? Bermuda? Why would you go there to record an album? Isn't Detroit or L.A. or Nashville or NYC good enough for the likes of you, country boy? Did you finally get a tan on that "white whale blubber belly" of yours?

To answer your question, Jodi is doing fine. She's great, actually. What was this crack about me renting a tux? She's not rushing me up the aisle, down the aisle or across the aisle. She's cool. I told you that. She already had her fiasco in front of a church, and she's in no hurry to turn us both into "unhappily ever after" married-types.

Now Gramps, he's a different story...He wants us to drive down to Florida for Christmas and see him get hitched. I keep telling him that it's better if he and Marjorie just live together since they're both on Social Security, but he insists on getting married. Call him old-fashioned he says. I just call him Gramps.

Jodi has got all these green things in pots around the house now—ferns I believe they're called. The hippie chick got married this past weekend (eloped is more like it) and they didn't have enough room for both his and her plants (he's an organic chemist) so Jodi took a few of the extras off their hands. She takes good care of them, which is great since I have the black thumb of death when it comes to vegetation. The house really looks alive like a rainforest and smells fresh and green like a salad, too. I swear it does. We have hanging ferns in the dining room and tall, potted ones in the front room and medium sized ones on the windowsill in the kitchen.

They remind me of when my grandmother was alive. She liked plants, too.

I'll sign off now…The boss is gone, it's almost quitting time and some kind of commotion is going on down the hall. Perhaps our resident unwed mother has given birth.

Later –
B

*****

"Get back y'all and give her some air!" Raheesha demanded with a wave of her long arms.

Brent halted dead in his tracks as he reached the cube farm. Babs knelt at the doorway of her neighbor's cubicle, cradling a pale face in her lap. A sharp, cold pang of fear stabbed his gut. Could he be psychic?

"Somebody get Jodi." Normally in-control Babs sounded like a lost child. Her lower lip trembled as she spoke. "Jodi had advanced CPR training when she was a lifeguard."

"What's going on?" Brent asked Lotus as she rushed past him with a wet cloth and handed it to Babs.

"Gabby fainted. Babs caught her before she could hit her head."

Jodi soon joined him and squeezed his arm. "I was on the phone when Mel grabbed me and dragged me in here. What happened?"

"Gabriela must have passed out. Is that normal for a pregnant woman?"

"No, it isn't." Jodi squatted down next to the unconscious woman, checked her breathing and held her wrist, frowning. "That's not right… Her pulse is very erratic. Somebody call 9-1-1."

"Right." Melody appeared and then disappeared in a flash.

Brent decided there seemed to be some kind of unspoken means of communication and delegation of tasks between women in a crisis. Keryn entered the cube farm and immediately went to work diverting incoming calls to the automated voice messaging system from Raheesha's phone. No one sobbed or went into hysterics like women did in the movies. In fact, they acted calmly and in control, which was more than he felt at the present. He stepped back and allowed the scene to unfold without his interference.

"Let's get her feet up higher. Lotus, can you hand me Rae's and yours phone directories as well."

Jodi accepted a thick tome and carefully placed the books under Gabriela's feet then let out a gasp. "Oh, my God… She's hemorrhaging. We need the paramedics now!"

"Can we move her?" Babs asked. "I'll carry her down the stairs if it means she gets to the ambulance faster."

"No, jiggling her about could cause her to lose more blood." Jodi bit her lower lip in thought. "We need to move her cube walls out of the way so they can get the stretcher in here easier and faster. Brent—can you help?"

Without a word Brent grabbed a front portion of the cubicle and pushed hard. What the hell? The thing wouldn't budge.

"It's tacked down to the floor. Let me try to loosen the pins up." Raheesha came around to his side and took her shoe heel to the clamping device head. "There. It should move now. Lotus, grab everything that isn't tacked down like the chairs and get them out of the way so we can shift this thing. Keryn, disconnect the cords and power strips so we don't get hung up on them."

Together they slid the first few cubicles toward the side wall creating a wide pathway to Gabriela's prone form. Brent noticed that her skin tone had changed from pale tan to ashen white in a short time. He swallowed hard, his stomach churning. A small puddle of blood was clearly evident on the carpet beneath her.

"Damn it!" Babs cursed. "Did Mel call 9-1-1 or not?"

Lotus knelt beside her and gave her arm a quick squeeze. "She did. She went downstairs to direct them to the correct office. They'll be here any moment now."

Minutes seemed like hours but the paramedics soon arrived. With the front set of cubes collapsed and moved out of the way, the EMS team easily maneuvered the stretcher to Gabriela's side and hoisted her on it as they prepared to take her down in the elevator.

Babs insisted on going with her to the hospital, but the police held her back.

"Next of kin only in the ambulance," a police officer informed her.

"She hasn't got anybody!" Babs cried. "It's just her and the baby...If she hasn't already lost the baby."

"Is the father nearby?" another officer quietly asked Jodi, glancing over at Brent. She shook her head. He turned his attention back to Babs. "All right then, miss. You can go with her."

"About time." Keryn tossed Babs her knapsack and jacket as she ran behind the stretcher.

Raheesha gathered up her things and pulled out her car keys. "I'll follow them to the hospital in my car. Flower Child, Mel, Keryn, Jodi—you want a ride?"

They each mumbled a yes. Brent remained frozen to the spot.

"You want to come along, too?" Raheesha asked him. "It might be a bit cramped, but we can squeeze you in."

"Hadn't someone better lock the office up…and what about the carpet?"

Six pair of eyes instantly zeroed in on the reddish-brown stain on the floor where Gabriela's cubicle once stood.

"Don't worry. I'll call the janitor on my cell and let him know," Melody said. "And then I'll call Mr. J at home, too. He should know where all his staff is going at fifteen minutes before five and why the calls are being diverted instead of answered."

"Good girl." Jodi smiled but her eyes never lost their concern. "Let me grab my purse and coat and then we can split. Brent, you want to go save your program and exit out of it?"

He stood statue-like. He couldn't make his feet move. He couldn't take his eyes off the spot…

"Brent? Are you okay?"

The blood on the rug seemed to be sucking him into a deep, dark vortex of death. Gabriela's blood became Helena's then became Jodi's and then became his. Death had followed him, trying to hurt all those he came in contact with…He felt sick and wanted to heave his lunch. Still, he remained motionless.

"I'm okay," he managed at last. He plastered an upbeat expression on his face. "You all go on without me. I'll catch up with you later."

Jodi opened her mouth to say something but hesitated. She went to collect her things and quietly exited with the others.

Brent finally forced his gaze away from the stain. He headed toward his office to finish what he had been working on when the disturbance erupted only to find his stomach diverting him to the men's room.

Chapter Sixteen

"Is Gabriela okay?"

Brent's voice sounded tight and strained. Jodi could tell how difficult it was for him to enter Missouri Baptist Medical Center, let alone stand in the emergency room waiting area. He clenched his fists repeatedly and took several ragged breaths. A thin sheen of perspiration dotted his colorless face.

"We don't know anything yet. Why don't you sit down?"

He sat beside her, stiff and mechanical, staring straight ahead at the door leading into the examining rooms as if they led to an execution chamber and not a place of healing.

"Where are the others?" he asked a moment later. "Didn't you all ride together?"

"We did. Raheesha and Mel went to the chapel to pray. Lotus is probably nearby meditating. Keryn started pacing the halls, trying to find out what's going on without us waiting for the official word. Babs went right in with Gabby, so I'm assuming she's standing nearby acting as her next of kin."

Brent swallowed hard. He looked like he was going to be sick. Jodi put an arm around his shoulders and squeezed. "It's okay. You don't have to stay and wait. I was elected to stick it out here in case we caught wind of something sooner rather than later. But it probably will be some time according to the desk clerk.

"It always is."

He turned to face her, a forced smile turning up the corners of his lips. Jodi could tell what a valiant effort Brent was making to appear nonchalant and in control.

"You ever sit in a hospital emergency waiting room before?" he asked.

Jodi shook her head. "No, I've never had the pleasure. Have you?"

"Several times…Gramps has a way of hammering nails into his feet or getting a hand caught up in a bicycle spoke and twisting his wrist."

"Ooo! Sounds painful. Poor Gramps. But you haven't had an accident that required a trip to the hospital yourself?"

"Not really. I had a couple of stitches put in my chin when I was four. I jumped off a platform at a church festival and busted open my skin. I don't really remember it."

She reached for his hand and held it. "You wouldn't being so young."

"Yeah, but my mother loves to tell the story over and over again to anyone who will listen. It's probably the reason I'm such a reckless person to this day."

"Sure you are." She placed his knuckles against her lips and kissed them. "You don't seem to take too many chances. You don't like rocking the boat at all, do you?"

"No, I don't. It's safer not to disturb the status quo…not to change things…to leave things as they are and remain content."

"You put up such a tough front that most people would say you're just plain ol' stubborn. But you're not so much stubborn as you are careful. Overly cautious to be precise…" Jodi tilted her head and sighed. "It's amazing how uninhibited you can be in the bedroom with such a cautious nature."

He waggled an eyebrow and leaned closer. "Well, it's easy to lose your inhibitions when you've got such a wonderful bed companion." He kissed her briefly on the lips. "That whipped cream stunt you pulled was phenomenal."

Jodi blushed. "Keep your voice down. We aren't the only ones in this waiting room. As I recall you enjoyed playing your part as the 'banana split'."

"What guy wouldn't with such a pretty cherry on top?"

Her cheeks warmed again. "Ahem…Down boy. I see Keryn coming this way. Act respectable."

"I ran into Babs in the hallway," Keryn announced, her heels clicking against the tile floor. "The others should be here soon. I told Lotus to round up Melody and Raheesha." She stopped and stared hard at Brent. "Glad to see you could make it. You look worse than some of the patients here."

"Thank a lot. Must have been something I ate."

Keryn rolled her eyes. "The case of Little Debbies or the truckload of Ding-Dongs? I've seen your trash can, Davison. They should pump your stomach. You certainly know your way around the junk food aisle."

Brent chuckled, relaxing his grip on Jodi's hand. "Hey, there are enough wine connoisseurs in the world already. Why not diversify my epicurean tastes into packaged snack cakes?"

"I told them and they're coming," Lotus said upon entering the waiting area. She paused and tilted her head. "You know, Brent, I've got some herbal tea that would do wonders for your pasty complexion."

"No thanks. I'll stick with Code Red. It goes better with Ho-Hos."

Melody and Raheesha turned the corner and stopped dead in their tracks.

Raheesha raised an eyebrow as they approached. "You feeling all right, Brent? You're pretty white even for a white guy."

He shrugged. "I forgot to visit the tanning booth this past week. That's all."

Jodi smiled at Brent's wisecrack. His cheeks actually had gotten some of their color back due to the distraction of his office mates.

"My mom's chicken soup can put the pink back in your cheeks—at least that's what she always says." Melody turned and spoke the question on everyone's mind. "Keryn, what's the news about Gabriela?"

The entire group stood huddled together. Keryn lowered her voice. "Babs said they're going to keep her here tonight and probably for a few more days after that. Then it'll be mandatory bed rest for the remainder of her pregnancy."

Melody sniffed back a tear. "But she and the baby are both going to be okay, right?"

"Yes, they say their prognosis is good. We did the right thing. We got her here before she and the baby could bleed to death. Babs says the doctors and paramedics alike were impressed with how professional we acted."

Raheesha sighed. "I just thank God Almighty that Gabby passed out at the office where we were there to help her and not at home all alone. Who knows what would have happened if she had."

"Oooo…I don't even want to think about it." Lotus cringed. "Did they say if we can we visit her, Keryn?"

Keryn shook her head. "No, not tonight. Babs says maybe tomorrow. She'll spend the night in ICU hooked up to monitors just in case something happens. It's still possible she could go into labor."

A group gasp echoed through the waiting area.

Jodi swallowed hard; her hands flew to her heart. "Gabby can't have the baby now—it's way too early."

Melody started crying in earnest now. "W-w-will they let Babs stay with Gabby through the night?"

Jodi noticed Keryn quickly dab at the corner of her eye with her finger. "Yeah, they said Babs could stay with her."

"Well, there's no use for us to stay around if we can't see her tonight." Raheesha pulled her sweater on and fished in her purse for her car keys. "Y'all are welcome to come over to my place. I'll fix us some supper. Any takers?"

Everyone nodded the affirmative except Brent.

"I don't think I'm up for a meal right now." He patted his stomach with a grimace. "But thanks anyway."

Raheesha chuckled. "Stay off the all-candy diet and your digestive system wouldn't play tricks on you like that. Jodi?"

Jodi looked out of the corner of her eye at her lover and knew where she was needed tonight. "I'll go home and look after the Cupcake Kid here. You guys will call if there's any news, right?"

They all agreed and went their separate ways. Even though Brent said very little on the drive home, Jodi sensed he felt better from the moment he stepped out of the hospital. When they walked through the back door she discovered the real reason behind his silence.

He pulled her into his arms and kissed her soundly and only let her come up for air a full minute later.

"I've been thinking of what I want to do to your body ever since we got into the car." He slid her jacket from her shoulders and began unbuttoning her blouse. His hands reached under her bra and easily undid its catch. "We have any whipped cream in the fridge?"

Jodi giggled. She tugged at his shirt hem and pulled his sweater over his head. They stood topless in the dark kitchen. They hadn't done it on her table since she had officially moved in.

"I think we're out of whipped cream," she murmured. "We may have some chocolate syrup, though."

"Hmm…a bit too sticky. You taste good straight up anyway."

Brent whisked her off her feet and then up the stairs. Jodi clung tightly to him, drinking in his masculine scent of sweat and cologne. He hadn't acted quite so frisky since she had moved into the house. She'd thought work and familiarity were the culprits that kept them apart, but perhaps something else had been at fault.

He laid her across the large bed that had been his grandparents' and helped her out of her slacks and shoes.

"It's so good to be away from that death place. It's good to be alive with you, Jodi."

She understood his sudden desire for closeness now. "Yes, it's good to be alive with you, too, Brent. I don't think I've ever felt so alive than when I'm with you, in your arms., You and I connected body and soul."

He tossed the remainder of their clothing aside and lay down beside her, caressing her mound while his tongue danced across the hard peaks of her breasts. "Let's not waste another moment then. I want to feel alive. I want to be inside you. I want you to carry life."

Their lips met again before Jodi could react. *What did he say? Could it mean…?*

She sat up and quickly took a ragged breath. "Brent, do you mean you want me to have your child?"

"Yes." He pulled her back down to him and began nibbling on her earlobes. "I agree with Gramps. The family tradition should continue. That old blue tricycle needs a new owner."

Jodi squealed then began some nibbling of her own. Her lips and tongue danced across his broad chest, twirling around his pebbled nipples. He groaned.

"You know, Brent, Gramps expects us to do things in the proper order. You realize what that implies, right?"

"Yes. To quote the old jump rope rhyme, 'First comes love, then comes marriage, then comes baby in a baby carriage.'"

Marriage? "You mean want to…?"

"Eventually. No, soon. Let's get married with Gramps and Marjorie. A double wedding on the beach. They'd love it. Sounds romantic, doesn't it?"

"Yes, it does." Jodi's heart soared. Their lips melded together in a kiss of promise.

"How do you know that old verse about love and marriage?" she asked, coming up for air. "Don't tell me you jumped rope when you were a kid."

"All the time. The cutest girls were always jumping rope at recess. I wanted to hang with them so I learned how to jump. I quickly became the girls' favorite."

"I bet. That explains a lot about your skill with women."

She allowed her lips to wander south and soon his erection stood at attention. "I hung out on the playground with the nerd boys and played the latest Japanese card game craze or other such nonsense. They never even noticed me."

"Blind fools."

She reached over to the nightstand to retrieve a condom from the box in the drawer. He pulled her to him and kissed her before she could pull one out..

"They were idiots. They don't know what they're missing. And I know I don't want to miss any more of life."

Brent wrapped a hand through her curls and

brought her lips to his, entering her before she could reply. Jodi sighed and arched her back, drawing him deeper within her body. It felt so good, so right...She'd never experienced such a feeling of togetherness before. Brent wanted to marry her and have a baby with her... Nothing else in the world could ever top that feeling.

Each thrust zinged energy through her. Her womanly muscles wrapped tightly about his cock as she began to grind her hips in a circular motion. Brent gasped and grabbed hold of her buttocks, deepening his penetration.

"Yes, yes..." he groaned. "This is madness. I won't last much longer if you keep that swivel hip action going."

She chuckled, low in her throat. "How about I go a little faster then?" Within seconds Jodi realized she had made the wrong move. "Oh, my...yes."

Stars blazed before her eyes as tremors rocked her body. She threw back her head and screamed Brent's name. He responded by driving himself hard inside her until the overwhelming sensation of soaring through space and time took hold as wave after wave of orgasmic ecstasy washed over her.

"Had enough yet?" he asked, panting.

Floating on a cloud above her physical form, the world spun around and around. "Enough of what?"

Somehow they had rolled over until Jodi found herself lying on her back with Brent kneeling above her. He cradled her buttocks and lifted her hips to afford deeper access then plunged inside, pounding her hard until she came once more. Relentlessly he plunged into her until with a great shudder his seed filled her, his cries mingling with hers.

They lay in each other's arms, content to make love again and again through out the evening and late into the night. Somehow Jodi knew that tonight they had created a new life.

TO: ShaynaE@wazoo.com
FROM: jbaker@hit-on-us.com
SUBJECT: A hunk by any other name?

You call your new flame "Bobo"???

Is that like "Bobo the Clown"? How do you find these jokers? No, I take that back – they seem to find you, don't they? ☺

But a pop-country singer? I thought you were too bright, too academic to fall for a simple musician – even if he's an up and coming star. The impromptu way he serenaded you at the restaurant sounds very romantic, though.

So...you were just sitting there celebrating your friends' engagement in this ritzy restaurant when this "Bobo" person strolls by and starts singing? He must have noticed you the minute you walked in the room, girlfriend. Of course, with those big brown eyes of yours and that sexy wiggle, how could any red-blooded male not notice you?

And he's dedicating his first album to you and you just met? He's fallen for you in a big way. I mean, think of all the starlets and back-up singers he must have fooled around with on his way to the top. If he's saying that you are the only woman for him forever then it must be the real thing. Grab him tight and hold on for the ride.

Well, your excitement there Ms. Shayna the Gorgeous is on a completely different plane than the excitement here in everyday St. Louis. Gabriela is out of the hospital, but it's still somewhat iffy about the baby making it to term. She's on complete bed rest. That means no lifting, no walking, no standing, no nothing. It's a miracle what all pre-natal surgeons can fix nowadays my mother tells me. If she had suffered this same thing even twenty years ago she would have lost the baby. He truly is a miracle child.

Yes, it's a he. Gabby says the ultrasounds all indicate it's a healthy boy. If she can just keep things together a few more months, he'll be born okay. It's a relief to hear that. Things are still tough for Gabby. But she's moved in with Babs and it seems to be working quite well. Babs has enough energy to take care of a sick mother and hold a job and fight off the idiots of the world so Gabby can rest and keep calm. Babs is the ultimate she-woman, man-eating tigress if you ask me.

The main idiot I'm talking about is Harrison Platte. He found out about Gabby's almost-miscarriage via the grapevine. Amazingly, it seems to have knocked some sense into his thick, "poor little rich boy" skull. He's actually talking about caring for the child financially. I don't think it involves wedding bells, but at least it's a start.

Maybe the whole Platte family is mellowing out? They seem to have fallen in love with Lotus. Of course she and Max are the world's most perfect couple. They listen to the same folk songs, attend the same political rallies, dress like they time-traveled from the original Woodstock. They couldn't be happier. Keryn and Peter (whom she lovingly refers to as "Pointdexter") seem to be growing closer, too. Pete's practically moved all his things into Keryn's place according to Lotus. At least the honeymoon couple has a bit more privacy now.

Raheesha and Darnell set a date finally—next June. They want a big church wedding with all the trimmings. It should be spectacular. Darnell isn't just a lowly undertaker—he owns the funeral home. He's probably worth as much as the Plattes. I didn't realize this until the other day when Rae made the comment that she planned on leaving Hit-On-Us right before their wedding and their month-long honeymoon to Hawaii. I know she loves to work, so I figure she's going to join the family business and work with her new husband. In the office pushing paper, of course. I can't imagine Rae working directly with their "clients" for some reason.

Everyone seems to have it together here somehow. Gabby has Babs and the baby (that sounds weird, but it's true) and Lotus Blossom has her Max the Plant Man. Rae's got her Darnell and Keryn and Pete seem to be an item, too. Melody's hanging in there with Barry...She's really trying to learn more about weightlifting, but it's not really her thing. She acts like a big girl now, and if it doesn't work out, I don't think she'll fall apart like she used to.

Brent is fine. We're fine. We've got some news, but we're keeping it a secret a little while longer. Don't worry – you'll be one of the first to know. You got some frequent flyer miles saved up? I have a good use for them around the holidays! ☺

Catch ya later – Jodi

P.S. You will let me know if you're eloping with this Bo guy, right? Who says I can't attend a secret wedding? I've always wanted to be your maid of honor – country music at the wedding or not! ☺

*****

"Come in." Mr. Johansson nodded to the empty chair in front of his desk as he put down the phone. "That was Brewster. He can't make it to the Reno IT show."

"That's too bad." A sudden sinking feeling hit Jodi square in the stomach as she sat down for their regular afternoon meeting. "How come Brewster can't go?"

"He just found out about a big sales conference going on in Los Angeles the same weekend. Since he's our regional sales manager for the west coast I gave him permission to attend that event instead. It makes better sense in the long haul."

"I agree. So who's going to attend the trade show?"

"Brent was—but since he couldn't find a train fare that cost less than an airline ticket I asked Brewster if he could go. He had no conflict until today when he heard about the other thing."

Mr. Johansson shuffled some papers around on his desk then cleared his throat and looked her straight in the eye. His attitude had taken on a seriousness she had seldom witnessed before.

"Jodi, I want you to talk Brent into attending the trade show as we originally planned."

"Me?"

Jodi felt her cheeks warm. She fidgeted in her seat. How in the world was she going to talk Brent into getting on an airplane? He hadn't even stepped across the threshold of an airport terminal since Helena's death.

They had planned on using up two full days of their Christmas vacation to drive all the way down to Florida for Gramps' and Marjorie's—and their—wedding on the beach. If Brent wouldn't even consider a short hop in an airplane for such an important event there was no way he'd fly cross country.

Mr. Johansson smiled and pointed a finger directly at her. "Yes, you. You two are an *item* now, aren't you? I listen to the break room gossip on occasion. I know you two are living together."

"Uh…well, we, uh…both needed to save money on rent and it made sense."

"I'm sure it did. So who else but you can talk some sense into Brent? I don't buy his claustrophobia reasoning for not wanting to fly."

"It's not quite the reason why Brent doesn't like airplanes..."

Jodi felt at a lost for words. She didn't want to blithely reveal Brent's dark, deep fears to their boss, but there seemed to be no other way. How could she get Brent out of this situation without compromising his secret?

"I'll attend the IT trade show if you let me, Mr. J."

One gray-tinged eyebrow shot up. "Are you certain? It's not in your area of expertise any more than it was in Brewster's, but we need a presence there to convince the market we mean business. You sure you wouldn't rather talk Brent into going?"

"No, this way is much easier. I don't mind attending the show. It's only for two days, right?"

They talked on about the IT world and sales figures, but Jodi only half-listened. What had she talked herself into? She had kept Brent from climbing aboard an airliner only to volunteer to fly in his place. Another girlfriend taking a flight without him...

Would he understand the sacrifice she was making for him—for them? And if he found out would he ever forgive her?

Chapter Seventeen

TO: MrBoJangles@crapster.net
FROM: bdavison@hit-on-us.com
SUBJECT: the last single man in America?

Dear Mr. Bobo…

Tell me more about this new woman in you life. I assume she is drop dead gorgeous – that's a given – but what else does she have going for her? Just because she says she's a graduate student doesn't mean she's got all her marbles upstairs. Is she a bookworm or a computer geek? An eternal college student? At least when you make it big time in the music biz she'll have someone to foot her tuition bills…after you've paid off all your college loans.

At least you've finally found a woman who can teach you how to write properly. I can barely understand some of your emails. Inventive spelling went out in first grade, buddy. Use your spell check. ☺

And you're the last guy I would have expected to fall in love at first sight. I mean you've only slept with most of the single females between the ages of 18 and 25 in the Eastern time zone… Why this sudden need to settle down now? Could it be the Bo-meister has finally grown up?

I know – I'm one to preach. Jodi and I have decided to tie the knot. Gramps and current events have really driven it into my head that it's better not to wait and plan a big, elaborate church affair. Skipping all the fancy stuff saves money, too.

We're planning a double wedding ceremony on New Year's Eve with Gramps and Marjorie down in Florida. Jodi likes the idea of a beach wedding. It's supposed to be a big surprise, too. She's not telling any of her relatives or friends until Thanksgiving. I figure it's because she doesn't want any of them talking her out of it. (Working in the travel business has its perks – she can get them all deeply discounted airline tickets. We're driving, of course.)

Yes, I know I'm one hell of a lucky guy. Just keep this info under your hat for a few more weeks and then you can blab it all you want.

Before I forget…I wanted to tell you that your lyrics about the rich dude who leaves the poor girl knocked up are really good. You can't use the asshole's real name, though. He'd sue your butt off. But if you can find another word to rhyme with "Platte" then you're good to go. He'd never recognize himself in the song. Screwing and dumping ordinary folks is an everyday occurrence for those mega-millionaire types.

I'm out of here now. Jodi and I have a little shopping to do tonight after work. I wish I had your dough – I caught this ring in a jewelry store window I want to buy for her. Of course, she'd need a forklift to pick her

hand up while wearing it, but it's the thought that counts.
B

*****

"Let's stop off at Walgreens first." Jodi sounded uncharacteristically out of breath on reaching Brent's car in the parking lot. He opened the door and helped her slide inside. "I need to pick up something important."

Brent glanced at her from the corner of his eye. Jodi had been acting tired all day. There were even dark circles under her eyes, and she appeared a bit pale and worn. Hopefully she wasn't coming down with something serious. He wanted his bride to look healthy come their big day.

"Sure, we can go drop by Walgreens. Can't it wait until after we go to the jewelry store?"

She shook her head. "No. I need to get this thing now. Tonight. It's important–very important. I want to make sure of something before I have to go out of town tomorrow."

"All right."

Brent started the car and headed toward home. Even though there were a million and one Walgreen stores in the St. Louis metropolitan area, Jodi always shopped at the corner store nearest to the house. Women like familiarity he reckoned.

He lost Jodi somewhere near the toothpaste section and wandered over to the photo area to check out a few prices. They'd been discussing buying a bunch of disposable cameras for friends and family members to take pictures of the big day on the beach. Professional photographers didn't come cheap.

According to Melody, even with paying for the plastic cameras and film development they'd come out ahead. She got the idea from a magazine. According to Jodi, Melody had been reading a lot of bride's magazines lately…But whether it was for her personal benefit or because of Raheesha's upcoming big deal as she insisted, no one knew for certain.

"Okay, I got what I needed. Let's split."

Brent's eyes widened. Jodi looked like death warmed over. In her white hand she clutched at a small plastic bag. She must have paid for her purchase at the back register near the pharmacy department.

"You sure you're okay? We can always go look at rings another time."

"No, I want to have our rings picked out before I go to this sales meeting…" She grimaced and patted her stomach. "I just wish I hadn't eaten that taco for lunch now."

He took her by the arm and led her out to the car. When they reached the jewelry store Jodi asked for a stool and a glass of water. The saleswoman was more than happy to provide them.

"A short engagement, right?" The motherly-looking woman smiled at them both upon her return. "Still, our engagement and wedding band sets are the best value for the money. Here, let me show you…"

Ring set after ring set materialized on the glass case countertop. Jodi seemed to perk up a little as she tried each example on, *oo-ing* and *ah-ing* at the brilliance of the metal and stones.

"Oh, Brent...I like this one the best." She sighed and held up her hand for his closer inspection. "What do you think?"

Think? They all looked like gold or silver circles with a few diamonds tucked in for good measure to him. He'd be happy wearing a cigar band or a Cracker Jack ring. But there was no way he'd voice that particular opinion out loud.

"It's beautiful. The swirl part on the solitaire is lovely. It looks like your golden curls. It fits you perfectly."

"But do you care about the wedding band being a rather plain gold band with just a little of the filigree detailing?"

He shrugged. "Tradition. There's no need to break with tradition."

Her smile practically split her face in two. "Right. We'll take this set, please."

"Very good choice," the saleswoman said. "Let me get the paperwork for you to sign."

Jodi began to slip the engagement ring off her finger, but Brent caught her hand in his.

"Leave it on. It looks good there."

She tilted her head and gazed up at him, smiling. "I thought we wanted to keep our nuptials a secret for a few more weeks?"

"To our parents maybe—but I think it's okay to tell the gang at the office. Maybe Mr. Johansson will stop looking at me like I'm the scum of the earth if he knows we're engaged."

Jodi blinked and practically dropped her jaw. "Oh... Mr. J doesn't give you the evil eye like that–

does he?"

"Occasionally. Ever since he heard on the grapevine you moved in with me he's been acting like your father. I think he thinks I'm not good enough for you."

"Really!" She laughed. The color returned to her cheeks. "You're so funny at times, Brent. Whatever gets into a guy's head sometimes?"

After signing away his next month's paycheck as a down payment they headed home. The moment he opened the door Jodi rushed up the stairs and ran into the bathroom, slamming the door behind her.

"She must have the flu or something. I hope she feels better so she can drive to that sales meeting."

*****

Jodi's hand shook as she held the test strip up. Ten minutes. In ten minutes she'd know whether or not she was pregnant.

The signs were all there–the missed period, the tender nipples, the queasy stomach and general fatigue–along with that annoying feeling that a small alien from outer space had invaded her body. She mentally congratulated herself on filling the small, empty plastic container this morning and secreting it under the sink cabinet. A woman's early morning urine revealed more accurate test results according to the pregnancy test kit's web site. Thank heavens Brent never seemed to look under the sink for anything.

She really should call her mom and dad and let them know about the baby–and the wedding, too. They'd be happy about it happening sooner rather than later if they knew they were about to become grandparents.

Jodi slowly sipped a cup of water and checked her watch again. Seven more minutes until her fate became clear. Should she tell Brent? He had a right to know, being the father and all, but was this really the best time to tell him?

She was leaving tomorrow for Reno. Leaving on a jet plane…and she hadn't said much to Brent about the nature of her trip yet. All he knew was that she was going to a conference out of town. She told him she was driving since it wasn't that far away. Brent had assumed she was going to Evansville since Mr. J had talked about a regional sales meeting on the same weekend the trade show in Reno took place. As far as Brent knew, Rich Brewster was attending the IT event.

"It's just a little white lie, baby," Jodi said, patting her tender belly. "I know it seems like I'm doing the same thing Helena did–but I'm not. She didn't tell him she was flying because she didn't want to upset him about her job interview. I'm not telling him I'm flying because he doesn't like the idea of anyone he loves getting on an airplane. It's not quite the same thing, is it?"

Jodi bit her lip. Who was she trying to fool? Her actions almost exactly mirrored Helena's. She was withholding information from the man she loved because she didn't want to worry him.

She glanced at her watch again. Four minutes.

Sighing, Jodi slumped against the back of the commode tank. So…what if she did come clean and tell Brent about her flight to Reno tomorrow? Would he forbid her from going? Would he call off their engagement?

And what if she turned out to be pregnant? Would he keep her from flying in order to protect their child?

"An-ti-ci-pa-a-tion," she sang softly. Two minutes to go.

To tell Brent about the baby or to not tell Brent about the baby...That was the question. Well, it really was a moot point, wasn't it? The pregnancy hadn't been confirmed yet. And even if the test strip did indicate a positive result, it wasn't conclusive. It took a doctor to give an official thumbs up, right?

Jodi picked up the test stick. Two pink lines. Okay...so the pregnancy wasn't a moot point anymore.

"Melody–she has Mr. J's home phone number on her cell. I'll call her and then call him and tell him I have to cancel. Hit-On-Us just won't make an appearance at the trade show this year. There's always next year."

A sudden urge to empty her stomach contents suddenly forced her to hug the porcelain bowl. As soon as she felt somewhat normal she was going to call Mr. J. Yes, being honest with her boss and with Brent would solve everyone's problems.

*****

"But Mr. J I don't feel so hot. Can't you talk Brewster into going again?" Frowning, Jodi lowered her voice to a whisper. "And I can't tell Brent about how easy flying is on a pregnant woman compared to driving. He just wouldn't understand. Trust me."

"Jodi, you've always acted professionally," Mr. Johansson began slowly and deliberately. "It's your best business trait. Now's not the time to stop."

She moaned but said nothing as her boss continued to lecture her.

"I felt tempted to fire Brent when he told me he didn't fly, but I realize his IT skills are too valuable to the company at this point in the game. But sales managers are a dime a dozen. Brewster has left for L.A. already. I can't order him to Reno at this late date."

Jodi sighed. "I know."

"Buck up–sip some clear soda and snack on crackers. It's how my wife always handled her morning sickness. Don't disappoint me."

"Yes, sir. I'll go to Reno. I won't disappoint you."

She clicked off the cordless phone and closed her eyes, resting her head against one of the fluffy couch pillows. There was no way she was getting out of this business trip. She had better inform Brent. First, however, she would simply lie still and gather her courage.

"Here's some chamomile tea." Brent's baritone broke into her dreams. "My mom always swears by it when she's feeling cruddy."

"Oh, thanks." Jodi sat up, shook her head and blinked several times. "Hmmm... Did I sleep for long?"

"I don't know. I was out in the garage looking over my old tricycle when I came back inside and found you snoozing on the sofa." He sat down beside her and gently pulled her into his lap. "You feel well enough to travel tomorrow?"

"I guess. Mr. J didn't leave me any choice in the matter. I go or I walk. Pretty simple."

Brent kissed her forehead and held her close. She rested her head on his chest, enjoying the sound of his heartbeat and his masculine scent. Perhaps the baby was doing the same thing even now?

"I can't believe Mr. J would fire you because you're sick and can't attend some dumb sales meeting. Can't they reschedule?"

"No, I'm afraid not. That's the duties of a regional sales manager–I have to be one whether I feel like it or not."

"But he was so understanding when I told him I wouldn't fly."

"Yes, but you have certificates hanging on the wall. I don't. There's the big difference."

Jodi slowly sipped her tea while Brent flipped TV channels with the remote. Everything seemed so right, so perfect. It would be a sin to disturb such domestic tranquility with the double announcement that she was pregnant *and* she had to board an airplane tomorrow.

Her mind made up, Jodi decided to postpone telling Brent about their unborn child until she returned from Reno. After a weekend apart he'd be more than happy to see her again. Any irritation he may harbor about her flying would be forgotten in the thrill of impending fatherhood. And then they could celebrate the good news in bed.

*****

TO: ShaynaE@wazoo.com
FROM: jbaker@hit-on-us.com
SUBJECT: Wish I were there

Whoa…Girlfriend you are moving sooo fast!

You're moving in with this singer dude? You've only known him for such a little while. Don't you think that's a bit precipitous? I knew Brent a lot longer before we started shacking up. How do you know your darling Bobo isn't an ax murderer? I mean apart from the fact he carries a guitar around with him instead of a chain saw?

Oh, well. You're a big girl. I suppose I have to let you make your own decisions. Just stay safe, okay? ☺

Here I am in Reno at the IT trade show. Yawn! I'm glad I borrowed a laptop computer from work and this place has wireless Internet so I don't totally fall asleep. This show is just lots of geeks and computer gurus shuffling around trying to impress the hell out of each other. I'm mostly handing out flyers about Hit-On-US and our new travel booking system that "eliminates the middleman while still maintaining that personal touch" or some such bullshit. I think the advertising and promotions firm we're working with is third rate. No one is even looking at our free mouse pads or squeegee balls with our logo on them. I hope Mr. J isn't too mad when he realizes exactly how much money he wasted.

I took that little home test you suggested. Uh-huh. You were right. Heartburn and nausea together is a good sign. I haven't told Brent yet since I'm here and he's there…I can't wait until tomorrow morning when I hop on that jet for home.

Will Brent be happy? I think so. He's the one who said he wanted another owner for his old blue tricycle. And yes, you guessed it why I told you to keep New Year's Eve open. I'm not going to buy a fancy outfit–and now that I'm a few pounds heavier, it's probably going to be difficult to find an outfit that's not too revealing anyway.

You can wear what you like as my maid of honor. It's a "beach wedding" so casual is in. Gramps says he and Marjorie were planning on wearing white slacks with matching cotton sweaters. I'm thinking of something along the sundress line – maybe in white, maybe not. What would folks think if I wore a tropical print in vivid red? Hey, they'll be counting the months backwards soon enough…

Oops–I see some geeks heading this way. Time to put on my best sales smile and do a little schmoozing with potential customers.

Talk to you soon–
Jodi

*****

"What do you mean my flight's been delayed?" Jodi gritted her teeth and blinked back tears. "I've got to be home by seven o'clock. I promised my fiancé my car would be in the driveway by seven."

"I'm sorry, ma'am," the pleasant-sounding, smiling airline clerk said. "There's been general delays across the board due to some fog in Atlanta and heavy rains at LaGuardia. Once those major hubs get backed up, it's only a matter of time until the rest of the airports in the country feel the brunt of it. Two hours isn't too bad, all things considering."

Jodi stormed away from the ticket counter and headed to her gate. She was going to have to break down and call Brent. He'd worry if she didn't.

It had been difficult to talk to him the night before when she called home briefly to let him know she was okay. There had been "trade show" types of noises in the background and so she had cut the call short. She wasn't supposed to be at a trade show but a quiet, orderly sales workshop. She had used her cell phone, praying that the caller ID didn't say something about her roaming charges on their read-out at the house.

Jodi plopped down into a lounge chair and mentally sorted through her options. She could either call him and tell him she was stuck in the Reno airport, or she was held up by something at the workshop and would leave about two hours later than planned, or she could simply not call him at all. The last option was tempting–as it meant she didn't have to lie to him–but she knew it wasn't fair.

Brent worried about little things like not arriving home on time. Gramps had told her how he felt like a teenager whenever he waltzed in late. Brent would stand there at the front door, frowning, shaking his head and saying things like, "You could have been run over for all I knew."

Jodi sighed. She had to call. She rummaged through her purse for several minutes before locating and extracting her cell phone.

"Hello." He answered on the first ring.

"Hi there…Um, I'm running a bit late. I should be home by nine or nine-thirty tops."

There was a long pause then, "I thought you said this workshop finished by three-thirty. It shouldn't take you that long to drive back from Evansville even with construction traffic."

Jodi bit her lip. She felt a nervous tickle of sweat slowly dribbling down her spine. "Uh, I was off on the times. It ended at five. And some of us want to go and grab a bite to eat before we go our separate ways. That's why I'm a bit iffy on exactly when I'll arrive home. I'm sorry."

"Yes, I bet you are. Hardly anything is affordable that's halfway decent to eat in an airport terminal."

Airport? Did he say airport? Jodi froze. How did he find out? What could she say? How could she rectify the situation?

"Will Ms. Jodi Baker please report to the Southwest Airlines ticket counter…" the P.A. monotone droned. "Jodi Baker to the Southwest counter."

"You'd better answer your page, Jodi." Brent's voice sounded flat, controlled. "They've probably found a quicker flight back to St. Louis for you."

"What…?" She swallowed and began again. "How did you know?"

"Melody slipped up Friday morning while

handling a call for you at the front desk. I happened to be walking past when I heard her tell someone you were at the trade show in Reno. I called Rich Brewster and discovered he was in L.A. It doesn't take a rocket scientist to figure out you lied to me."

The soulless P.A. announcer repeated again, "Will Jodi Baker please report to the Southwest ticket counter."

"You'd better go the ticket counter. You do want to come home, don't you?"

"Of course I do." Suddenly a rush of emotion filled her tired bones. She felt angry, betrayed, confused. She gathered up her things and marched toward the ticket counter.

"I didn't lie to you, Brent," she said, breathless as she threaded her way through the crowds. "Mr. J said I had to attend the trade show in Reno and so I did. I need to keep my job to afford raising our kid in this day and age. Diapers and runny noses don't come cheap."

"How long have you known you were pregnant?"

Jodi stopped dead in her tracks.

"I…I'm not exactly sure. I haven't seen a doctor yet or anything…I wanted to tell you when I got home so you wouldn't worry about me traveling in this condition."

"Thanks a lot. Now I have to worry about the two of you."

"No, you don't." She started walking again. "There's nothing to worry about. We're both fine. F-i-n-e, fine. It's ridiculous to totally freak out about another person's safety."

"So you think it's ridiculous for me to act concerned? I should care less that the woman who's bearing my child is about to step onto an airplane?"

Jodi reached the back of the ticket counter line and deposited her briefcase and tote bag at her feet. "In a word, yes."

"You don't see any risk involved in flying?"

"Risk? *Risk*?"

Brent Davison totally exasperated her at times. Her volume rose along with her frustration. "Of course there's a risk. There's a risk every time you step into the bathtub that you'll slip on the bar of soap and hit your head and drown. There's a risk any time you eat that you'll die from food poisoning. There's a risk you'll die in an auto accident every time you climb behind the wheel. In fact, you're more likely to die in a car than an airplane."

She took a deep breath. "But, most of all, Brent–and this is the important part–I'm not planning on dying today."

"Neither am I," a roundish man in a black suit sporting a red nose and the distinct odor of alcohol answered her. "Today's not a good day for dying. It's always more expensive to die on a weekend."

Jodi glared at the nosy drunk, covering the phone with a hand. "Do you mind? This is a private conversation."

Brent sighed. "You'd better get back to your seat mate, Jodi. I'll see you when I see you."

A cold shiver coursed through her veins. "What's that suppose to mean?"

"It means that funeral homes and hearses charge

more to pick up a deceased loved one on the weekends than they do on normal business days," the stranger explained. "So, if you were choosing a day to die on, I'd pick Tuesday around mid-day. It's like flying–you get a cheaper rate in the middle of the week."

She spun around to avoid the buttinski's rude attempts at conversation. "Brent, please don't be angry. Chill out. I'll be home later tonight. We'll talk then, okay?"

"Whatever."

The phone went dead. His words sounded final. He sounded hurt.

Blinking back tears, Jodi stepped up to the ticket counter. The pleasant, smiling customer service woman took her boarding pass and handed her a new one.

"Good news. There's an earlier flight to St. Louis that we can get you a seat on. You'll only be about an hour later than planned. Is that satisfactory?"

"Yes, thank you." Jodi took the boarding pass and shuffled toward her new gate number. The need to return home on time didn't seem all that important anymore.

Chapter Eighteen

TO: ShaynaE@wazoo.com
FROM: jbaker@hit-on-us.com
SUBJECT: Boss happy, me miserable

Hey there,

Not much to say here. The boss is happy that I attended the trade show and made a good impression on people in the industry. Personally, I'm a miserable, upchucking mess. Being pregnant isn't for sissies.

Everyone at the office is laughing at my predicament behind my back…I can tell. They all think it's funny that I'm knocked up. I'm the last person they'd ever figured would be in this situation. Miss Cautious Jodi Baker who wouldn't let a man into her heart–or bed–again after she was jilted at the altar. I certainly fooled them, huh?

I shouldn't complain. My doctor says I'm in great shape and can pretty much go about my normal routine. Gabriela is still on bed rest, but she's making the most of it. She's doing some work from home. Keryn set her up with a decent computer. Mr. J was nice to let her do that. Most bosses would have simply laid her off.

Brent still isn't really talking to me. I thought after a

week he'd get over it, but he hasn't. I came home safe and sound–what's his problem? I may have rocks for brains, but there seems to be more to his pouting than just me getting on an airplane. I'm still wearing the ring, however. He hasn't asked for it back. But we haven't talked much about the wedding plans. Gramps will probably call tonight. I guess I'll find out what Brent feels about the subject then.

I'm glad to hear your thesis project is going well. Colobus Monkeys and Their Swinging Sex Habits *definitely is a catchy title. I'd pick it up and read it.*

Sorry to hear your dear Bobo is back in the recording studio and you miss him. That's the life of a vocal artist for you. They can't lie around and compose personal serenades 24/7 or else they wouldn't be able to afford those big cars and bigger mansions. Don't worry–he won't forget about you. How could he forget the woman who inspired the title song of his first album?

Yep, you've got yourself a good-looking guy, and you're on your way to a graduate degree. Stop hogging all the good luck, will ya?

(Oooo…I got heartburn bad. And I have to go potty again. I've gotta stop it with the tacos for lunch.)

Grumpily yours,
Jodi

*****

"You wanna go to happy hour with the gang at the Zodiac Cafe tonight?" Melody asked as Jodi stepped out of the ladies room. "For old time's sake?"

Why not? It wasn't like she and Brent talked much. He had planned on staying late to work on a project anyway. It would be nice to get out with the girls and chat a little, dance a little, drink a little…Okay, she'd just chat and maybe dance a little–if she felt like it.

"Sure, I'd love to go." Jodi smiled. "Just as long as I get home by eight. We're expecting a phone call from Gramps and Marjorie then."

"The way we've all been dragging lately we'll probably be done by seven." Melody plopped into her desk chair. "I'm feeling pretty beat myself."

"What's your problem, Mel? It's only me and Gabby who are in the family way–right?"

Melody blushed. "I certainly hope so. I don't think it's contagious."

Something didn't quite add up with Melody's mannerisms. The youngster of the office seemed to be withholding information. Jodi parked herself in front of the receptionist counter, determined to get to the bottom of things.

"Has Barry popped the big question yet?" Jodi noted a marked increase in Melody's fidgeting and shuffling of papers.

"Question? Oh…you mean has he asked to marry me yet. The answer is no, he has not. And why should he? It's not like we're dating anymore."

"You're not seeing Barry?" This was news. Melody, who found it difficult to keep Krispy Kremes in the break room a secret, had never acted so tight-lipped before.

"No, Barry and I broke up a few weeks back. He...he just didn't do anything for me anymore. But Lionel..." She sighed, dreamily twirling a lock of brown hair in her fingers. "Lionel is just dreamy."

Jodi blinked and stared. Melody's radiant face positively glowed with a look of pure contentment. It must be love–or a recent trip to the tanning both.

"So, tell me...who is this Lionel person? Why have you been keeping him a secret? Is he a hotty? Lifts weights like Barry?"

Melody shook her head and grinned. "No, he's not into weigh lifting. Thank goodness. Barry was always preening and worrying about his weight and his muscle mass gain. Lionel is a real man. He's strong–but he's not vain. He's gentle and kind and has a lovely tenor voice."

Jodi experienced a pang of jealousy. Since she'd moved in with Brent and stopped commuting with Melody she really hadn't kept up with her office mate's love life. Jodi made a silent vow not to let things slide between her and her girlfriends after the baby arrived.

"A lovely tenor you say? Where exactly did you meet him?"

"At church. Raheesha's church. She invited me to a revival there. I just adore their gospel choir. She introduced me to Lionel after one of the services. He's Darnell's younger brother."

Gasping, Jodi's jaw dropped open wide. "You've been double dating with Raheesha all this time and neither one of you let on? You dirty dogs! Here I've been puking my guts out all week, and this tidbit of news would have distracted me from my misery. Why didn't you tell me?"

"I-I didn't mean to hurt your feelings, Jojo." She pouted momentarily then grinned. "But I'll let you in on everything so far. We've only gone out once or twice. Lionel is sort of shy. Like me. It's tough for him to meet understanding women, being in the business he's in and all."

"What business? Oh… I get it. He works in the family business with Darnell."

Melody nodded. "Uh-huh. He gets a lot of razzing from people. Girls have told him he was downright creepy for studying to be a mortician. But it's an honorable profession. Darnell has done quite well working in the field."

"I'm sure he has." Jodi rested her chin on her hands. "You and Rae planning on a double wedding by chance?"

"No, we're not. Rae and Darnell are going to have their big spectacular ceremony, and Lionel and I will…Well, I guess we'll be wedding attendants together."

"Sweet. Has Raheesha picked out her wedding colors and bridesmaid dresses?"

"No, not yet. That's why I've been going through bridal magazines. There's a lot of stuff to choose from. And you wouldn't believe the price tags. Get a load at this outfit…"

Melody retrieved a magazine from under her desk and showed Jodi several styles of bridesmaids' gowns. Jodi bit her lip to keep from groaning. All she planned to wear to her own wedding was a simple off-white sundress with a flower tucked behind one ear. It wasn't quite the storybook wedding in a huge cathedral she had always imagined she'd experience someday. Too bad she had sold her formal wedding dress on eBay after the debacle with what's-his-face.

"What are you two looking at?" Babs paused at the counter to shoot an envelope into the *To Be Mailed* bin behind Melody's head. "Yessss…Two points–I score! The crowd goes wild." She began to strut about and make roaring crowd noises.

Jodi rolled her eyes. "Uh-huh. Wanna look at bridesmaids' dresses, Ms. WNBA?"

That stopped the Sports Queen in her tracks. "You're not still thumbing through bridal magazines, are you, Mel?"

"Sure I am. There are tons of them on the newsstand. Some are better than others. Look at these cute strapless dresses."

Frowning, Babs tilted her head as she viewed the photo spread. "I'd look like a first class dork wearing one of those things. I suppose we'll all have to buy one to be in Rae's wedding, though, huh?"

"You wouldn't if you helped serve punch or something," Melody said. "You could get away with a dressy pantsuit number in that position. How's that?"

"Much better. You in the wedding, Jojo?"

"It's news to me if I am…I'll be rather on the large size by June. I won't fit into anything but a burlap bag."

"At least Gabby will be thinner. By the way, she says she wants to come to happy hour with us tonight.

I'll go home early and pick her up and bring her over for a little while."

Melody's eyes widened. "Should she get out of bed like that?"

Babs nodded. "The doc says it's okay provided she doesn't stand up too much or jump around. She's okay to attend sit-down functions for short periods."

"The doctor probably meant a baby shower–not a loud, smoke-filled night club." Jodi sighed. "But who am I to talk? I said I'd go tonight for a little while myself."

"The mommies can talk shop then." Babs laughed, giving Jodi a light punch on the shoulder. "Don't it beat all? Out of seven females in this office, two are *in the family way.*"

"And one is married and two are engaged," Melody reminded her.

Babs nodded. "Wow, some year it's been at Hit-On-US. Who will be next in the stork and-or wedding bells club?" She grinned and playfully wiggled a black eyebrow at Melody. "Any ideas?"

Melody blushed and slouched down behind her magazine. "No comment."

"You're just not trying hard enough," Babs teased, walking backward toward the cube farm. "Landing dates seems to be a cinch these days. I'm even seeing someone I picked up at the gym."

"A Martian or a Venusian?" Jodi asked.

Babs grinned. "That's for me to know and you all to find out later."

"That girl is incorrigible," Jodi said, shaking her head. "I guess I'd better get back to my rock pile, or else I won't make it to happy hour."

"Oh, Brent's invited to come tonight, too."

Jodi froze in mid-step. "Did you ask him already?"

"I didn't, but someone else may have mentioned it to him."

Jodi frowned. "He probably wouldn't want to sit around and yak with a bunch of Venusians when there's work to be done. But I'll let him know."

As Jodi slowly walked back to her office she considered how things had changed since late spring when Brent arrived on the scene. Amazing what one guy could do to an office full of females…Once the match had been lit, the entire office seemed to go up in flames. People and relationships changed rapidly. No wonder it was always males who started wars–women never acted impulsively or irrationally except around men.

Jodi strolled past Keryn's office. The door stood slightly ajar, and the tone of her phone conversation was unmistakable.

"Grab whatever you like for dinner tonight, Peter. I'm going out with the girls for a short while after work. I won't be out too long. We'll have plenty of time to plan our little romantic trip later, okay?"

Jodi despised eavesdropping, but she found she couldn't help herself. It must be her hormones she reasoned. She perked up her ears.

"Hmm…I can't wait to feel the sun on my face and the sand on my back, too, my little Peter, Peter, pumpkin-eater. Now be a good boy and get back to work. Your cuddly-wuddly Kerry-baby will be home soon. Kissy, kissy. Bye."

The world *had* changed...Nerdy Keryn Wiseman was making smooching sounds and babbling like a toddler, and Babs was seriously considering wearing a dress pantsuit to a wedding. If miracles like these could happen to her co-workers, surely Brent could forgive her for lying to him about flying to Reno?

A sudden abdominal cramp made Jodi double over and gasp.

"What's happening?" Keryn stepped from her office at the sound of Jodi's cry. "You didn't feel the baby kick or something?"

"It's way too early for that. I'm not sure what's going on."

"Let me help you to your chair."

Keryn helped her sit down and handed Jodi her bottle of water. "You want me to get Brent?"

Jodi frowned. They had barely grunted at each other all day. And Brent was super busy on another project that Mr. J had labeled "top priority". She shook her head.

"No, don't bug him. It's just a Braxton-Hicks contraction–a false labor cramp. All the books say these things can happen at any time."

"But you're not very far along. Are you sure you're okay?"

Jodi felt heartburn bubbling up her esophagus. She sipped a little from her water bottle and leaned back in her desk chair. "Yeah, I'm okay. I just ate something I shouldn't have. Spicy food. I seem to have cravings for Mexican food a lot. Weird, huh?"

Keryn shrugged. "I don't know. Mexican mothers

probably experience the same craving, too. Unless they have urges to binge on McDonald's or something equally nasty."

"So you've become a health food nut like Lolo and Max now?"

"Sort of. Peter is a vegetarian by default. Max will only cook vegetarian meals. Peter didn't like to act rude so Max gradually won him over. It's a healthier for you anyway."

"Maybe I should become a vegetarian. I doubt they suffer heartburn nearly as much as us carnivores." Another stabbing pain in her abdomen. Jodi bit her lip. "Ow."

Keryn picked up the phone and offered it to her. "Call your doctor, Jodi. Better safe than sorry. I'll get Brent."

Jodi waved the phone away. "Don't act like such a worrywart. I'm f-i-n-e, fine. I told you what it was–heartburn and normal uterine contractions. Like they say on those British comedies, 'There's no need to get your knickers in a twist.'"

"Right. I'll call Brent and he can take you to the doctor in person." Keryn punched in his extension.

"No." Jodi reached across the desk and pushed down the hang-up button before the call could go through. "He has enough on his mind. He doesn't need to be bothered about something so trivial."

"What could be more important to the man than his fiancée's health?"

"Yes, what could be so unimportant that you can't be bothered to tell your fiancé about it?" Brent stood at the doorway, arms crossed, frowning. "What are you keeping from me now, Jodi?"

*****

Jodi's bottom lip quivered. She looked like she was going to puke again. He'd never understand how on earth a baby the size of a dot could cause so much nausea.

"Morning sickness?" he asked.

"Heartburn." She glanced over at Keryn. "I'm okay now. Thanks, Keryn."

"You're welcome." Keryn narrowed her eyes, closely observing both of them. She quietly exited the room, shutting the door behind her.

Brent sat down in the chair opposite and stared across the desk at the enigmatic woman carrying his child. He loved Jodi–he lusted after her–but did he really *know* her?

"So?"

She frowned. "So what?"

"So, are you going to tell me what's really wrong with you?"

"I already did, Brent. I suffer from the common malady of heartburn. It happens. I have more volatile chemicals pumping around in my system than Monsanto's experimental laboratory. It's nothing for you to be concerned about. I'm fine."

"You're absolutely sure?"

Jodi groaned and spun around in her chair to face her computer screen. "Positive."

"Great." He stood. "Mr. J gave me a reprieve on the project I'm working on so we don't have to stay late tonight."

"We don't?" She bit her lip and turned back

around. "I'd planned on it, since I sort of promised the girls I'd go downstairs to happy hour with them. Gabby is going to be there."

"You guys are throwing a baby shower in a bar?"

She shrugged. "Why not? But this is more of a get-together than a shower. We're planning the official party after the baby comes so we know what colors to buy for clothing." A momentary grimace passed over her pale features. "It's better than buying everything in yellow unisex."

No matter how good an act Jodi Baker thought she was putting on, she couldn't deceive him. She looked sick. She needed to see a doctor.

"Get your jacket and purse and let's go."

"Go where? The doctor's? Brent, I told you already. It was just heartburn and maybe some false labor twinges. I'll feel fine in a few moments. Trust me."

"Trust you?" Brent's volume slid up the scale involuntarily. He clenched his fists and planted them both firmly on the desk blotter, his face inches from hers.

"Trust *you*? Why in hell should I trust your word about anything? You lied about going to Reno. You conveniently forgot to tell me you were carrying my child before you left. And I suppose tonight you planned to party without a second thought as to how it could compromise the baby's health."

She gasped. "Compromise the baby's health? What kind of monster do you think I am? I'd never do anything to hurt our child."

Yeah, right, Brent thought. Caustic rage and years

of frustration bubbled up from depths he had no idea existed within him. Women were all such selfish creatures. Always defending their rights to act as they deemed fit. Never acknowledging their efforts to destroy their supposed loved ones in the process. Finally his bitterness and disappointment erupted, spewing its vile verbalizations upon an unsuspecting Jodi.

"*Our* child?" He walked away from the desk and threw up his arms. "How do I even know that it's mine? Maybe you were just using me to get what you wanted without the baggage of marriage. Maybe what's-his-face didn't walk out on you at the altar. His dumping you at the last second could have been a part of your master plan to gain sympathy to lure the next guy into your bed."

Jodi rose unsteadily to her feet. Her eyes bore into his as her measured words sliced deep into his soul, ripping open the festering wound that lay hidden within his heart.

"Have you ever considered that Helena only boarded that plane to escape what she considered a fate worst than death–being married to you?"

Suddenly Brent's world turned cold and black and empty, an open throat of nothingness swallowing him whole. He ran from Jodi's office. He ran down the hall, past a gape-mouthed Melody at reception and out of the building. He ran to his car and got in and started driving. He had no idea where he was heading. All he knew was he was heading anywhere but home.

Chapter Nineteen

"Gabriela–you look fantastic," Lotus beamed. "The earth mother look becomes you."

Everyone around the back corner table at the Zodiac Café admired Gabriela's long, luxurious dark brown hair and amazingly long fingernails. The rosy color tinting her olive cheeks together with the roundness of her figure said "motherhood". Correction—it *screamed* motherhood Jodi thought, sighing. If Leonardo DaVinci were still alive he would have pleaded with Gabby to sit for a portrait of the Madonna and child.

Her friends' happy faces did little to assuage Jodi's twinges of guilt and self-loathing. Brent's horror-stricken face burned in her mind. She wished she could take back the horrible thing she had said earlier, but he had left the building by the time she'd gathered the courage to step out of her office.

What if he never came back? What would she and the baby do without him?

"I think you guys look terrific, too." Gabriela's gracious reply forced Jodi back to reality. It wasn't only her body angles that had lost their sharpness but her personality as well. "Hit-On-US employs the hottest chicks in the Westport area."

Everyone whistled, laughed and clapped in agreement.

"I'm so glad to get out of the house," she

continued, "even if I can't dance or drink. You don't know how stir crazy you get when you're on bed rest. At least doing some work at home takes my mind off my confinement." She smiled at their tech head. "Thanks for the computer set-up, Keryn. You've saved my sanity."

"You're welcome. And thanks for your feedback on what works and what doesn't work from home. We'll probably set up something similar for Jodi in the near future."

Gabriela covered her gasp with a hand. "Jodi, don't tell me…You're expecting?"

"So much for me telling my own bit of news." She wrinkled her nose and stuck out her tongue at Keryn then turned back to Gabriela. "Yep, I'm preggers, too."

"How wonderful. My little guy will have a playmate. Maybe we can talk Mr. J into letting us start up a daycare on site? What do you guys think?"

The talk soon revolved around bringing Gabriela's baby into the office and how the break room could be modified into a nursery. Babs volunteered to tear out a divider in the ladies' room to build a diaper station. Lotus knew of some natural herbs that would work as a good diaper pail deodorizer. Melody volunteered her mother to crochet a blanket for the bassinet that coordinated with the cube farm's gray color scheme.

Jodi plastered a smile on her face as her mind drifted elsewhere. Where had Brent gone? Why couldn't she reach him on his cell phone? Had she flushed their love down the toilet with her careless remarks? Would he ever forgive her for what she said?

"Now tell us truthfully, Gabby," Raheesha was

saying as Jodi's focus came back to the conversation at hand. "Is Harrison Platte really doing right by you?"

Gabriela shrugged. "We're talking–civilly. It's getting better. His family acts a bit more supportive of me, and we've signed some papers guaranteeing that Harrison will be a part of the baby's future."

Melody's eyes widened with excitement. "You mean…wedding bells?"

"No, I don't think so. Harry is a gorgeous hunk, but he's got way too much emotional baggage to ever make a good husband. Even a screwed up person like me can tell that much."

"You're not screwed up," Babs corrected her. "You've been screwed. But you're making the best of things."

Gabriela gave her roommate's hand a quick squeeze. "Thanks, dear. Harry is paying child support and starting a college fund for the baby. It's a start–and I have to thank Lotus and Keryn for all their help. I couldn't have done it without you two."

Lotus blushed and mouthed "you're welcome" while Keryn only shrugged.

"Hey, it was no big deal," Keryn said matter-of-factly. "We just sweet-talked the guys into putting a good word in for you with their cousins. Max and Peter are the real heroes here."

"Yes, my Max is a hero." Lotus sighed with a dramatic flourish of her hands on her heart. "And I don't think you minded sweet-talking Pete one bit, either, Keryn. Admit it."

"No, I didn't mind," Keryn said, grinning. "Pointdexter is one cool dude. He's renewed my faith in the male of the species."

"Here, here." Raheesha raised her glass. "My Darnell has certainly made me forget the fool I married out of high school. All it takes is one good man's lovin' to make everything seem all right in the world."

"Or it takes the love of one good Martian." Melody giggled. "Lionel says he likes being called a 'Martian'. And he told me since Venus is the goddess of love I'm very much a Venusian."

Everyone cheered and clapped. Melody's cheeks warmed. "Well, he does."

"Jojo…What do you say?" Gabriela raised an eyebrow and patted her swelling belly. "Does all it take is one good man's loving, or is loving someone else good enough to make everything work out right?"

All eyes at the table focused on Jodi. Tears welled in the corner of her eyes. A sudden sniffle made it difficult to breathe, let alone talk.

Oh, Brent…Is our love strong enough to endure both our fears of rejection?

Jodi blinked back her sobs and lowered her gaze. "I…I'm not sure yet."

Fortunately Babs' antics saved Jodi further interrogation. Standing on her chair, she whistled across the room. "Hey, Nick! Get over here. I want you to meet the girls."

Jodi relaxed as Babs' latest conquest approached. The topic of conversation quickly turned away from her muddled relationship with Brent. Babs jumped down from her perch and kissed a tall, dark and very Italian-looking stud on the cheek.

"Everyone, this is Nick. Nick, these are the girls I

work with."

Gabriela's eyes widened with recognition. "The pizza delivery guy?"

"Uh-huh." Babs slid into Nick's ample arms. He returned her quick kiss with a long and sensual one. Whistles and catcalls echoed throughout the café. Moments later they came up for air.

"Remember that night, Gabby, when we ordered pizza and breadsticks and thought we were short a few dollars but weren't sure? Nick here said he'd foot us the remainder if I went out with him the next time he was off. So, I did. And there you go."

Melody hopped out of her seat and shook Nick's hand. "It's very nice to meet you. I used to date a delivery guy, too, but he only delivered FedEx stuff. You look like you work out at the gym like he did."

"Sort of," Nick drawled. "I work construction for my uncle when I'm not carrying pizzas around."

"Construction work?," Keryn raised an eyebrow. "How come the second job?"

"I'm trying to save up enough money to build my own house some day–complete with a basketball court."

"Ahh..." Everyone nodded and smiled at the obvious mutual attraction. Babs at last had found her perfect man.

At Babs' instigation the more able-bodied Hit-On-US employees took to the dance floor. Raheesha stayed put with Jodi and Gabriela, insisting that her knee was acting up and she didn't relish wearing a brace on it for the trip down the church aisle.

Gabriela waved at their laughing co-workers.

"Well, I always wondered what took Babs so long to pay the pizza guy after that one time we miscalculated the bill. She always insisted on answering the door. Then we began ordering pizza about every other night. How could I've been so blind?"

"That Babs can pull a fast one on anybody." Raheesha chuckled. "Must be all the basketball training. She's quick witted as well as quick footed."

"Yeah, makes sense," Jodi agreed.

Max and Peter entered the café just then, joining Lotus and Keryn and the throng of happy dancers gyrating under the spinning lights of the disco globe. Jodi slowly sipped her soft drink, growing more melancholy by the second.

"What's up with your man?" Raheesha asked her at length. "He didn't accept the invite to come tonight."

Jodi shook her head. "No, he left work early. I guess I'll have to bum a ride home."

"That's fine." Raheesha patted Jodi's hand. "He'll be all right. It takes time."

"Time?"

"For him to heal some. You don't think we couldn't hear him blowing up this afternoon? Brent's deep voice carries–even through walls and closed doors."

"Oh…sorry." Jodi slumped in her seat and pulled her jacket over her face. "I'm so embarrassed."

"Don't be. You're just lucky Mr. J was out of the office at the time. He probably would have called the cops if heard Brent yelling. He acts right protective of his female employees at times."

"Yeah, Mr. J is sort of like the dad I never had." A wistful look misted Gabriela's eyes. "He certainly looked after me even when I've disappointed him on several occasions."

"Like any good father would. You're worth looking after, Gabby. Don't forget it." Raheesha gave Gabriela a quick hug before turning her attention back to Jodi.

"Now sit up, girlfriend, and act like the grown up, engaged, pregnant woman you are. Tomorrow is another day. You two will kiss and make up, and everybody will have a great time in the sun come New Year's Eve. You'll see."

Gabriela smiled. "I'm sorry I can't travel to Florida to witness your wedding ceremony, Jodi. I wish you and Brent every happiness."

Jodi nodded mutely. Their kindness was simply too much. The crying jag she'd been holding back all afternoon suddenly exploded in a rush of tears and sobs.

"W-w-what if he doesn't want to get married now?" She covered her red face with her hands. "W-what if I've screwed it all up by telling him to get over her?"

"Get over her?" Gabriela's jaw dropped. "Is that jerk-off seeing someone else?" She picked up a dinner knife from Babs' appetizer. "Why, we ought to cut off his balls and grind them into cat food."

"Calm down, honey child," Raheesha advised. "Jodi is talking about a dead woman." She wrapped a comforting arm around Jodi's shoulders. "I think he is over her. He's with you, right? He wants to have a baby with you...He's not stuck in the past anymore. He's planning for the future."

The future? Jodi had never thought about it that way. Brent wanted this baby...He wanted to make a life with her and their child. He was a man of principle and honor. Sure he had his down days, but he didn't just walk away and throw in the towel when the going got tough.

Jodi sniffed twice and dried her tears with her cocktail napkin. "You really think so?"

"Yes, I do."

Gabriela put down the dinner knife. "I'm glad. I don't think I have quite the strength to emasculate a guy in my condition." She chuckled low and leaned in toward them. "Of course, a verbal castration works just as well if not better on the male of the species."

Raheesha looked down her nose at her. "Now, now, mom-to-be." "All right. I'll watch what I say about Harry in front of my baby. But I don't want him to grow up thinking that humping and dumping girls is what it's all about. I want him to respect women and treat them like ladies."

Jodi grinned. "I have no doubt that you'll be successful, Gabby."

"Yes, your boy will turn out fine," Raheesha agreed.

Gabriela looked puzzled. "Why makes you two say that?"

"You have the courage of your convictions." Jodi squeezed her hand. "If all of us acted out of our courage rather than our fear, the world would be a happier place."

*****

TO: MrBoJangles@crapster.net
FROM: bdavison@hit-on-us.com
SUBJECT: lies and the lying liars who tell them

Sing me a sad song, Mr. BoJangles…

I'm feeling down. Actually, I'm pissed off–but it only makes me feel more depressed. I just don't understand women. They act like simple creatures and then they turn around and throw everything back in your face. They act like cold, calculating bitches–even the supposed kind-hearted ones.

They tell me that men are from Mars and women are from Venus. How true. Venus is a hot, hellish, acid-riddled world. What more fitting place in the universe is there for she-devils to come from?

I know you're not getting any of this. I'm sorry, man. I just have to rant a bit. There's steam pouring out of my ears…Email is a good way to let it out without throwing things. I snuck back into the office after everyone left for the day so I could email you in peace.

No, I don't want to go home. Jodi might be there. I can't face her now. But she's probably still out partying with the girls in the office. The very pregnant Gabriela was scheduled to be there. I don't understand this group bonding ritual of human females where they dress up and hang out at a club. Why can't they just watch the game on the tube and snack on junk food like normal people?

I tell you it's women who cause all the grief in the world. No wonder there are so many wars.

You're probably scratching your head (or your ass or both knowing you) about what I'm going on about…I'm still angry that Jodi got on that plane and flew to Reno and didn't even bother to tell me. Sure, I know the boss man sort of laid it heavy on her. And I realize I'm partly to blame since I was the one who was supposed to attend the trade show in the first place. But there are more important things in life than keeping your job–aren't there?

She's carrying our child. That's the most important thing in the world. Why doesn't she trust me enough to tell me what's going on with her? Why does she continue to risk her and our baby's health by ignoring symptoms that could add up to something serious?

I admit I tend to spout out a lot of nasty stuff when I'm pissed. I didn't really mean anything I said to her this afternoon, but I know I hurt her. Badly. I know Jodi didn't bail out of her last relationship. She didn't try to trap me into marrying her–I want to marry her. I'm just so screwed up about how to tell her that I love her and I can't live without her.

I know you're going to write back and tell me to stop acting like a pompous idiot, spewing gloom and doom all the time. But I can't take being lied to and treated like a helpless moron. I have feelings, too, although I don't always express them very well.

I'll end this tirade now and delete it. There's no need to bring everyone down with me. I'll call Gramps. Then I'm going over to the church and talk to Father Tim. He's cool. He'll listen.

*****

Jodi arrived at a darkened house around seven-fifty. She saw no signs that Brent had arrived home and left again. Sighing, she kicked off her shoes and curled up on the sofa. Ten minutes later the phone rang.

"Hello there. How's my happy couple?" Gramps' cheerful tone usually brought a smile to Jodi's lips, but tonight she could only feel her heart breaking.

"Gramps, did Brent call you earlier this evening by chance?" She closed her eyes and crossed her fingers.

"No, he hasn't called. Why? Was he supposed to?"

"Not really." She released her twisted fingers, sighing loud and long. "I was just hopeful."

"He's not there right now, is he?"

"No, he isn't here." Should she tell him about their argument? After all, if Brent wanted to call the wedding off then Gramps and Marjorie had the right to know.

"I know where he is then," Gramps said. "He likes to go and sit in the church whenever he's upset and can't talk. Sometimes he even talks to the priest.

Sometimes Father Tim can even talk some sense into that thick head of his."

Jodi felt some of the weight lifting from her heart. "How did you know Brent was upset? Are you psychic, Gramps?"

"Of course. It comes from years of living with Brent Davison. Brent is a simple enough man to understand. He expects things to be orderly and straightforward. When life takes a few hairpin curves and gets messy, he panics. But he calms down and gets his act together eventually. He gets his common sense gene from me, you know."

She grinned. "There's no doubt about it. And his good looks, too."

"You're darn right about that." Gramps chuckled.

Their conversation wound its way through Marjorie's pineapple upside down cake idea for the wedding reception to the trouble of locating matching beachcomber outfits in sea foam green for their nuptials to the possibility of hurricanes in late December.

"Is the boy back yet?" Gramps asked at last.

Jodi lifted the curtain an inch and peaked outside. "I don't see his car yet. Oh, Gramps! What if I really got him so angry that he decides he doesn't want to get married? What will I do?"

"Kick him out of the house."

"Kick him out? How can I do that? I don't own this place."

"Yeah, but I do. I can rent it out to whomever I darn well please."

That was comforting to know. "Thanks, Gramps.

You're a sweetheart."

"You're welcome. I can't have my great-grandchildren living on the street no matter how pig-headed my grandson is."

Great-grandchildren? Brent had told her to keep her pregnancy a secret until after the wedding...

"Gramps, you sure Brent didn't call you earlier today?"

He cleared his throat. "I refrain from answering that question on the grounds it may incriminate me."

So, Brent had contacted him. "Brent told you about me being pregnant, huh?"

"He did sort of let it slip. He was mad at you for not telling him and for going to Reno. What did you do in Reno? Win some money on the roulette table?"

She laughed. "Not really. I had to attend a trade show for work. Brent wouldn't fly, so the boss sort of made me go instead."

"Hmm...I thought as much. The boy acts like a dunderhead at times. He gets his thick skull from his grandmother. She wasn't always the sharpest tool in the shed."

"Gramps! How can you say such a thing?"

"Easy. She married me, didn't she?"

Jodi held her sides as uncontrollable laughter filled her frame. Tears rolled down her cheeks. Tears of sadness, fear, relief...and then joy. The front door opened.

"He's back, Gramps. Do you want to talk to him?"

"Yep. Let me holler at the boy for a moment and then I'll give him to you."

She held out the receiver. Brent accepted it as he

sat down beside her. After a few monosyllabic grunts and an "okay" and "yes, sir" he hung up.

Jodi clasped her hands and averted her eyes. "Brent...I just want to say that I'm sorry for what I said to you this afternoon. I didn't mean it. It just came out. Please forgive me."

"Same here." He gently took her hands in his and kissed her fingers. "I didn't mean anything I said, either. Can you forgive me?"

She nodded and laid her head on his shoulder. "Yes, completely."

"It seems both of us have hot buttons that blow up like time bombs when pushed."

"Don't we." Jodi chuckled. "I'm going to try from now on not to push any of your buttons."

Brent smiled and pulled her into his arms and kissed her forehead. "It's okay. They needed to be pushed. I needed to blow up–or blow off–some shit that had been bothering me for so long that I didn't know it was still bothering me."

"Huh?"

He took pity on her lost expression. "I had a long talk with Father Tim this evening. He made me realize that I hadn't quite let go of the past like I thought I had. But starting from now on, I'm going to make it up to you, Jodi. I'm going to make you the happiest bride, the happiest woman in the world if you let me."

"Well, I won't stop you from trying, but you really can't make another person happy. You can only love, honor and cherish them. The happiness will come of its own accord. We've got to have faith that it will. We both have to stop fearing a repeat of our previous trips to the altar. We both need to be brave."

"I'm a coward. I fear things that no sane person should at times. I fear I'm losing you because you are your own person." His lips met hers in a tender kiss. "But at the same time, I also like how you are your own person. You definitely know your own mind."

Jodi kissed him back, gently at first and then with more passion. "Hmm… I know what I want right now. And it's not tacos." She began unbuttoning his shirt.

"Yes, it's been a few days since we've made love, hasn't it? Amazing what anger does to one's libido." Brent reached for her bra catch and helped her wriggle out of her sweater top. "Ah, what a beautiful sight."

"But I'm retaining water. I've turned into one big, fat giant sponge." She pouted then reached for his belt buckle and zip. "I can barely squeeze into my everyday bras."

"Yes and it shows." He tenderly massaged her full breasts and sampled her nipples. Jodi groaned with pleasure, collapsing against him.

"Speaking of showing," she whispered with a nod toward the front window. "We're casting a wonderful shadow through the curtains for the neighbors."

Brent wiggled an eyebrow at her. "Really? Let's give them a real good show then."

"Why, you…" Jodi laughed and sprang to her feet, wiggling out of her pants. "I'm game if you're game."

Their remaining vestments vanished within seconds. Brent sprawled across the couch. Jodi lowered herself onto his rigid erection with a sigh.

"Oooo... It has been too long." She slowly twirled her hips around and around, pulling his shaft deeper into her hungry core. "You can bounce me as hard as you like. Give the baby a good bouncy ride."

"It won't hurt him, will it?"

"No, the doc says he or she is protected in a nice, little water balloon." Jodi corkscrewed her hips faster. She began to pant and move her pelvis faster. "Whew—whew—hey! Those breathing exercises work great for sex, too."

He took a nipple into his mouth and suckled until she squealed and her toes curled. "I'll say... I don't think I can last much longer."

She rocked and bucked faster, rubbing her clit in rhythm with his thrusts. He grabbed hold of her buttocks and squeezed tight. The stars exploded with one single mind-blowing thrust. Jodi threw back her head and screamed his name as the first wave of tremors crashed over her body, sucking her into its undertow. Brent pounded her harder, bringing about yet another earsplitting cry of ecstasy.

He laughed. "Louder! I don't think the neighbors can hear quite yet. Some wear hearing aids."

"Why you..." She ground her hips in a tight circle, willing her womanly muscles to contract tighter around him. He gasped, groaned and with a sudden, wild thrash of his pelvis his seed gushed forth, triggering in her yet another orgasmic contraction and another round of raucous cries.

Sated and spent, they kissed and caressed each other, oblivious to the time or their whereabouts.

"Oh, dear." Jodi moaned. "We shouldn't have

moved my sofa in here."

Brent sighed contentedly. "That's okay. What's a little stain on a piece of furniture? I'm sure we'll figure some way to get it out."

"It's not the sticky spots I'm concerned about." She lifted her head and then the end of the curtain behind them. "See for yourself."

Brent sat up and stared out at the red flashing lights parked across the street. Jodi began to laugh at the embarrassed look on his face. "Ah shit. The neighbors heard us after all."

Chapter Twenty

TO: ShaynaE@wazoo.com
FROM: jbaker@hit-on-us.com
SUBJECT: That was some wedding, huh?

You naughty girl!

Here you and Bo had it all figured out and you never bothered to tell us until the day of the wedding. Oooo – I could just kill you guys! ☺

I know Brent mentioned a frat brother named "Beauregard" or something like that once, but I never made the connection. He never once said that his good pal's girlfriend was a graduate student. He just referred to you as the "smart woman who finally bagged his drinking buddy." Well, you "bagged" him all right. Dr. Easton, you are one savvy and sexy chick! He's totally hot for your bod–and your beautiful mind, of course. We both appreciated the lovely ballad Bo sang (with your inspiration) at the reception. It was the perfect gift.

You know, I thought I wanted a big wedding with a long dress and the veil and the fifteen attendants, but now I'm glad we didn't go that route. The beach at sunset was beautiful. Marjorie and Gramps in matching sea foam green sweaters with sailboat appliqués were cute, too. I'll never forget the look on the minister's face when he told them they could stop kissing. Even Brent and I took him seriously during the ceremony rehearsal and kept our "you may kiss the bride" kiss to less than two minutes. I was sure that someone was going to get a hose and squirt Gramps and Marjorie to break it up after five! ☺

It was so fun having all our friends and co-workers there. Even Gabriela got to attend in a way–Babs had her cell phone with the built in video camera on the entire time. Imagine the phone bill! The atmosphere was so laid back and I could tell everyone enjoyed the sun and the fun.

Even our parents didn't seem like their usual harried selves. Brent smiled when he saw his folks together for the first time in a long while. That's a first according to Gramps. Now that Brent is healing inside, other hurts from the past are healing, too. My mom got critical about my hair again, though–"Why don't you put it up in a chignon? You've got to do something with those frizzy ends of yours." But other than that, we communicated better than we have in years. A new beginning all around, you could say.

And everyone appreciated the great discounts I got on their airline tickets. Brent handled himself well on the plane trip. The motion sickness pills worked well. He only squeezed the circulation out of my hand during take-off and landing. At least he's willing to fly again. That's one small step for his career–one giant leap for my man.

Okay, it's time for me to paste the photos in my wedding scrapbook and get to work on my next project–setting up the nursery. It's six months until "B-Day", the invasion of the latest alien to the Davison household.

Is it from Mars or Venus, you ask? I can't say. The ultrasound gave the doctor a pretty good picture, but I told him I didn't want to know the baby's gender. I like surprises. Good surprises, that is.

I'm not so fearful about the future anymore. I'm not worried about being left behind somewhere like at the altar or at a dead end job. I've got my man and my little alien and my nice house in the suburbs and a little blue tricycle. Life is good.

Let us know what date you and Bo pick for your big day. Please say it's at least six weeks after I deliver. I want to look halfway normal in a bridesmaid dress. ☺

Forever your friend,
Jodi